W9-ACG-202

The Philip G. Brown fund

little alternative, and they presented the plan to her parents as a
fait accompli. They accepted it with mixed feelings : on the one
hand they were pleased that they would not lose their daughter
so soon; on the other, the procedure—after all, it was a big
thing, expecting Mother to travel so far alone—seemed rather
irregular. Nevertheless they still did not enquire into Father's
circumstances : his reasons seemed quite sound. In any case it
would have been far too late for that.

Father returned; a little afterwards I was born, sickly and
premature. Mother waited : I grew stronger. The money arrived,
each month, from New Zealand. Father worked to get the farm
ready (whether 'ready' meant suitable, and livable, for a woman,
or just a paying proposition, I have never discovered) but of
course it was never really ready. It was all he could do to send
off the money to England every month. Finally, in desperation,
he took out a second mortgage on the farm to pay Mother's fare
to New Zealand. Clutching me, Mother embarked at Southampton full of new fears and hesitations. She wept; her parents
wept. I wept for no precise reason, and was curious.

But Mother's nightmare journey (at least that was the very
conventional way she always described it) only really began when
our ship docked at Auckland. Father was not there to meet us.
Instead, he sent his brother, the waterfront worker, with a message. It is difficult to know which shocked Mother most : the
fact of Father not meeting her, or the fact of his brother being a
labourer. There had been recent heavy floods, and Father was
having difficulties with the farm. It proved impossible to leave it
in the care of a neighbour, as he had hoped, so that he might
travel down to Auckland to meet the ship. So there was his
brother, hands and hair still whitish from unloading a phosphate
ship that morning, to meet us. He put us on the train north,
since Mother wished to leave immediately for the farm, and sent
off a telegram to Father. The journey was long and slow; our
carriage was one of two second-class carriages attached to the
rear of a goods train, and filled, to Mother's surprise and alarm,
with Maoris—tattooed, pipe-smoking old women, and loud
young men with cases of beer. Mother remembered quite distinctly that one of the young men held an uncapped bottle

directly under her nose, offering a drink. The old women clucked
and the young ones became drunk and noisy. They had all been
to a large tangi near Auckland, and now they were returning to
their tribal country. It was a humid summer, and the inside of
the carriage was hot and sticky; the landscape jolted past, losing
its green complexion for the bleached, brown colours of the
summer north. We survived to the end of the train journey,
where the bus-ride began. The bus was ramshackle and bumped
over stony, uneven roads. We were finally deposited in the
shambling little river-town which Mother came to know so well
and hate so much; wooden and sprawling, the old houses were
scattered along a bush-laced finger of land, and its shops, about
the crazy-shaped jetty, were stilted out over the water. The town
stood near the end of a long harbour; on each side, creeks fed
through grey mud-flats and thick forests of mangroves. For
Mother, as we stood upon the jetty waiting for Father to appear,
we might well have been looking out, across that wildness and
loneliness of landscape, at the end of the world. But I cannot
imagine that she displayed any emotion, certainly not to the
lazy-voiced inhabitants of the town, the Maoris squatting in the
shade of pepper trees, or the roll-trousered launchmen and half-
caste fishermen lounging and yarning about the jetty. Her kind
had been tested by worse than this before; and survived.

Father appeared, at length, in the launch of a neighbour. His
trousers, Mother remembered (she always had a fine eye for
certain detail), were milk-stained and patched; he wore gumboots and a torn flannel shirt. Possibly there was some mild
display of affection on the jetty that day—after all, it was nearly
five years now since they had last seen each other, and Father
had never seen me before—but the memory escapes me, and in
any case it was not the kind of detail Mother was inclined to
remember. We were introduced to the neighbour, a broad-
featured Maori in a wide-brimmed hat, a Mr. Patera; our trunks
were loaded, and the town and jetty dwindled into the distance
behind as the launch puttered up-river, zagging back and forward to avoid the shallows left by the out-going tide and sliding
under steep banks hung with obstinate bush. The wake of the
launch sent small waves sipping over the glistening mud and

through the tangled roots of the mangroves. I must have been delighted and excited by the new sights; for I can remember, very clearly, Mother telling me to contain myself. Eventually the engine-sound ceased and, in sudden queer silence among the sounds of cicadas and bush birds, we glided up to a fern-fringed jetty, a rickety structure made of twisted manuka trunks. In those days there was no road to the farm; the only access was by way of launch and horse. The trunks were lashed to a konaki, which Mother discovered was the Maori word for a horse-drawn wooden sled; Father helped Mother side-saddle on to a placid-natured horse, and sat me forward on the saddle of his own. Mr Patera followed behind with the konaki. In this way we travelled a mile back into the hills, along a horse-beaten track, and the long journey, really begun that summer so many years before when Father and Mother first walked together in an English garden, was at an end.

Paint peeled from the house; broken windows were covered with sacking (again Mother's memory for detail comes to my assistance). The corrugated iron roof was bright with rust; the guttering in some places had come adrift altogether, and rattled in the wind. Still, the place, a pioneer structure, had a fine solidity about it; it stood, aloof and strong and independent of the landscape, planted down on a rise in the lee of a great hill. Norfolk pines stood to the front of it; a grove of cabbage trees, at the rear, screened off the milking-shed and the hay-barn. The long verandah, with its convoluted mock-iron cornices, over-looked the valley, the widening and winding tidal creek running shining to the sea, and the hazy blue hills shouldering tall bush to the skyline.

But Mother would naturally have been more concerned with viewing the interior of the house. And the interior, she always said, altogether beggared description; so I must take her word for it. Apart from Mrs Patera, who in kindly and neighbourly fashion had sometimes come to tidy and clean for the lonely man on the farm, the place had not seen a woman for years. First with the four brothers, and then with Father alone, it had been an exclusively bachelor domain. But there and then, in the chaos and filth, among the broken sticks of furniture, she set about making a home.

She forgave Father in the end, of course. For he had, as she said, not an ounce of deceit in him; he was a fine man, even if rather limited. It simply hadn't occurred to him that she might expect to find the farm, the house, any different. And, she added generously, he always meant things for the best; after all, he had tried, quite wrongly, to save her from it as long as he could.

She forgave Father; but not the country. How could she forgive the country for being so utterly, so inexplicably, different from that which she had expected? No, it was the country itself which had deceived and betrayed her; there could be no forgiveness. And when she said Father was limited, she meant simply that Father failed to share her anger at the cruel trick played on her. 'You know,' she would tell me, 'your Father has no real affection for England at all. None at all. He might as well never have been there.' This actually, so far as Mother was concerned, was his greatest limitation.

So the strangeness of soil, water and light in time bred a sickness of despair in her. Her life became an unwilling, lonely pilgrimage over a terrain littered with stunted hopes and forlorn memories. Even I, to whom she could confide, was lost to her on those days when Father mounted me, with my neat lunch-packet secure inside my school-bag, on the konaki beside the cream-cans and took me, with the cans, down to our jetty, there to await the cream-launch which carried me down to the little riverside school. It was of course shock enough to have to lose me at all: it was even greater when she realized I should have to share a tiny schoolroom and a solitary teacher with some thirty other Maori, half-caste, and pakeha children. 'How can she learn there?' she would demand of Father. 'Under those circumstances?'

'My school was no different,' he replied cryptically. 'I learnt.'

'And besides,' Mother said, 'they all go barefoot.'

'So?' Father said. 'Do they keep their brains in their feet?'

'I should like,' she would often repeat, 'to see Bridget go home to finish her education.'

'Yes, dear,' Father would say, rising, methodically hitching his trousers, and finding something to occupy him in another part of the house.

There were neighbours. The nearest were the Pateras: they could be reached on foot. They were members of an old well-known Maori family, descendants of the chief Hone Heke who had repeatedly chopped down the British flagstaff at the new colony's capital of Kororareka, in the Bay of Islands. Mr Patera was a man of raw speech, rough gestures, and quite marvellous natural intelligence; his talent for invention, his affection for even the simplest piece of machinery, was exceeded only by his talent for producing and entertaining a houseful of children, and his affection for his wife. Mrs Patera herself was an astonishingly delicate woman, of slight bone and thin flesh; through years of child-bearing and work, she had somehow man-aged to retain the impression that she must once have been a singularly handsome woman. She had received a good education, and could quite well have won a prominent place for herself somewhere in the European world, or even in the twilight world of Maori politics; but, instead, she accepted young Kiwi Patera, and was taken to spend her life above the placid tidal creek. Children seemed compensation enough for whatever she had lost, if indeed she had lost anything; though in her middle years, as if stirred by conscience, she began to play an active part in tribal affairs, and her voice was heard with respect by the elders.

Kiwi, in the hard years after the war, became Father's closest friend; it was entirely natural that I should become friendly with the Patera children. But relations between Mother and Mrs Patera were never natural. Mother could not conceal an over-whelming self-consciousness when with a Maori; and the fact that Mrs Patera was both educated and intelligent only seemed to aggravate her feelings. It was almost as if some incipiently hostile part of herself was announcing: it is all wrong; they should not be like this; this man should not speak so casually to my husband; these children should not play so freely with my child; this woman should not sit so much at ease in my house. When she first met Kiwi, that day we arrived on the town jetty, she misunderstood the nature of the introduction and assumed he was a labourer of Father's and therefore had not shaken the friendly hand he offered. It was a handshake of a kind, with a man, with a country, she was never to make.

Then there was Mrs Benjamin. If Mother found a real friend at all, it was Mrs Benjamin. She was a member of the third generation of a famous pioneer family, and lived, with her taciturn husband and sullen children, in a large and prosperous white homestead near the town. The homestead was quite famous in itself; and was often visited by those who wished to find an authentic colonial atmosphere. Its interior was still cluttered with heavy polished furniture, and decked with pioneer knick-knacks; in that sombre, rather gloomy place, only the people had changed in the past hundred years. Mrs Benjamin had never been to England; yet she spoke with an artificial, sometimes comic, English accent, and received *The Tatler* and *The London Illustrated* regularly. She liked Mother to talk about England. 'This, of course,' she would confide to Mother, 'is a second-rate country, my dear.' It was enough to win Mother's affection; enough even to overcome her aversion to Catholics, for Mrs Benjamin, though not a very devout Catholic herself, liked to make much of the fact that an ancestor of hers had been present at one of the first Catholic masses celebrated in New Zealand.

The Benjamins visited us on Sunday afternoons. Their large, brightly-painted launch would be tied up at our jetty; Father and Tom Benjamin, who did not really like each other, would be wandering about the farm, talking in a desultory fashion; and, from a sense of duty, I would be playing with Millicent Benjamin, a sulky, rather fragile child, while Mother entertained Mrs Benjamin in the drawing-room.

'I hope, of course, to be able to send Bridget back to England to finish her education,' Mother would tell her. And if Mrs Benjamin found any incongruity in this thin, pale woman on a poor farm (it was the depression then, and Father's mortgages were causing him sleepless nights) speaking of sending her child overseas for education, she certainly did not show it; another point, of course, in her favour.

'That is the ideal, naturally,' she said. 'I mean there would be so much for her there. So much that she would never find here. Everything here is so, well, so—' (a pause and then, for want of another, the tired old word would be paraded once more) '—so absolutely second-rate.' But Mrs Benjamin had more realism about her own children. 'I simply couldn't bear to lose Millicent,' she sighed. 'I mean even the thought that she might go down to Auckland university worries me. But then Millicent isn't really a terribly scholarly child, you know. Your Bridget has the advantage there.'

'Well,' Mother said modestly. 'I only do my best, you know. I supplement whatever Bridget learns at school as best I can. Every little helps, I imagine.'

'Of course, dear. You're really a quite, quite remarkable woman. To manage it among—well, among all this.' And the flattery would be spread with an all-inclusive but entirely genteel sweep of the arm. 'It's quite remarkable.'

Then there were the people of the town and the farms along the creek.

'They're buried here,' Mrs Benjamin would say. 'Simply buried. And so cut off from everything.' She meant, of course, that they did not receive *The Tatler* or *The London Illustrated*; but only the *Herald* and the *Weekly News* from Auckland. 'And the most terrible thing about it is that they just don't seem to care.' There would be, perhaps, a brief but meaningful silence while Mother and Mrs Benjamin meditated on the idlers and drifters about the pub and the jetty, who ventured away from the town only on fishing expeditions to the harbour heads.

'Now take the Larkins,' Mrs Benjamin added. 'There *is* a peculiar family for you. Well-educated too, I might say. But what is the difference between them and the Maoris? I ask you, dear.' The Larkins had a farm on the creek not far away from us. It was once quite large in size, but second growth and aspiring new bush had effortlessly found its way back down the upper slopes while the useful pasture diminished. Like his father before him, Cecil Larkin, a freethinker, was less interested in large-scale farming than in the business of quiet living. Luxuriant sub-tropical growth rioted about their creeper-entwined old bungalow down above the creek; olive, fig, and uncertain banana trees grew crankily in the gardens. The children ran as wild as the bush which encroached on them. 'But there you are, dear. The blood will out. Cecil Larkin's mother was a Potoki, you know. A half-caste. It's what I always say. Mix the races, and the seed goes bad.'

Then there were the Maoris themselves.

'Of course they're very different from us,' Mrs Benjamin said.

'Yes,' Mother answered; she could never show great enthusiasm for this subject.

'They have, well, different—different outlooks on things.'

'Yes,' Mother said.

'Morally, I mean.' Mrs Benjamin began working hard to ignite a spark of interest.

'I can imagine that,' Mother said. 'After all, they've not long been in touch with civilization, have they?' She was prepared, despite the vague promise of spice, to let the subject rest there; but Mrs. Benjamin was clearly determined to pursue it.

'I mean we have to be tolerant,' she said. 'Their minds work differently.'

'I imagine they do.'

'I mean it's common knowledge about what happens at the pa when there's a big hui. There's always too much liquor there, and the boys and girls mix freely. Really, if you were to think about it, you just wouldn't credit that it's a hundred years since the missionaries first came.'

'No,' Mother said. There was a silence.

'But,' added Mrs Benjamin, 'there are other things—other things that aren't such common knowledge.'

'Oh?'

'Other things—well, you could only call them unnatural things.'

This time there was a quite definite silence.

'Mind you,' Mrs Benjamin went on, 'I shouldn't normally breathe a word of this outside the Church. But I do happen to know that often when priests are coming to work among the Maoris they're given, well, certain advice. To prepare them for what they might hear in confession, you see.' She paused. 'I mean if they come out with it in confession, they must know it's wrong, mustn't they?'

'I imagine they must,' said Mother coolly.

'But there you are, dear. They're only savages, really. It only goes to show. They know quite well now the difference between right and wrong, and yet they're still not prepared to observe common decency. I mean if you were to think about it, it'd make your flesh creep. You wouldn't credit it in this day and age. Older women taking young ones and initiating them—'

At this point Mother must have observed, through the french windows, Millicent and me sitting within earshot, dangling our legs over the verandah rail; and gestured for silence. For when Millicent and I re-entered the drawing-room they were talking about something else altogether.

Friendship with Millicent was urged on me : I disliked her. My real friend was always Ruia Patera. Ruia was a tall, slender, fast-growing girl, striking in appearance, and two years older than myself. She, alone of all her football-crazy brothers and dreamy sisters, seemed to inherit her mother's aptitude for learning; for she always headed her class at school, and her mother and her teachers early foresaw the day when Ruia would go to Teachers' Training College at Auckland. For she showed ability both to acquire knowledge and to impart it; in her last year at the little riverside primary school, she often helped the sole teacher with his infant classes. But our friendship was not based on learning, at least not on the schoolroom kind; in any case, probably because the conflict between home and school confused me, I was not a scholar of particular promise even if I did read, hungrily and redeemingly, books of haphazard and erratic choice (even Father's tracts on the monetary theory of Douglas Social Credit, which attracted him in the worst period of the depression, did not escape my attention).

Our friendship, at the beginning, was a casual thing, as casual as the lives of the people of that town through whose dusty streets we dawdled on Saturday afternoons (when we went down the creek for a movie matinée); but it grew with us. Ruia was not only clever, but beautiful; and, for some reason I have never properly

understood attractive girls, in adolescence anyway, invariably
seem to acquire plain girl friends. I was the plain friend, an awkward, rather plumpish ugly duckling; and we walked together,
her brown beauty shown to advantage beside my pale drabness
of figure and feature. By this time she had finished with the
riverside school; each morning she continued her journey on the
cream-launch all the way down-creek to the high school in the
town, where again she began to head her classes. I was lonely
then, without her in the schoolhouse and playground, and I
counted the months to the time when I should begin to travel
with her to the high school.

It seems now that my life, from the age of four to seventeen,
lacked any sense of permanence. It was all a kind of giant holiday until the real business of life, in England, began. Perhaps
that was why I thought I could afford not to take school too
seriously : it was the mood Mother encouraged in me. One day,
not far distant, I should return to the country where I properly
belonged. I shared in her fantasy. I took it as something natural,
inevitable. And Mother, pleased, could regard with amused
tolerance my affections for the farm, the animals, my surround-
ings; and for Ruia.

'But a girl like yourself can never really feel at home here,' she
said. 'I know you will love England.'

I used to talk of it with Ruia.

'But when you go to England,' she said once, 'what will you
do?'

It was the end of a warm summer day; we lay on a grassy
cliff-top overlooking a huge expanse of twilit sea. In the school
holidays we often excursioned, on horseback, to a coastal farm
belonging to her uncle, where we spent lazy days before returning. All this particular day we had spent some distance from the
farmhouse, by a quiet and sheltered tidal lagoon, shut off from
the roar of the Tasman by barriers of rock and hills of sand. We
collected mussels and pipis in flax kits, swam naked in the heat
of noon, picnicked in the shade of a crimson-blooming pohutu-
kawa grove, and sunbathed the afternoon away. In the cool of
dusk we were making our way slowly home along the crumpled,
crumbling coastline, pausing to rest now and then.

'Yes,' she repeated, plucking at blades of grass when I was silent. 'What will you do?'

'Well,' I said, 'I expect I shall study and learn and—'

'But I mean,' she said, 'afterwards.'

'Well,' I said uncertainly, 'I expect I shall travel about a bit. Mother wants me to see as much of England as I can.'

'But you can't do that all the time,' Ruia pointed out, very sensibly. 'You going to live there? You going to work there?'

I was slow answering. Mother had never been very explicit on those points. 'I expect I shall,' I said.

She was puzzled. 'Won't you get lonely? Won't you want to come home?'

'But England is my home,' I said.

'What you talking about? Home is where your folks are. That's what I always thought.' She paused. 'What about your Mum, anyhow? What about her when she hasn't got you, eh?'

'I expect she'll come and see me,' I said. 'For holidays and things.'

'For holidays and things?' echoed Ruia incredulously. 'But England's a long way. It costs money to go there. A lot of money.' Even Ruia had the imagination necessary to see that. 'I reckon your Mum must really be pretty rich, that's all.'

But she made no impression; my fancy had already darted away. 'Perhaps you can come too, for a trip,' I said.

'And stay with me,' I added grandly. 'I shall have a house in Kensington.'

Ruia laughed. We picked up our kits of mussels and pipis, and went on our way again.

It was during that same long summer that we first talked about Ed Larkin. Ed was the youngest of the Larkin boys. The others had gone away to get education, had found manhood, worked for a while, and sooner or later seemed to tire of the city, for they returned, one after the other, to the tranquil Polynesian life of the farm. They farmed after a fashion, fished, played football, drank beer, went to country dances, and dissected Social Credit and talked Communism with their father on Sundays. Ed was young, vigorous, and studious, a contrast to his lethargic brothers; that summer he finished high school, and was preparing to begin

a law course at Auckland university. Ed was always friendly
with the Pateras; in childhood he often squatted, along
with the other children and myself, around Kiwi Patera and
listened to his stories. With the pride and self-knowledge of adolescence, he grew a little aloof and away from us all while he
attended high school. But at school dances, that final year, he
began to notice Ruia again. They often danced together, and
once he took Ruia outside to sit some distance from the hall, on
a hill looking down on the town and the interwoven tidal rivers.
If they kissed and petted, Ruia never told me; she only told me
how they sat there together not speaking, arm around arm,
watching the scattered lights and shimmering water in the blue
evening.

'I think maybe I love him,' Ruia said, as we lay once more
upon our favourite high cliff-top above red rocks, yellow sand,
and blue sea.

And so we talked of Ed Larkin.

Ed was tall and stringy, fair-haired and brown-faced. He wore
glasses sometimes, mostly when he read, which gave him a
scholarly appearance. He was captain of the high school's first
fifteen in his final year, and played cricket for the town side as a
star spin bowler. In the weeks before he went away to Auckland
Ruia and I often used to watch him play; we admired the casual
way he polished the ball against his shirt and spun it from hand
to hand before he flicked back his hair and made his slow,
ambling run up to the wicket. We could not foresee the time
when the ball which curled so slowly, so accurately, through the
air would become instead a grenade; or the time when one such
grenade, inexpert in construction, would blow off his hands and
most of his head on some Middle Eastern battlefield. It was mid-
summer, warm and blue, and the players were white on a green
field, the beer passed about in the shade of the pavilion, and
families lunched in and about the marquee down under the
willows by the river; and there were mild explosions of applause
for Ed Larkin when he took another wicket.

Ed came back for vacations in May and August. Once or twice
he took Ruia to country dances, but always they were along with
a crowd. By this time, however, Ruia was generally acknowledged

as Ed's girl. All this happened at a remove from me, since I was still only fifteen and in my second year at high school, and there would be plenty of time, in Mother's view, for dances when I was older. To find out about Ed I had to question Ruia. He was dissatisfied with university, and at Christmas he returned to announce that he despised law as a profession, and was now going down to the South Island, to study medicine at Otago university. He took Ruia out again, though not regularly, during that Christmas vacation; and the Saturday night before he left for Otago he kissed her goodbye. I had difficulty persuading Ruia to admit that he had; for she was growing more and more reticent about Ed and herself.

That year Ruia should have gone away herself, to Training College at Auckland, but some small initial difficulty over admission decided her to leave it till the next year, and to spend the intervening time helping her mother on the farm. Ed was too far away now to return for mid-year vacations; Ruia wrote several letters to him and once received one in reply, written about the middle of the second term. He said he was well and liked Dunedin. He hoped Ruia was well.

That was the year I first remember people talking about men called Mussolini and Hitler; and about another, more obscure, called Franco. But only Father, who told Kiwi Patera that international bankers were plotting a new war, and the Larkin family became really excited about what was happening on the other side of the world. The eldest of the Larkin boys, who had briefly been a member of the Communist Party in Auckland after the unemployed riots in 1932, left his family island of quiet in uproar when he went to fight in Spain. Mrs Benjamin, who thought Franco a Christian gentleman, thereafter avoided the Larkins, whom she had always thought subversive anyway.

It was the year I turned sixteen, and Ruia eighteen. My birthday was notable only for the reason that for the first time I saw fit to argue with Mother about being forced to invite Millicent Benjamin to my party. Ruia's party was notable because of Ruia. Kiwi Patera, deciding that this, perhaps the last birthday party she might have at home for a long while, deserved special celebration, called in relatives and friends from miles around. The party was in early December; and the summer was already warm.

Father took me; Mother pleaded a headache, and remained at home. We broke through a periphery of whooping children and pushed through an overflow of guests to get into the house; then Kiwi took us, and steered us to Ruia. She was dressed in a gay Mexican skirt, gaudy colours woven on black, and a crisp white blouse; a simple silver necklet lay against her dark skin. Wine-glass in hand, she stood erect and contained, with the assurance of a woman, among a crush of young men. She made me aware of my own inadequacy, made me feel my own incoherence of poise and gesture. Suddenly I could have fled from my first adult party; fled from her, as from a stranger. But as soon as she saw us she broke away from her admirers.

Kiwi led Father to the keg; and I was left, bewildered, with this new, dazzling creature. She took me aside and told me glee-fully that Ed had finished his exams, and was on his way north for the vacation; in fact, he was expected that day, but so far there was no sign of him. The Larkins were all at the party; but they had left a note at the homestead in case he should arrive.

The old Patera house shuddered with noise and movement; the floorboards creaked and bent under the slamming feet of the dancers. The Potoki boys hammered the piano and banged the drums; Keith Larkin played the saxophone. Kiwi rolled in new kegs from outside. People were still arriving from the other side of town : the newcomers drank to Ruia. She was caught, dance after dance, by eager young men. I sipped cautiously at beer, and found it bitter. And about midnight, long after Mother had instructed Father to bring me home, Ed Larkin appeared, still dusty and red-eyed from travel. His appearance was quiet, almost unnoticed. He already had a glass of beer in his hand when I first saw him standing quietly in the doorway; he was looking across the room at Ruia. Eyes brilliant, hair cascading, she was giving herself entirely to the dance, to the discovered rhythm of her body. Probably I was the only person in that room to notice Ed. He was changed. He seemed older, taller; he wore an open-neck check shirt and a zip-up jacket. The expression on his face seemed to me very odd; but only because then I knew too little about people to recognize it. He stood there watching, waiting, altogether patient and sure of himself; and when the time came, when the music paused, he moved across the room to Ruia.

At three in the morning guests were beginning to depart; launches were throbbing on the creek, and horses thudded off into the night. Father belatedly remembered his promise to Mother. 'Time to go, girlie,' he said, fetching my coat from a darkened room where one of the Potoki boys had pitched a girl, in unequivocal fashion, upon the bed. At the front door we found Kiwi dismayed. Ruia was not there to say goodbye to her guests. No one knew where she had gone. Someone had seen her on the verandah with Ed Larkin not long after midnight; then she vanished.

I heard later that they did not re-appear until breakfast time, when they came walking down from the hills hand in hand, as if an early morning stroll were, for them, as natural as the day. I say that I heard advisedly, for it was not Ruia who told me; I did not see much of her that summer. She was rarely home when I called. And not once did we ride out, as we always had in summers before, to her uncle's farm on the coast. She was with Ed Larkin.

I also heard, in the usual way one heard things along the creek, that Ed and Ruia were near to being engaged. Towards the end of the school holidays Mother prevailed upon me to accept Mrs Benjamin's invitation to holiday with Millicent at a cottage in the Bay of Islands. Millicent, lipsticked and perfumed, dragged me out on expeditions to attract teen-age boys also on holiday. When I returned Ruia had already gone to begin her studies at Auckland Training College. After I was home a day or two Ed left for Dunedin. No one knew anything about an engagement.

That was the beginning of the year of Munich; but, so far as I was concerned, it was the year I finished high school and, above all, the year I learned the truth.

I was not, after all, going to England.

'You might as well know it,' Father said angrily one day in the middle of the year when I had ridden out with him to mend some boundary fences. 'Your mother's been filling your head with a lot of damn nonsense for years.'

He calmed quickly. I felt the anger had been more directed at himself than at anyone, or anything. 'She doesn't like to admit that she's beaten,' he added quietly.

But it was Father who had been beaten. The land had sapped him, thinned him to dry, lean middle-age; the farm, he realized now, would never be the one he wanted. Already erosion had claimed the land he had taken from the bush in the four frantic years after the war. The pastures were still not rich, but sparse and hungry. The farm would never run a large herd. Always there would be the monthly struggle on small cream-cheques.

'You'll have to face it,' he said. 'The damn idea's always been impossible.'

'Then why,' I cried, 'haven't you ever said anything?'

He finished working the wire-strainer, and surveyed the line of the fence. 'Because,' he said, 'I wanted her to have something— even if it was only a dream of something she couldn't have.' He finished with the fence, and we walked back to the horses. 'And once I thought it mightn't be so impossible myself,' he added.

'There's never been much for her here, you know,' he said. 'I've often thought it was a mistake, bringing her—' He checked himself suddenly; and, tight-lipped, swung up into the saddle. It was too difficult to quickly dismiss twenty years, and a marriage.

'Anyway,' he said, 'forget it.'

The hills were bleak that day, I remember, and the sun was watery in a grey sky. The creek was swollen and ran a muddy brown. I felt shrunken and defeated, at one with the misery of the winter landscape; I seemed cheated of myself, of all the sixteen years of my life. Everything had been taken, suddenly, and nothing given back.

It was some time before I could bring myself to talk to Mother. I expected a painful scene. Instead she was so calm, so philosophical, that I was too astonished to be angry. After all, she had months, years, to prepare herself for this eventuality; and, moreover, an excellent excuse was near at hand. 'It's probably all for the best, dear,' she said 'There might be a war, you know. While things are uncertain it's better that you stay here.'

Sitting on our verandah idle, somehow emptied of myself, I watched the slow change of the seasons, saw the colours of spring begin to freshen the hills. At school I worked without effort, and sat matriculation. I knew I had done satisfactorily; well enough to have passed. But it seemed pointless : it did not concern me, one way or the other. I was oddly friendless too. Millicent came and went, prattling about what she intended to do when she went to Auckland next year. She was in love with the son of a Waikato racehorse owner. There was a letter from Ruia. She did not mention Ed, but this was not significant, since she had been secretive about him a long while now. I replied to say that I too might be going to Auckland next year; I would stay with my uncle, the watersider, and if Mother and Father could manage it, I would study at university. I wrote these things down coldly, as if they were facts about another person, not myself.

I was aware of the strangeness, the lassitude that spent itself in vague yearnings; I wandered through bush lit with rata flower, and meditated by the creek. Change had overtaken me mysteriously; my childish plumpness was gone. But even that seemed somehow not my responsibility.

I had no boy friend. But at the end-of-year school dance there was a boy who seems, in memory, strangely faceless; he danced with me, and I allowed him to lead me outside. We drove in his car to the top of the hill above the town, and parked off the road. I remembered how Ed and Ruia had escaped from the dance in the same way, to look down at the lights and the silvery water. I wondered what Ruia had felt then; for I felt nothing.

He was very nervous. He offered me wine. He held me clumsily and kissed me. It all seemed an awkward business. I was afraid of crumpling my frock, and smearing my lipstick.

I feel absolutely nothing, I told myself. And we drove back to the dance.

Summer came, and with it Ruia. But I had hardly time to see her before I was whisked off to Auckland for Christmas. Mother had judged the time convenient to discuss my future stay in the city with my uncle, who had just acquired a pleasant beach cottage at Takapuna. Kiwi and his sons looked after the herd while we were away. Ruia, I gathered, had enjoyed her first year at Training College; again she did not mention Ed. But I still presumed this was because they were to be engaged soon.

Father returned to the farm first. Mother and I followed, two days before New Year. The first morning home I walked over to the Patera farm; though the sun was not yet high in the sky, the day was thick with heat. I met Ruia just emerging from the house. She had a towel slung over her shoulder. 'I'm going to cool off,' she said. 'Coming?' She went back into the house and fetched another towel. We walked to the back of the farm, to a place where a fresh-water creek spilt down terraces of rock to form deep, clear pools of dawdling water; it was a pretty place, set about with bush and fern, and clamorous with bellbirds. As we undressed Ruia asked how I'd enjoyed Auckland. I asked, more pointedly, how she'd enjoyed Christmas, since I knew Ed had been back some time.

'Oh,' she said vaguely, 'it was all right.'

We were lying naked now, like two long lazing sunlit fish, near the surface of the water, rolling gently, from side to side, in the cool sway of the circling currents, so that now and then our flanks and our shoulders touched. The sky was vivid, the air motionless. The drooping leaves of the nikau palms sprinkled a confetti of sunlight on the fern and moss of the banks above us.

'Have you seen much of Ed?' I said finally.

'I expect I'll be seeing him tomorrow night,' she said. 'At the barbecue. You'll be coming, won't you, Bridie?'

'Yes,' I said. It was only afterwards I realized she had not answered my question.

She slid away from me, turned sideways, and wriggled to her feet. Water showering from her dark skin, she waded up to the waterfall at the end of the pool; she stood there erect and smiling, the diamonds of spray glittering down her. She seemed very cheerful. She looked down at me.

'You've grown up, Bridie,' she said. 'You've got a good figure now.' She laughed softly, as if the thought had just come to her. 'You got a boy friend yet?'

'Not really.' I still found the memory of that clumsy night in the car an ugly thing.

She laughed, that soft laugh again, and splashed down beside me. Her long hair fanned loose and silky in the water, flowing across my shoulder.

'What is it like,' I asked cautiously, 'when boys kiss you, and things?'

'Oh,' she said. 'It's funny.'

'Sometimes I wish I knew. Sometimes I don't think I'll ever know.'

She agitated the water gently with her long legs. 'Oh,' she said. 'You'll know all right. You wait till you get to the city. All the boys will be after you there. Wait and see.'

'Were they after you?'

'They would have been. If I'd let them.'

'Didn't you because of Ed?'

'Yes,' she said, and was suddenly reticent again.

'Anyhow,' I said quickly, to end the silence, 'I don't think they'll be after me.'

'Why?' she said. 'You scared, Bridie? Why shouldn't they be after you?' She touched me lightly on the breast with a tentative finger, and withdrew it quickly. 'You're pretty, Bridie. And you mustn't ever be scared. Ever.'

In the hot day, floating weightless on the cool water, I felt, in place of apathy, a curious excitement begin to stir my body. Ruia was crooning softly to herself; her eyes were closed. A new listless breeze rattled the nikaus; a chittering fantail flickered in and out of sunlight.

Then I was afraid. I slipped from the water and began to towel myself. Ruia, eyes open in surprise, followed. We talked again.

'So,' she said, 'you're not going to England now.'

'No.'

'And you're not the English girl any more.'

'I don't suppose so.'

'Don't look so sad,' she said. 'Is it very terrible, being a New Zealander like me?'

'I don't know.'

'How do you mean you don't know?'

'Well,' I said miserably, 'I don't really know what it feels like yet.'

'Then you better hurry, eh?' she laughed.

We dressed and walked downhill, hand in hand, along a narrow bush track. It was time for me to go home for dinner. We said goodbye and arranged to meet and go to the New Year barbecue together. I was surprised that Ed wasn't taking her, but I said nothing. After all, their arrangements always did seem terribly casual; there was nothing unusual about him promising to meet her there.

The barbecue was held on a sandy spit about a mile, by water, from the place where the town met the tidal creeks; there the creeks became sea, and the sea swelled out to the harbour heads. It was chosen first because it was a respectable distance from town, and beer could be sold there illegally and the local policeman kept pacified; and second because it was actually a very pleasant place.

The moon was rising as we arrived, and there were fires lit all along the beach, under the pohutukawas. Parties with rugs and beer and guitars were strewn in the gay yellow light. Here and there sucking pigs turned, crackling, over glowing pits. There was even a crude dance-floor erected for the night a little back from the beach. There were parties spread there too, in the shadowy light, on the sparse grass, among the lupins and the dunes.

Ruia and I wove in and out around the fires, saying hello. We met some of her cousins who had come down from an up-river timber mill, and who insisted we sit with them a while. They were rowdy, good-natured boys. When we declined their beer they triumphantly produced some sherry from a Dalmatian vineyard which they had kept aside for just this possibility. We sang with them and they took us to dance.

'Why you no with t'at pakeha fullar Ed tonight?' one of the boys asked Ruia, throwing an affectionate arm around her. 'What's a matter? Don' you like him no more, eh?'

'When you goen to be te big-time schoolteacher?' asked

spin her round in wild, stampeding dances. Her hair tangled down her face, and her blouse became undone at the top. She was barefoot now, and her red skirt and white petticoat swirled about her legs. The circle had grown about our fire; there was a chanting, a twirling, a clapping of hands. The bare feet stomped the sand, and Ruia was flung from partner to partner. Sometimes she was lost in shadow; then she emerged, high-stepping and erect, head snapped back and body thrust forward, colours boiling and flashing in the orange of the dying fire. Always there were new arms to receive her, new partners to spin her onwards.

Then it was midnight, and the dance was joined: it became confusion. We danced till we were exhausted; until, dropping coupled to the sand, the boys claimed their New Year kisses. I picked myself up, retrieved my dignity, and saw Ruia still dancing. When she fell, at last, there were willing arms to receive her; and again she was thrown, hot and full-lipped, from partner to partner, this time enacting with each a parody of passion. I was bewildered and a little horrified.

From the platform above the beach voices still proclaimed the birth of the year: it was nineteen thirty-nine.

And then Ruia was suddenly in my arms, and weeping.

We were given a ride home in a launch which belonged to a young married couple who lived at the top of the creek. We left early, soon after midnight, and the lights and singing were lost across the shining water. It was not cold, yet Ruia still shivered against me as we held to each other at the back of the launch. The wine, and a sadness for Ruia, still sang in my head. Perhaps too there was a faint premonition of the time when we would watch the boys swing, bayonets flashing, down crowded, streamer-strewn streets towards the grey waiting ships. For our youth was ending even more quickly than we knew: fires of another kind would greet the years ahead.

The launch nudged up the creek, waves washing the wiry mangroves in the moonlight. The Patera jetty came into sight, round a turning. Ruia stiffened. 'No,' she whispered. 'I don't want to go home.' She was afraid of being alone. The solution seemed perfectly simple. 'Come home with me,' I said. She held

another. 'When you goen to start given all te kids te whack, eh?'

'One and one are two,' a couple started to chant. 'Two an two are four . . .'

'One an one are three!' cried another. 'You don' know your sums, ehoa. Don' you know t'at one an one makes te little one. Ehoa, you don' know nothing at all.' He guffawed.

'I don' t'ink you like t'at pakeha fullar no more, eh?' said the first. 'I t'ink you like t'is fullar best, eh?' He tightened his arm around her possessively.

'I like everyone best,' Ruia said non-committally, her eyes dancing mischievously in the firelight.

'You better watch out, ehoa, or she be given you te whack.'

'How you know, boy? How you don' know he might like Ruia given him te wackety-whack. Oho, maybe he like te wackety-whack from Ruia. I wouldn't mind her given *me* te wackety-whack.'

There was no sign of Ed. That was when I had my first feeling of something wrong. It was getting late, after eleven, when I at last had a chance to ask Ruia, 'What time did Ed say he'd be here?'

'He didn't actually say,' she answered vaguely.

'But he's coming?'

'I expect he is,' she said, even more vaguely.

'How do you mean—you expect?' At that moment I felt an urgent desire to shake her, to shake away her slowness and stupidity about a thing of such very great importance.

'He's been with his family ever since he got back,' she said finally.

So that was the truth of it, I saw suddenly; she hadn't seen him at all. She had been confidently waiting out the days for him to come to her once more, in his casual fashion. Only this time he hadn't come. I was silent. There was nothing to say.

In a little while I wandered off and found Keith Larkin on the dance-floor, where he was playing the saxophone. 'Ed?' he said. He looked at me curiously. 'He was here early, but then he shot off back to town in the launch. Had to meet someone off the night bus. Why? You want to see him or something?'

'No,' I said. 'It's nothing.'

It wasn't long after that when I heard the launch. Its wake, phosphorescent in the moonlight, was chalked erratically across the sea. Presently the engine quieted, it drifted a while, and then an anchor splashed. A dinghy slid out from the shadow of the launch, and I saw Ed was rowing a passenger ashore. Ruia, beside me, had grown very still and quiet. The dinghy beached some distance from us: the two people, Ed and his passenger, were hidden behind one of the fires.

I turned to Ruia urgently. 'Hadn't you better go and see him?'

'I expect I'll see him in a little while,' she said placidly.

She began to annoy me again. There was a lot of noise coming from that part of the beach where the dinghy had been drawn up. I heard Ed's name shouted several times.

'For heaven's sake,' I cried. 'You haven't seen him for a year. And you just want to sit there.' But she said nothing. If he came, her mild face seemed to say, he came; if he didn't, he didn't. She was not the same girl who had floated beside me in the pool yesterday, and told me not to be afraid.

I became impatient. The noise drifted off towards the dance-floor. I went angrily across the sand, away from Ruia. Looking back, I saw her half-risen to her feet. Confused, shamefaced suddenly, she followed, tripping and sliding in the sand in her haste to catch up with me. She clung to my arm as we went up to the dance-floor. The crowd was thick there. Then I felt her grip tighten on my arm: she saw Ed first. He stood in the centre of a laughing group. His shirt was unbuttoned down his chest, his trousers were rolled above his bare ankles, and his hair was awry. He swayed on his feet: he was very drunk. People shook his hand, slapped him on the back. He smiled slow-wittedly as he accepted their congratulations.

And I saw the reason why Ruia might wait, but Ed would never come to her, not ever again.

The girl was dressed in a tight black sweater and dark slacks. She was short and blonde, not particularly pretty. She had an affected voice and a hoarse laugh. Holding a glass of beer in one hand and a cigarette in the other, she seemed entirely at ease; on the third finger of her left hand an engagement ring glittered. She was talking to Ed's brother, the one who had been to Spain.

'I've been so keen to meet you,' she said. 'Ever since Ed fi[...] me about you. I was terribly thrilled when he told me I'[...] you along with the family when I came up for New Y[...] course I've always been too busy passing exams to be [...] Party myself, but I was all on your side over the Spain [...] I imagine you must find all this rather limited after all th[...] ment you had over there. Tell me, do you think there's [...] be a war?'

'There's always been one,' he said shortly. 'Some way [...] Can I get you another beer?'

I didn't like her: I didn't like her, or her tight sweat[...] zipped slacks, or the way she held her beer and her ciga[...] such ease. She was a stranger, a foreigner speaking [...] language.

People were still jollying Ed, shaking his hand, sl[...] back. Before Ruia could slip away unseen, one of the [...] saw her.

'Hey, Ed!' he cried drunkenly. 'Come an say hull[...] You mus' say hullo to Ruia.' Ruia, still clutching [...] away. The Potoki boy led Ed towards her. The cro[...] very silent: they wheeled about, forming a long pa[...] staring faces. At the other end of it the short, bl[...] slacks looked on with curiosity. Ed shambled up t[...] looked at her. In the silence someone giggled. I [...] fluttering at the corner of Ruia's mouth.

'Hullo, Ruia,' Ed said at last. His eyes were quit[...]

Then he backed away, releasing the tension, grin[...] and calling for another drink. Someone announc[...] dance platform that it was just thirty minutes to mid[...] back to our place on the beach blindly, stumbling [...] not daring to look at Ruia. The boys, oblivious to v[...] pened, were scattered about the fire, eating pork [...] more beer. They must have thought we had esca[...] they received us with jubilation. Prancing about u[...] wine, urged us to dance. I emptied most of m[...] sand; Ruia drank hers. Her eyes were perfectly c[...] lingly bright; too bright. Whenever I looked a[...] smiled and raised her glass. She drank more, a[...]

to me gratefully, forlorn and strangely flimsy, as I called to our
friends to keep on going, past the Patera jetty; to our own. Little
distance separated the two jetties : soon I was helping Ruia up on
to the rickety landing, and we were waving goodbye as the
launch chattered away up the creek.

We turned and walked towards the homestead, through the
silvered bush, and over the blonde grass; the nikau palms and
cabbage-tree groves stood vivid in the night. The moon was cold
and high. Everything glistened, faintly luminous, and larger than
life. We walked slowly, resting now and then, over a world become oddly unfamiliar, unreal. Animals stood frozen and statu-
esque in the drenching white light; cicadas sang thinly; a
morepork called from up the creek.

We crept across the creaking verandah and through the french
windows into my room. Quietly we undressed and slipped into
my bed while the world outside blazed with the pale fire of the
moon. Ruia lay quiet, breathing evenly. She no longer wept; she
seemed almost to have become herself again. But something—the
deadness of Ed's eyes, Ruia's dance, the voices calling, the fires
vanishing across the sea—had disturbed me, and left a profound
ache of disquiet : it was my turn, now, for tears. The sobs rose
huge in my throat. I wept for no reason and every reason. For
Ed gone, for England gone, for the years betrayed. Ruia's arms
slid around me.

'What is it?' she whispered.

She took my face between her hands. 'What is it?' she repeated. 'What is it, quiet one?'

But it was no use. The storm had come at last : the storm,
and the shelter of Ruia's arms.

Awakening was a slow sliding upwards through liquid layers of
web-thin sleep, a tender surfacing in a strangely new world.
I could hear birds singing in the bush. I loosened Ruia's arms
and slid from the bed gently, so as not to disturb her. Then I
padded across the floor to the open windows and, suddenly conscious of my long bare limbs, gave myself to the morning. I felt
perfectly calm; and bruised with a kind of wonder.

It was the hour before dawn, the hour before the first sunrise of the year. The turning earth unrolled a pastel sky. The moon, and the milky transparent night, were gone; already fresh, soft colours lighted the land. The dew scented the morning, and the air was cool and still. A stranger to myself, I had a longing to walk barefoot, clean-limbed, through green forest where clear waters fell: to tread softly banks of moss dappled with new sun-light: to bed in silver fern with the slender fronds tickling my cheeks: to sleep flesh to flesh with the warm earth.

I felt an immense peace, a drowsiness of spirit within a tranquillity of body; and when the moment of revelation overtook me, I felt faint, and I reached out, to the side of the window, and held myself steady.

I should never go to England.

I should never go to England; and I was glad.

And I was no longer afraid.

At first I thought I only imagined it: but then I heard, clearly across the calm morning, a launch idling up the creek, guitars strumming, and voices singing. The Potoki boys were only just returning home from the barbecue. As their launch passed below the farm, the distant voices rose in flawless Maori harmony.

I turned slowly from the window and walked across the room, as if in a haunted dream in which all that was old and known—all the paraphernalia of my seventeen years, the pictures, the books, the clothes, the brushes arranged before the mirror—had risen vivid and marvellously strange. Pausing, standing in the centre of the floor, I felt my heart hammer in its cage of cooled flesh. Everything swam, settled, solidified again.

I went to the bed. Ruia was still asleep, her arm curled limp where my body was printed on the sheet. I bent towards her and lifted her arm and kissed her on the cheek. She stirred and murmured but did not waken.

Then I lay beside her and waited for the day.

AFTER THE DEPRESSION

THE NIGHT had come and almost gone again; now, when the rough sweep of his large hand gashed the mist of the carriage window, he was able to see, beyond steep yellow clay-cuttings crested with damp green bush, the brightening grey of the morning sky. His view was obscured for a moment as steam from the engine, shredding and spinning, gusted past the window. But he had seen enough : he sighed, stretched, yawned, and sat back in his seat.

The guard, his cap awry, picked his way through the swaying second-class carriage, carefully avoiding the pillows, heads and legs which jutted into the narrow, dirty aisle. He called the name of the next station, a one-minute stop. His voice in the dim, sleeping carriage was loud, without apology for intrusion. There was an angry mutter from one awakened passenger; but the rest, apart from the tall man stiff in his seat, stirred sleepily, adjusted their pillows, and slept again. The guard left the carriage, slamming the door after him : and once more there was only the sound of iron wheels racketing on uneven rails, and teacups and saucers rattling beneath the seats.

The tall man, who had sat sleepless through the travelling night, gashed the healed mist of the window again. But his view of the dawning sky was gone; in its place was a swift, gloomy blur of thick bush tangling close to the track. Weak spots of light flickered on his face : a face with a coarse, grainy quality; the spare flesh bleak and unhealthy. The features, though, were firm, the eyebrows dark and heavy, the eyes sharp blue, the nose slightly hooked, the lips dry and pale; there was a faint blackish stubble on his thin, pointed chin. He wore a tight black suit that had probably been too small even when it was purchased from a cheap ready-made store six years before; it was frayed at the

39

cuffs and food-stained on the lapels. His thick, broken-nailed fingers and flattened thumbs had by degrees loosened his brown, imitation-silk tie: it hung askew, proclaiming its unfamiliarity with his sinewy neck. The top button of his shirt was undone, and the twisted collar grubby with travel.

He occupied a double seat, his back to the engine. He hesitated a moment before waking the woman and child who slept in the seat opposite.

The woman was upright, her head against the window: a woollen jersey packed between the window and her head served to cushion her from the monotonous violence of the train's motion. Her face was young and pale, verging on plumpness; it quivered with the movement, and her mouth had fallen open. The lapels of her shabby grey coat were drawn up to cover her white throat. Her figure was short and mannish, and her dumpy legs barely touched the floor. The child, cocooned in a faded tartan blanket, slept with his head against her thigh. He had the fresh, sexless face of a three-year-old; the features girlish and delicate, like those of the woman. A cream beret had slipped to the back of the head, releasing a small cascade of uncut crinkly blonde hair, streaked with brown.

The man reached forward, finally, and touched the woman gently on the arm. She woke with a jerk, her eyes fluttering open: finding herself in the gloomy, jolting carriage, she was, for a moment, bewildered. Then she saw the man and smiled sleepily.

'Nearly there,' he said. 'We're nearly there.'

'There?' said the woman, vaguely. 'Already?'

'It's morning,' he said. 'Look out the window.'

'Ian,' the woman whispered. 'Ian, wake up.'

The child woke and murmured. The woman stood, replaced the lapels of her coat, shook out wrinkles, and bent to the child. Uncovering him, she folded the blanket and put it away.

The train, hammering along a flat stretch of track now, had begun to slow. While she whispered placatingly, the woman fastened shoes on the child; the man removed luggage from the rack above their heads. There was a hoarse whistle: the train shuddered with a prolonged clashing of couplings, and was still.

The three descended from the stuffy warmth of the carriage

into the chill of a sunless, misty morning; they were the only passengers to leave the train. His thick dark coat flapping obstinately about his legs, the man carried two heavy suitcases alongside the stationary, hissing carriages. The woman followed, carrying a small case in one hand, and guiding the slow child with the other. Their feet made crunching sounds on the raw gravel.

The station consisted of a square, broken patch of concrete, a set of hand-operated signals; and a dully reddish waiting-room, an uninhabited box of feeble yellow light. The buildings of the settlement around were dark and obscure in the mist.

'It's early yet,' the man observed, as he set down the suitcases in the waiting-room. 'We can wait here.'

The room smelt of soot and urine. They sat on hard wooden seats, the child's feet dangling above the filthy, paper-strewn floor. The woman blanketed the child and drew the coat-lapels over her throat again. The man sat hunched forward, his large veiny hands dangling fidgety between his knees : he looked at his hands, turning them over for inspection, as if seeking some answer there.

'It'll be all right this time,' he said at last. 'I know it will.'

The woman was silent.

'I got a good feeling about it,' he said, still looking at his hands.

The woman remained silent. The child was once again asleep against her thigh. The man became annoyed with looking at his hands, and suddenly thrust them deep into the pockets of his coat. He discovered, as if by accident, a tin of tobacco and began, laboriously, to make a thin cigarette.

The engine whistled : the shrill, imperious sound echoed and re-echoed against hills hidden in the mist. There was a renewed hissing and lurching, and a long line of unlit carriage windows streamed past the waiting-room.

A solitary railway employee, walking homeward, looked into the room. He was puffy-eyed; and under his railway uniform a pyjama-top showed. 'Anything I can do for you people?' he asked.

The man looked up. His eyes were sharp and hostile. 'We're just waiting here,' he said aggressively. 'No law against waiting, is there? That's what this place is here for, isn't it?'

The railwayman was startled. He blinked. 'Don't get me wrong, mate. Just wondering if I could help, that's all.'

'You can't,' the man said.

'Strike me dead,' the railwayman said. 'No need to bite me head off, mate.' He retreated, still astonished, and strode off; his feet crackled away into the quiet, grey morning. They were alone again.

'He was only trying to be helpful,' the woman suggested timidly. 'You could of been nicer to him.'

'Helpful?' The man laughed. 'Nicer?' He stopped laughing suddenly. 'I pick his sort a mile. Bloody snoopers everywhere.'

The woman shrank from him. The child stirred and murmured.

'Sorry,' the man said. He seemed dismayed. 'You're right. I don't know.' He shook his head. 'There wasn't no need for me to go crook like that. I'm just a bit jumpy about everything. I didn't sleep. I suppose he might of been all right.' He drew hard on his cigarette, but it had burnt out. He threw it away in disgust, then reached in his pocket, took out a soiled paper bag, and tore it open. There were three stale-looking refreshment room sandwiches inside. He offered them to the woman. 'You hungry?'

'We can wait a while,' she said. 'You eat.'

'I'm not hungry neither.'

The woman looked sick with tiredness; she touched his arm hesitantly. 'Where are we?' she asked softly. 'Do we have to go far?'

'This place here's a timber-milling outfit,' he said, pointing out the door to where mist still curtained the landscape. 'The mine's a couple of miles or so from here. There's a road down to the mine, and a railway track. Don't know how the locos run from here down to the mine. That's what we got to find out.'

'You could of asked that man then,' the woman pointed out cautiously. 'He could of told you how the locos run.'

The man sighed. 'I could of,' he agreed. 'I just wasn't thinking. When I seen him come along I was thinking of other things.'

The woman seemed altogether satisfied by his reply, by his admission that he had been wrong. It was an event of a rare kind, and she could afford satisfaction. He sat forward, looking out the door, thinking of his other things again.

The light outside was now quite bright. The mist, retreating from the settlement, fled up the sunlit flanks of the hills. In the waiting-room, the child slept against the woman, and the woman against the man; the man was awake. He at last reached for a sandwich and began to eat it slowly and thoughtfully. His movement woke the woman, then the child.

She took the child to a tap outside the waiting-room and washed his face with a dampened handkerchief. Then she set the beret squarely on his head and led him back into the room. She took a bottle from her case and poured some cream-flecked, sour-smelling milk into a peanut-butter jar that now saw service of a different kind. She gave the child the milk and a sandwich. There was one sandwich left. She looked at her husband, then at the child; and her hand darted out, as if of its own volition, and carried the sandwich quickly to her mouth. She ate almost guiltily.

The man stood. 'I'll find out what time a loco runs down to the mine,' he announced. He went out of the room, across the tracks, and into the settlement, walking with an abrupt, jerky stride. Presently he returned.

'There's a loco comes up about ten,' he said. 'It don't go back again till about one. That's five hours yet.'

'We can wait,' the woman said patiently; she fingered back her limp, wisping hair.

'Wait?' he said. 'I'm sick and tired of waiting. It drives you up the wall. We can walk to the mine. It's not far.'

'Walk?' the woman said faintly.

'All right?' he said briskly, but gave her no time to answer. He took up the two large suitcases. 'Let's go.'

They walked over the tracks and through the settlement. Along a single stony road, pooled with rainwater, there was a store and post office combined in an ungainly wooden building with unpainted weatherboards; one or two early-morning loungers watched the three strangers go past. Further along there was a string of old houses, knotting at the end into a cluster of ramshackle single men's huts. The timber mill, which stood at the end of the settlement, was already alive with grinding, tearing noises.

'Hell-holes, them places,' the man observed.

'They couldn't be much worse than mines,' the woman said; but he didn't seem to hear.

An articulated timber-truck, unloaded and jerking, rumbled past, splattering them with mud. The man spat after it. 'Could of given us a lift,' he said.

'He mightn't of been going the same way as us,' the woman observed.

'How does he know till he's asked us?' he demanded. He spat again, at nothing in particular this time.

'Anyhow,' she said, 'there wouldn't of been room for the three of us in it. Not in the cab.' She was right in defending the driver; she knew she was right. But this time, she knew also, he would not admit it. So she added appeasingly, 'It doesn't matter much, does it? You said it wasn't far.'

'No. It's not far.'

They walked in silence. His pace, even with the two heavy suitcases weighting him, was too brisk for her and the child. Soon he was several yards ahead.

'Wait,' she called, her voice mild with an old despair.

He sat on his cases and waited. She expected irritation in his face, but found only concern. 'I'm sorry,' he said. 'I keep forgetting him.' He pointed to the child. 'Let's have a rest.'

The child's face was still sleepy, and bewildered; the woman sat him on her case. 'Where we going?' he said.

'I told you before, sonny,' the woman said, sighing. 'We're going to a new place.' She was tired of the question.

'Why?'

'Shush, Ian,' she said with annoyance. Then, repenting, she straightened the cream beret on the small head.

'Why?' the child repeated.

'Because,' she said, raising her eyes in appeal to the man. 'Because Daddy's taking us.'

'Why Daddy taking us?'

The woman didn't answer: she didn't look at the man. He knelt beside the child; the child surveyed him gravely. 'We're going to a new place because it'll be a better place,' he said simply. 'That's why.'

The sun warmed the pale sky, lighting a landscape stripped and harsh. On the upper slopes of the hills, where here and there limestone outcrops stood gaunt against the sky, were long-dead trees, tangled and whitened, and giant ulcers of erosion scabbed with weeping crusts of clay and papa; on lower ground lank wire fences straggled about small, pine-sheltered farmhouses. The pasture was a dead green colour, and loose-bellied cows grazed. The road unwound slowly, a thin strip of clay and bluish metal edged with ti-tree and gorse. They came, at length, to a crossroad, and a signpost which said: FERNDALE MINE 2/$\frac{1}{2}$ M.

'I thought you said it wasn't far,' the woman protested.

The man didn't argue. 'It was a bit further than I thought, that's all.'

'We should of waited. We should of waited for a loco.'

The man seemed to agree. 'I just wanted to get there. I just don't like hanging round.' He paused. 'I didn't think it'd of been so far. I'm sorry.'

She was placated; she nodded, as if she too well understood his impatience. 'I don't like hanging round neither,' she said. 'But we should of waited.'

They came to a rise. The man, walking ahead, crested the rise first. He stopped and set down his suitcases. 'There she is,' he said, pointing as the woman and child came up beside him.

The mining settlement discoloured the end of a tawny valley; the hills around were lacerated with black weals. Two groups of buildings made the settlement, one group large and dark and tightly gathered, the other small and white and more scattered. The large dark buildings belonged to the mine; the small white ones, a little distance removed, were the miners' homes. Above and beyond the valley were hills tall and blue and remote.

'What that?' the child said.

'That's where we're going,' replied the man. He said it almost with pride, sitting on a suitcase and rolling a cigarette. 'Might as well have a rest now,' he announced. 'It looks pretty good to me.'

Sitting beside him, the woman looked down the valley with a pensive expression. He touched her playfully under the chin, tilting up her face. 'What do you think, mother?' he said. 'Look good to you?'

'Any place,' she said. 'Any place looks good.'

'I think you'll like it here. I just got a feeling.'

'I'd like it anywhere. It doesn't matter where. Just as long as it's somewhere.' She continued to look pensively down the valley.

'I don't want to go,' the child said. 'I want to go back.'

'We can't go back,' said the woman, softly. 'We can't ever go back.' She didn't look away from the distant settlement.

'Why?'

She didn't seem to hear.

'Why?'

'Shut up,' she hissed suddenly, jerking her eyes to the child. Astonished, he began to whimper; she softened. 'Shush, Ian,' she whispered. 'We're going to a new place. A nice new place.' She pointed. 'See?'

But the child couldn't see; his eyes were filled with tears. 'My feet are hurty,' he complained.

The man picked up his suitcases. 'Let's go,' he said jubilantly. He set off with a jaunty stride, humming a tune.

The sun grew hot in an empty sky. A few hundred yards down the road they came to an old wooden bridge which spanned a clear, glittering stream. Upstream a little they could see a sandy place, like a miniature beach, strung around with toi-toi and flax, and shady with willows.

They made a halt on the bridge. 'It's a pretty place,' the woman murmured. 'A pretty place.'

'That'll be nice in summer,' said the man, pointing across the glittering water to the place of sand and shade. 'We could have picnics there. And swim. And eat our lunch under the willows.'

'Yes,' said the woman doubtfully. She had heard all this before. But there had never been picnics.

Their halts along the last circling stretch of road became more and more frequent. The child whimpered with hurting feet while the woman became tired and ill-tempered. The man, however, only seemed to increase his pace as they neared the settlement.

It was late in the morning when they came to it. The white miners' homes, so attractive from a distance, were now small square boxes, crudely built and ugly, crammed together as closely as houses in a city suburb; they looked as if huddled for protection in the bare valley under the burnt sky. Each had a black strip of garden and a green patch of lawn.

The man nodded towards one of the homes. No curtains showed in the window; no smoke wisped from the chimney. The lawn was long-grassed and unkempt, and weeds grew in the garden. 'That one's empty,' he said. 'That might be the one we get.'

The woman looked at the place wistfully.

'Like it?' he said.

'There'll be a lot of work to do,' she said. 'I expect the inside's a mess. And the garden. But heaven couldn't be better.'

'I knew it was going to be good,' he said with satisfaction, spitting on his parched palms and gripping the suitcases again. 'I knew it was going to be pretty good here. I had a feeling we was going to like it.'

This too she had heard before. Reluctantly, she turned her eyes from the house, took the child's hand, and followed the man.

Beyond the store and post office they found the settlement's most imposing structure, the mine office; a squat grey building. 'Wait here,' directed the man. 'I don't think I'll be long.'

The woman and child sat outside while the man went into the office. She removed the child's shoes and massaged the small, blistered feet. 'We'll be all right soon,' she said.

'Why?'

'I know,' she answered, confidently.

The reception office was a small, gloomy room. Beyond a

dark counter were two desks. At one a grey-haired woman sat typing. At the other was a clerk, a slight mousy man of about fifty. He had a shiny bald head with a slender periphery of silver hair; steel-rimmed glasses sat on a thin, bony nose. His face was dried-up and humourless. He worked in a limp black smoking jacket. Just beyond him was a door displaying the sign *Mine Manager*.

The clerk looked up from his papers, apparently to ascertain that the visitor was of not much account, and then bent to them again. His pen scratched briefly, and he rose without haste, fastidiously flicked a spot of dust from his papers, and minced slowly to the counter.

'Yes?' he said. 'Anything I can do for you?'

'I'm here about a job. I wrote a letter—'

'The name?'

'Morrison's the name. William Morrison.'

The clerk screwed on the top of his fountain pen; he began to twirl the pen slowly in his fingers. 'Ah, yes, Mister Morrison,' he said. 'I remember.' His expression was pained; the pen twirled.

'It's all right, isn't it?' the man said. 'You said in your letter—'

'There were two letters actually, Mister Morrison.'

'Two letters? I only got one. You said there was a job for me here.'

'It's apparent you couldn't have received our second letter. We only posted it two days or so ago. We hardly expected you would turn up here so soon. You see, there was some mistake.' The clerk smiled blandly.

'Mistake?' His voice trembled. 'What do you mean a mistake?'

'About the job. An error in the office here. Really most unfortunate. What it amounts to is that there isn't really a job here for you at all.'

'But you said—'

'As I explained, Mister Morrison, there was a mistake. We tried to tell you in our second letter. Unfortunately you set off before that letter arrived.' The pen still twirled between nervous fingers. 'The whole thing is really most unfortunate.' He shook his head. 'I'm so sorry.'

The man's eyes flickered, and were suddenly sharp. He slammed his fist on the counter. 'Don't lie to me,' he snapped.

'Really, Mister Morrison. Please.' The clerk retreated from the counter; he gave a small, despairing shrug.

'I don't want none of your bloody lies.'

The grey-haired woman, startled, looked up from her type-writer. The clerk appeared to wither before the prospect of further violence of language. 'Please, Mister Morrison. Please. There's a lady present.'

'Tell me the truth,' the man demanded.

'I'm afraid I don't understand,' said the clerk weakly. 'I've explained all there is to explain.'

'Let me see the manager.' The man pointed to the door beyond the clerk's desk. 'Maybe he'll have some truth.' He went round the end of the counter, but the clerk blocked his way.

'He's a busy man. He wouldn't want to be disturbed. He really—'

Shoved aside, the clerk fell back against the woman with the typewriter. She gave a cry, and was just in time to prevent her typewriter crashing.

Without knocking, the man pushed open the door of the manager's office. This room was bright after the gloom of the other; too bright. He could not see at first. Sunlight fed through a long window in the opposite wall, silhouetting the desk and its occupant. The walls were cream-coloured, and there was now a thick green carpet beneath his feet. This room was not only brighter; it was luxurious by comparison. There were leather-covered chairs and light-varnished filing cabinets.

'My name's Morrison,' he announced.

He could see the occupant of the desk now, as he rose slowly to his feet, removing his thick tortoise-shell glasses. A short stocky man, moon-faced, in a pepper-and-salt suit; a gold watch-chain was looped across his waistcoat. He was a man with every appearance of assurance. He looked mildly puzzled.

'I beg your pardon?' he said.

'I said my name's Morrison. William Morrison. I want to

know why I can't have a job here. After you people said I could have one. And I don't want none of your bloody lies.'

'A job?' the manager said. He resumed his seat and began, methodically, to clean his glasses with a white handkerchief.

'The job you people promised me. Now your bum boy out in the office tells me I can't have it. I want to know why.'

'Why?' the manager repeated. He seemed amused. 'You want to know why?' He coughed significantly, and added, 'There was a mistake. No doubt you've been told that.'

'I told you I don't want no lies. I'm sick of these kind of lies.'

The manager replaced his glasses and studied the man before him. The glasses seemed to give him added assurance.

'Well, Morrison,' he began casually, 'if you must know—'

The clerk put his head cautiously around the door. 'I tried to stop him coming in,' he started to apologize.

'Get out,' the man said. 'Leave us alone.'

The manager appeared to agree: he too irritably waved the clerk out. The head vanished and the door closed softly.

The manager straightened a file on his desk and closed it. 'Now,' he said slowly, fingering his lower lip. 'Your name is Morrison. William Morrison.'

'That's right. And I'm proud of it.'

'I daresay, Morrison. I daresay.' He slipped the file into a wire basket and drew out another one. The item he wanted was near the top of this file. He coughed before he spoke again. 'You're the Morrison who was gaoled for sedition three years ago, aren't you? You seem to get around quite a lot. And everywhere you've been there seems to have been trouble. Strange how trouble follows you around, isn't it?'

'I'm not ashamed of it. None of it. I've never caused no trouble. It's you people make the trouble. No, I'm not ashamed of nothing.'

The manager coughed with certain delicacy. 'That, of course, is no concern of mine, Morrison. My concern is that we don't have trouble here, or trouble-makers. Up till now we've been free of trouble. The management's on excellent terms with the men. We wouldn't like any change. We want to keep things pleasant here.'

'Keep them down, you mean. I know your kind. I suppose you run the union too, eh?'

'I don't want to hear speeches. Speech-making might be part of your business. Listening to them is not part of mine.'

'You won't get away with this. You can't victimize—'

'No one, to my knowledge, is being victimized. No one is being discharged from employment here. There was just a mistake, as I told you. In any case, I'm sure if I discussed this thing with the men they would certainly prefer to be without your company.'

'Or else,' the man said with sarcasm. 'I know your stunts.'

'They would,' the manager repeated, 'certainly prefer to be without your company.' With an expression of innocence, he held up his hands. 'The clerical error which led us to advise you that we had a job offering is, of course, most regrettable.' He laid his hands flat on the desk, as if to signify he was finished with the subject.

'Bloody lies.'

'If you persist in seeing things in that light, Morrison, then of course there is simply nothing I can do about it.'

'If everything's so sweet here, what are you scared of? Eh?' He didn't give the manager time for reply. 'You know as well as I do. This place is known right up and down the country as rotten, isn't it? That's why.'

'If it's as bad as you say,' said the manager calmly, 'why did you come here, Morrison? Why don't you,' he added deliberately, 'go to Russia?'

'You really want to know. Because I don't like the likes of you. Because I got a kid I want to bring up decent here. Because I'm not a Russian.'

'Just as well for you,' observed the manager. 'They'd shoot you.'

'And you.'

'I've a considerable amount of work to do today,' the manager said abruptly. 'I'm sure we could have a most interesting discussion some other time.'

'Like hell. Scared, aren't you? All your kind.'

'If you'll excuse me, Morrison.' The manager opened a new file. 'I have work to do.'

'Take a good look around you sometime.' The man pointed out the window. The colliery workings, the mine shaft, blackened sheds, rakes of coal-trucks shunting, were all visible against scarred hillside. 'One day that's not going to belong to you. Or any of your kind. One day this country will belong to the people who sweated into it.'

'Get out,' the manager said.

He strode out of the mine office into the street; a door slammed behind him. He went past the woman and child, as if he had not seen them. The woman ran after him and caught at his sleeve.

'Where you going?' she said. 'It's all right, isn't it?'

He stopped to look at her; but his face was remote and expressionless. He hesitated, turned, and walked silently back to the suitcases. He lifted the sitting child aside, and took up the two large cases again.

'It's all right, isn't it?' the woman said, still plucking at his sleeve. He shook her away and began to walk. She picked up her small case, took the child's hand, and hurried after the man. 'Where we going?' she pleaded. 'It's all right, isn't it? There's nothing wrong? You got the job, didn't you?'

He stopped walking suddenly, and let the cases fall heavily. 'No,' he said. 'They knew. They found out.'

Her eyes trembled. 'But the letter,' she said. 'The letter. They said you could have—'

'They must of found out after they sent the letter.' He was not looking at the woman now. 'They said it was a mistake. All a mistake. Bloody liars.'

Her shoulders quivered; the child began to whimper in sympathy. The man took her by the arm. 'Stop it,' he said. 'Not here.' He looked up and down the deserted street, but there seemed, at that moment, no onlookers. 'Not here,' he repeated.

'Where we going?' she whispered. 'Now?'

He avoided the question. 'We'll wait,' he said. 'Until the men come up from the pit. The day needn't be wasted.'

The woman gave her attention to the child. 'Shush, Ian,' she said. 'He's hungry,' she appealed to the man.

He wasn't listening: he had taken a letter from his inside suit pocket and was shredding it. 'Liars,' he said, more quietly now. A light breeze fluttered the torn paper from his hands; confettied, it whisked a little distance along the street and then lay still, like a thin paper-chase trail. 'Well?' he said at last. 'What are you waiting for? You can get something to eat from the store, can't you?'

In the late afternoon a low siren moaned: echoes circled the valley. Thick wire rope strained against turning winches: the cage from the pit screeched and rattled to the surface. Presently men emerged, dusty and blackened, in scarves and helmets, with eyes negro-white, through the colliery gate. They carried lamps and lunch-boxes and blinked against the bitter sunlight.

On one side of the gate they saw the short woman, drab and pale, with a child and some suitcases; on the other, the tall gaunt man in evangelical black. They were distributing leaflets with huge, exclamatory headings. The woman gave out her leaflets almost apologetically; the man was confident, entirely without apology, and called friendly slogans to the miners as they passed. 'The truth,' he said. 'Get the truth, comrades.'

Puzzled, most of the miners accepted the strange, rustling sheets of paper with urgent words; though some, as if fearing infection from a malady which they themselves could not properly define, side-stepped the outstretched hand, the humourless slogan, and hurried away. Some accepted only to repent, crumpling and discarding the leaflets as they walked with quickened step towards the safety of their homes. One or two stopped to talk briefly with the gaunt man in black; one pressed money into his hand. And then they were gone, all of them, into their square ugly homes with strips of garden and patches of lawn: the streets were empty again.

The man, moving slowly now, gathered up the remaining leaflets and packed them into a suitcase glutted with pamphlets, books, and other leaflets.

'How we going to get back to the station?' the woman said, as though waking from deep, dreamless sleep. 'Can we catch a loco?'

'Walk,' said the man. 'The way we came. There's no loco back now. It's too late in the day.'

'Walk?' the woman said.

They walked. The sinking sun coppered the land; the valley was still and quiet, dry and dead. The road had whitened, and their feet swirled pools of dust.

'Where we going?' the child said.

'Shush,' said the woman. 'Daddy's taking us.'

The sun sank; the valley was shadowed. In the east the clouds were pale and curdled; in the west they were gold and pink.

'Why?' said the child.

Dusk smoked, fine and blue, from the land. When they reached the rise in the road from which they had first seen into the valley, they paused and looked back. An island of weak lights had grown under the brightening evening stars. The child was tripping and crying.

'Why Daddy taking us?'

'Shush,' said the woman, patiently.

The man set down his suitcases and took up the child gently. 'He's tired,' he said. 'Poor kid.'

'Why?' the child said, stubbornly.

THE STRANGERS

I

THE SUN of a hot summer cooled in lightening blue skies. Along the trees of the front driveway the leaves withered and twisted into their autumn colours. Sudden breezes showered them down, paper-chasing them across the grass; afterwards, in the calm, their browns and reds and golds speckled our paddocks brightly.

Sometimes, feeling the new chill in the air as I walked back to the house after putting the cows to pasture for the night, I would see the yellow light from the kitchen window slanting out into the deepening blue twilight, and I would consider, almost with surprise, how tightly the nights were gathering about the days: I was still young, and had yet to learn by heart the farmer's story of changing seasons, birth and death, growth and decay; of the gay, sad dance of natural things.

And with our household milk slopping noisily inside the billy which swung from my hand, I would hurry to get inside. Already the final dusk song of birds would have thinned and faded; there would be the steady rustle of cicadas and perhaps from far back in the bush a morepork would begin to utter a single, plaintive cry. My gumboots swished quickly over dewy grass and made small rubbery clumps up the steps to the back porch. Always I remembered first to strip them off and wipe my bared feet on the doormat, as Mother had taught me. Then, opening the door, I moved swiftly inside, clicking it shut against the cold and darkness and damp-earth smell of evening. The house was always filled with the fragrance of cooking food, stew bubbling or sausages frying. Padding through to the warmth and brightness of the kitchen I came upon my father stooped over our huge old iron stove, feeding wood into its hungry mouth; or

55

turning and stirring food with a fork folded into his large, worn hand. And while he worried and muttered I made haste to prepare the table before he put out steaming meat and vegetables on two warmed plates.

But of all those autumn evenings there was one to remember clearly, a different end to a different day. Since morning there had been the promise of rain; grey clouds built on the hills, growing darker and finally smothering the weak sun. We hurried through our evening jobs. But it wasn't until we were about to sit down to the meal that we heard the falling patter of rain on the iron roof. Shortly afterwards there was a faint rapping on the door. Looking surprised, Father rose to answer it.

—I didn't hear any car, he said.

We were out in a lonely part of country and didn't often have visitors. At that time it was an even more pleasant surprise than usual to have them, because Father didn't always know quite what to do with himself in the evenings the first year after Mother died. Most nights, if he couldn't find something to keep him busy, he'd fall back in his favourite easy chair, put up his stockinged feet on another chair and balance his steel-rimmed reading glasses on the tip of his nose. There would always be a big pile of newspapers for him to read; always too many, for all the time new ones arrived at the farm. Now and then, with sudden resolution, he threw out all those unread and began again with the very latest issue. But the pile grew again. Because some nights, too tired to work or read, he just rested in his chair and looked up at the ceiling through half-closed eyes. If I asked him anything, while I read or puzzled over homework, he answered only with great effort.

And, after he'd sent me to bed, the living-room light would burn till late: from the warmth of my blankets I saw its reflection under the bedroom door. Sometimes, when I was awake longer than usual, I slipped from my bed, opened the door quietly, and tip-toed over the cold floor down the passage to the living-room. Often I found him still in his chair, sprawled asleep, the glasses balanced precariously on the tip of his nose while he made loud snoring noises in his mouth. Timidly, I moved closer and touched him lightly on the shoulder: he always woke with a jerk, and stared at me with wide-open tired red eyes as if I were a stranger, as if he had expected to waken somewhere other than under the cold glare of light in the living-room, with me standing before him small and frightened in my tight, outgrown pyjamas. Presently he seemed to recognize me. Then, slowly and deliberately, he removed his glasses and said :

—You ought to be in bed. Asleep.

It was a stern voice, one that made me scurry back to bed. In a little while I heard the jangling of easing chairsprings as he lifted himself up. He went through to the kitchen, and presently the kettle hissed for his suppertime cup of tea. And suddenly my door swung open and the light behind showed him tall and upright. Bending, he gave me my glass of milk and a thick slice of fruitcake.

—And after this you better go to sleep.

And before he left he reminded me :

—Early to bed and early to rise makes a man healthy, wealthy and wise. Goodnight, boy.

—Goodnight, I murmured through my mouthful of cake.

And after a while I'd hear the rattle of his cup and saucer as he finished his tea, the splashing of water as he washed himself, the lights clicking out one by one, his feet whispering up the passage to his bedroom; and, finally, the slow grating as he wound his shrill-voiced alarm clock, and the wirewove of the big double bed straining as he eased his weight on to it. But I rarely heard him begin to snore, for I was tired too.

—I'm damn sure I didn't hear any car, Father repeated.

I followed him from the table. He opened the back door, and light played faintly on the damp face of a young Maori with a swag on his back. He smiled cautiously, as though uncertain of his welcome. The rain whipped under the porch roof and stung our faces. Father quickly invited the young man inside and closed the door. Still surprised, he asked :

—How'd you come?

—Walked from town.

The stranger spoke matter-of-factly, as though there was

nothing interesting in the fact that he'd walked fourteen miles. He hastened to explain :

—Heard you might have a job going.

—Well, Father said. Well, yes, I might have.

He paused thoughtfully a moment.

—Well, dump that swag of yours. Tim boy—run and get the young man a towel to dry himself.

The stranger eased the load from his shoulders.

—It don't matter. Don't fuss me. I don't want to be no bother.

As I fetched the towel, Father said :

—Don't suppose you've eaten.

—No. I was walking to beat the rain.

—Well, you can eat with us then. You're pretty lucky. We was only just starting on the tucker.

Father spooned out some new stew and potato on a new plate while the stranger dried himself. I set another place at the table, and we all sat down.

—My name's Tui, he said. Tui Waritene.

—I expect you know mine already, Father said. Anyhow I'm Ned Livingstone and this is my boy Tim. We run this place between us, Tim and me.

—Yes, Tui said. They told me your last man left quite a while back.

Father frowned. Just as if nothing had been said, he asked :

—What part of the country you from?

Once that question was asked he could talk for hours, contrasting different places. Tui explained that he'd come up from the south lately, and liked the look of our district. When Father began to talk my eyes stayed on Tui. Even to me he didn't seem very old. His skin was the rich brown full-blooded colour, clear and smooth; different to Father's wrinkled, weathered face with its greyish stubble of beard which he never seemed able to shave cleanly. He smiled with brilliant teeth and a friendly twinkle in his eyes; his voice was soft and pleasant and made me think of quiet restful places with cool shadows, deep grass, and running water. He was very careful with his table manners and listened attentively to all Father said. It didn't seem Father would stop talking. And the more he talked, the more carelessly he ate. Stew splashed off the plate and soiled the table-cloth; little bits of food clung to the corners of his mouth. When he tried to eat and talk at the same time he never had good table manners: when Mother was alive she often reproved him for them after visitors left the house. Now, seeing his bad manners, I felt embarrassed and uncomfortable and responsible. I shifted in my chair, trying to catch Father's eye while I rubbed industriously away at the corners of my own entirely clean mouth. I desperately hoped he would see my meaning. When he at last took notice he regarded me sternly, the food still clinging to his mouth, and demanded:

—What's the matter, boy? Eh? You got St. Vitus' dance?

He glared as though ashamed for an idiot son. Tui was smiling at me in a friendly way, but I wasn't prepared for that yet, and lowered my eyes.

After dinner Father went out and Tui helped me with the dishes, drying while I washed. He wanted to know how I liked living on the farm. I told him I wouldn't ever want to live anywhere else. Did I like school? Not much, I said, because I'd sooner be with Father than sitting in class. And Tui said it was a great change to hear a boy talk that way. After a while Father came inside the house again, his clothes spotted with rain, and took Tui through to the living-room and said for him to make himself comfortable while they had another yarn.

I was sent to bed early. They talked till late. Or at least Father talked. I could hear his voice rising and falling, like the sound of sea, as he told Tui about the farm. One of the last things I heard was Tui asking about the job again. Father said, well, they could sleep on the subject and see about it in the morning. I was sure then, by the agreeable tone of his voice, that he already intended Tui should have the job. But it was Father's belief that you should never make things too easy for anyone. They never appreciated it, he said. And before I fell asleep I thought about the last man.

He was a Mr Smith. He arrived in winter, not long after Mother died, and left just before Christmas, staying nearly six months altogether. He was a young man too; but pale and thin and awkward in movement, much different from Tui. He was very quiet; he spent most of his spare time reading in his small bedroom and smoking cigarette after cigarette, so that for a long time after he left the stale nicotine smell haunted the room; and the smell, together with the tattered jumble of detective novels in the corner, infected it with the memory of his presence. Mr Smith rarely spoke to me; often he didn't acknowledge my existence. Father liked him, though, and slapped him on the back and called him Bill; I wasn't sure whether to like him or not. And it wasn't just because he passed me by without a flicker in his bleak eyes; or because of the times when he threw stones at friendly birds or kicked and growled at the cows when Father wasn't looking. I was always noticing things about him, like the way his lips trembled and his eyes shifted when someone spoke suddenly; or the way he sat out on the porch looking at nothing, his eyes growing big and watery while he smoked a damp-ended cigarette. They were things Father didn't notice. Though Mr Smith never said much, his clumsiness let Father make up his mind that he was a city man seeking a clean and decent way of life by working in the country. He was pleased to have such a sensible chap; he was very pleased with Mr Smith. Until one day, when we went to town, we returned to find that Mr Smith had left suddenly, stealing thirty pounds. Father stood in the kitchen, bewildered.

—No. It can't be. It can't.

A ripple of looseness went through him, and he slumped to the kitchen table, his head in his hands. And he said the words I could remember him saying, over and over, from the time I began to remember.

—There's no one you can ever rely on. Only yourself.

And, in a voice a whisper :

—Don't you ever forget that, boy. Don't ever forget it.

A little while afterwards the police called at the farm; they had been seeking Mr Smith for some time, under his real name, and for reasons of their own.

I knew how difficult the stolen money made things. Though we'd been working hard, the cream-cheques were poor, and there had been all the expenses for Mother's funeral. Not to speak of the thing called a mortgage which worried Father so much. And it was nearly Christmas.

—It's a day for those with money, boy. Not for us.

But it seemed to make no difference, for when I woke in the grey early light of Christmas morning I found at the foot of my bed, brightly wrapped in red cellophane, the model railway set I'd always wanted. I began to play with it. Then, suddenly, I saw his bare bony feet splayed on the floor and, looking up slowly, I realized he had come softly to stand above me. He was still in his sleeping shirt, his legs pale and hairy, the sleep clinging to his eyes, the rumpled hair falling over his face, and the faintest of smiles playing about his lips. Presently he squatted on his haunches, farmer fashion, and while he rolled and lit his first cigarette of the day advised how to lay the rails properly and wind the toy engine.

Later in the morning he went to a rarely-opened cupboard and removed a single bottle of beer. It had gathered dust with time, and he polished it against his shirt and uncapped it with ceremony. He poured a few drops into an eggcup for me, and filled a large glass for himself. The beer frothed a cheerful smell.

—And go easy, boy, he said, raising his glass. Learn to be moderate. Cheers, now.

He drank while he prepared dinner, and presently he even began to whistle tunelessly. I couldn't remember having heard him whistle for a long time, not since before Mother died.

When we were about to sit down to the meal, he suddenly remembered something. He went from the room and returned with three coloured-paper party hats. They were hats we'd used for Christmas dinner for years; Mother had always carefully folded them each year and put them away for the next Christmas celebration.

Standing before the laden table, he peeled off one of the hats and gave it to me; he watched with a smile as I put it on my head. Then he lowered his eyes and the smile slowly went from his face as he separated the two others in his hands. He took one for himself, then seemed to become rigid as he looked at the other. With a queer expression, he crumpled it in one hand, and threw it away. He sat down heavily, and I could see the big vein at the side of his temple beginning to throb.

—Eat, boy. Eat. Go on. Don't sit there like a ninny.

He forced the hat on his head: it ripped. Obediently, I began to eat. There was a fowl which he had killed, cooked, and dressed; it had somehow burnt in the oven, but there was still enough of the novel poultry taste to be enjoyed. And Mrs Fletcher on the next farm made a Christmas pudding as a present for us, filling it with surprise threepences. Father ate in silence. Astonished at my own boldness, I said:

—I bet I can find the most.

—Most what? he growled.

—Threepences, I said timidly.

He looked at me, startled.

—You do, eh?

—Yes, I said.

He seemed almost to smile. In no time at all he discovered four threepences. I found only one.

—What happened to you, eh? he grinned in triumph. You swallow all yours?

He stood up and looked at himself in the mirror. The torn hat was askew on his head.

—Don't I look stupid?

He grinned, and we laughed. For the rest of the day everything was all right. We spent the afternoon chopping out a rebellious patch of scrub and gorse. Father said people like us couldn't afford to be idle, not even on Christmas day. Besides, he added, idleness led to the habit of slackness, and if there was any such thing as sin, then slackness was the worst sin of all. He explained I should be glad to learn this so early in life. Some people went all through life without ever learning it. So many in fact, he hated thinking of them all. It wasn't, though, that he was afraid for their souls; he said he wasn't worried about nonsense like after-life. It was just that he didn't like the thought of them going into the darkness without ever knowing.

The sun baked the sky, and stung the sweat from our faces. We worked all afternoon, till our backs ached and hands chafed, and then it was time for the evening jobs. After tea he took me to the living-room, where he spread the railway set on the floor. But soon I wilted with tiredness and fell asleep when I should have been watching him explain something. He must have taken me up gently and carried me to bed, for I remembered nothing more until I woke with the morning sun shining through my window.

One night not long after Christmas he jumped from his chair, waving a newspaper.

—My God, he said. They got him.

—Who? I said.

—Him. That Smith joker. They got him.

He pointed to a news item.

—Two years they give him. There, he said with satisfaction, they got him all right.

He fell back in his chair, reading the item again.

—Yes, he said. No doubt about it, eh?

He was silent a while. The newspaper rustled to the floor. Then his voice was changed.

—The poor young devil. Two years.

Presently he added :

—He probably didn't have a chance. It's just the way it is in them cities. It's the way people get.

He rose and paced about the room.

—I liked that young joker. I had faith in him.

He paced about for some time. Then he halted, stiffened.

—But there's no one you can ever rely on, he said. Only yourself.

He turned to me, and his face was hard.

—Remember that, boy.

2

Now the cold wet night of the young Maori stranger had come and gone, receding beyond the days of deepening autumn and approaching winter. Tui slipped so quickly into our life that it was hard for me to remember back to the time when he was not on the farm. One day Father took me aside and told me how pleased he was that Tui fitted in so well. But that day too had come and gone, merging into the grey twilight of the season. And there was only the present, the cold morning awakening, the beginning of each day. When Father and I stepped out on the back porch, Tui would emerge from his little room, washed and dressed and ready for work. There were brief morning greetings and Father and he talked as they walked down to the cowbails with me trailing behind. Sometimes the farm was under a slow-dissolving fog, which might in time lift to reveal a sullen, weeping sky. Other times, those which fastened on my memory, a heavy white dust of frost covered hillside and flat, icy grass crunched under gumboots, and warm breaths bloomed steam in the clear air as sharp voices crackled through the brittle silence. Above, beyond the eastern hills, there was the first glow of sunrise. Threads of mist hung in hollows and folds, soon to be warmed away by the risen sun. But always, rain or fine, there was that brisk morning mingling of awakened voices; and, later, while Father brought our antiquated milking machine racketing and chugging to desperate life, Tui's voice bursting into song above the noise. He had a good voice, and I loved to hear it. He said he reckoned the cows gave up their milk easier when you gave them a little song. Though Father never said anything, he liked the changed atmosphere too, in his own way. Afterwards Tui was left singing by himself while he cleaned the separator. Father cooked breakfast and I got ready for school. Every morning after breakfast I had to excuse myself, pick up my schoolbag, and hurry to the door while the two of them still relaxed at the table, lingering over steaming cups of tea, rolling cigarettes and talking. I felt badly about leaving them, but there was nothing I could do about it, and so I'd be walking quickly down the driveway, turning now and then to look back at our old unpainted house, tiny behind the trees, with its dull redbrick chimney curling a faint blue wisp of smoke into the morning. Father and Tui usually came to the window to wave goodbye. Satisfied now, I'd run the rest of the way to the gate, where presently the school-bus would call to take me the long miles to the classroom.

I liked being with Tui. Towards evening, while the shadows merged and deepened through our valley, we winterfed the cows with hay from the barn while Father cooked a meal inside the house. Sometimes we chatted as we forked.

—Your Dad's a great man, eh? Tui said.

—Yes, I said, pleased.

—Yes, Tui said, he's a great man on the work. He never stops. All day and half the night. He's a great man on the work all right.

—He works pretty hard, I said proudly.

—Too much work's no good. What d'you think, eh?

Surprised, I only said :

—It makes you pretty tired.

—Too right, Tui said. Too right it makes you pretty tired. All work, no play, eh?

—Yes, I answered; though I still couldn't see whatever it was he meant.

—You got to have fun sometime, eh? You're a long time the corpse.

Paused in his work, leaning on his fork, he looked down at me as if he expected an answer. But I didn't know what to say.

Through autumn and winter, as the cows dried off and things became easier, Tui and I shared our spare time. On fine days we went for walks. Climbing the hills which rose steeply from the back of the farm, we came upon the sight of bushland tumbled out in a carpet, blurred and crumpled, of brilliant browns and greens. In the distance, greys and blues washed the purple line of the horizon. It would be strange then to look back and see the valley so naked where Father had burned and axed to sow pasture. As if flung back by storm, the bush hung ragged on the hills around. Burnt, sunwhitened stumps jutted from the torn earth; second-growth manuka strung itself weakly on erosion-veined slopes; bracken, fern and toi-toi clung weakly to weatherworn limestone cliffs. Thickening, the bush fell back over the hill-crests to flourish, lush and tall-treed, circling the valley. When an inflamed winter sunset lit the valley, it seemed an island in a wild sea.

While I skipped and scrambled along beside him Tui told me the names of trees and birds, and old Maori legends and tales about them. Guiding me by the hand, pointing things out, he explained how easy it was to live off the bush if you wanted, eating eels and birds, fernroots and berries and the juicy white insides of nikau palms. He told me his own adventures in the bush. And one day he let slip that his great-grandfather was one of the old chiefs who fought the pakeha in the Maori wars. After that I made him tell new stories, stories he had heard long before from the old men. The thing that caught my imagination was not so much the actual resistance to the pakeha, but the picture of the brown men after defeat, fleeing through the bush before the clumsy advance of the redcoats. And his slow voice made the picture come alive, so that sometimes I could almost imagine that these things were still really happening, so that I could see the long-dead tattooed men fleeting softly and shadowy through the contorted bush, playing the final act in the drama of dispossessed landowners and defeated warriors.

He would tell the stories reluctantly. At times like these we would have halted our walk. I would sit on something, perhaps a fallen treetrunk, while he stood and talked before leafy curtains of evergreen. Sometimes startled wood-pigeons flapped heavily away at the sound of his voice. The sun, shafting thinly through the trees, streaked the fern and moss and maidenhair of the bush floor; and touched him, here and there, with its dusty pale lemon-colour as he moved talking, somehow sad and solitary, in and out of shadow.

Father didn't mind Tui spending time with me. He seemed pleased with everything Tui did. He said he was a pretty good sort of Maori. He worked hard, never complained; he was a big help around the farm. Pretty educated too, and sensible. Not like some of the Maoris who went gallivanting round spending all their money and having a good time. No, Tui worked hard and saved his money. He expected Tui was doing it with the idea of getting married, or something. Anyhow, whatever it was, he hoped Tui wouldn't leave us too soon; even a couple of years would be too soon.

The idea of Tui getting married interested me; I remembered it one mid-winter day when we were out fishing. The frost had melted from the grass, the sun was warm, and long white clouds feathered the sky. Below us the cold-running creek sparkled as we waited for eels to swim into the trap Tui had shown me how to make.

—When you going to get married, Tui?

He laughed.

—Married?

—Yes.

He laughed again.

—You get some funny ideas, he said.

I thought of when Tui and I went down to the town together. Maori girls, shy and hopeful, or haughty and proud, would often look at him as he walked the street. And I remembered that Tui never seemed to notice them at all.

—Aren't you going to? Not ever? I said hopefully.

—Sometime I might. No big hurry, eh?

—I just thought you might be going to.

—No fear. Not me. Not yet for a long time.

—Dad thought you was going to.

I spoke as though that somehow proved he really should be getting married.

—Hah, Tui said; his smile was big. Why, eh?

—Because you save up your money.

With his hands behind his head, he lay back and closed his eyes.

—Well, he said, you both thought wrong, eh?

There was a silence.

—Then why do you save up?

—To get money.

—What for?

—So I can do things.

—What kinds of things?

He rolled on his side, took out a tobacco tin, and began to make a cigarette. After a while, reluctantly, he said :

—Things I want to do.

—What kinds? I persisted.

—Well, he began. Then he fell silent, licking the tissue paper around the tobacco, and lighting the finished cigarette.

—Well, there's lots of things I want to do. Around the
country. Like a bit of shooting. I need a good new rifle.

—That'll be good fun, I said.

I began to get excited at the prospect of all the good times
we'd have together. But he didn't seem to hear what I said; he
was still talking about the other things he wanted, for hunting
and fishing.

—Gosh, I said. You want a lot.

—I want things like that. And money to keep me going. For
clothes and food and smokes and stuff. I'm spoilt now, eh? I
can't go living off the bush for everything.

I was slow to see his meaning. Bewildered, I asked:

—Then won't you be stopping at our place?

—No, he said. Think I'll have to be moving on for that. For
what I'll be going to do. Don't think your Dad would like me
spending all my time having fun, eh?

There was a long silence. The creek rippled, and the wind
murmured; and a bellbird sang. I looked at Tui.

—You never ever told me you'd be going away.

—Not right now, he said.

—Don't you like it here?

—I like it all right. I like you and your Dad all right.

—Then what d'you want to go away for?

He sat up and folded his arms around his legs.

—I just think I'll have to be moving on one day.

Then he rose to his feet.

—We better have a look at that trap.

We raised it. There were five eels; three big, and two little.
Tui let the little ones wriggle back into the creek.

—They'll be big next year, he said.

—Will you be here next year?

He shrugged.

—It depends, he said.

Things I'd been about to say fell back into my mind, like drops
of water softly into a brimming pool; I was sad. Tui, singing,
dropped the threshing eels into a sugar bag and slung it over his
shoulder; as we walked home, I wondered if he might stay long
enough for me to leave school and go away with him. But then

I thought of Father lonely by himself on the farm : and I didn't know.

Presently we mounted a ridge and saw the trees and buildings clustered tiny on the green valley floor. We could only just distinguish Father's distant, solitary figure as he moved about the backyard, close to his workshop. He began to hammer at something; the hard, rhythmic sound rose up to us.

—He's a great man all right, Tui said. A great man on the work.

He paused, and added :

—You better not tell him what I been telling you. He mightn't think it's a good idea, eh?

3

Spring had already slipped behind us now : the stirring and change, the sogged paddocks drying, the cows coming into milk, the calves tottering spindle-legged, the awakening green of the bush, the flame of rata blossom, the pink of puriri, the sharp new clamour of birds. And there was Tui, restless and alive, moving abruptly away from his work to stare at the slim crest of bush along the enclosing horizon : staring, and then walking away, quickly, with me following until he tired and sat in silence. If we talked, the conversation circled slowly to alight on the things he would do when he left the farm, while his eyes lit and I wondered.

Then summer was upon us; summer with the sun stinging out of baked blue sky. Though we didn't know it yet, ahead were rainless months while the sun browned and killed the grass and dwindled the creeks to trickles; while fire crackled through the hills to bloom blue-grey smoke and send cinders falling like rain. Father would afterwards recall that we only came through that summer by the thinnest skin of our teeth.

—If that much, he'd say.

But the future was still preparing to burn its way through the present into the past; and at night Father, settled comfortably in his chair, talked to Tui about this summer, next autumn, next winter, and about bigger cream-cheques and a smaller mortgage.

—It'll be a great thing, he said, when a man can go out there and plant his two feet down and look around and tell himself it's all his, eh?

—Yes, Tui said. It'll be a great thing, all right.

But he would seem somehow uncomfortable in his chair; he shifted, and rolled another cigarette.

One evening after milking, while the farm was alight with a cool orange sunset, Tui came into the kitchen and told Father he wanted to leave.

Father was bent over the hot stove. He turned stiffly at the sound of Tui's voice. In a slow, bewildered way, he drew the back of his hand over his sweaty brow. Tui's eyes were dark and apologetic.

—Well, Father said at last. I'm sorry to hear that, Tui. I am sorry.

Tui was silent.

—I thought you'd be with us a bit longer.

—I think I'll have to be moving on, Tui said quietly.

—Well, I don't expect there's anything can be done about it. If you want to go, you'll go, and that's flat. I couldn't make you change your mind, eh?

Tui shook his head.

Father turned awkwardly to the stove again.

—I knew you'd be pulling out one day. The only thing is I didn't pick it'd be this soon.

Tui went to bed unusually early that night, leaving Father with his newspapers. Sitting near him with a book, I looked up suddenly at the sound of his voice. Then I realized he wasn't talking to me, but to himself.

—He must be going to get married. It's the only thing. That's why he's been saving so careful. Been putting away every penny. Probably counts on getting himself a bit of land one day too.

He was silent, and I began reading my book again. Presently there was a small rustle of paper and, looking up, I saw a newspaper slide from a limp, dangling hand. He slept with his mouth fallen open, and the deep lines on his brow relaxed. Moving softly towards him, I saw his face as older than I had ever seen it before, and I noticed the new grey hair patching the side of his head. Gently I removed the glasses from his nose and set them quietly on a table. Then I switched out the light and went to the kitchen. With the least possible sound, I set the kettle to boil for his suppertime cup of tea. While I waited I opened the window and, resting my arms on the sill, looked out into the mild summer evening. Stars peppered the sky above the dark hills, and from somewhere deep in shadow a morepork called, its cry prolonged and lonely.

It was another clear day, that Saturday, and I was home from school. The sun, climbing clear of the hills, had still to smother the clean smell of morning. I sat on the porch. Tui was singing as he packed in his room; Father was out in the backyard, tinkering with the engine of our battered old Ford. He had promised to run Tui down to town, but the car had broken down earlier in the week and he wasn't able to get it running again. He made a lot of apologies to Tui, but Tui just said not to worry, he was used to hiking, and anyhow he really liked it better that way. It made no difference, though, because Father kept apologizing and making Tui more embarrassed.

Father was still swearing and muttering at the engine when Tui came out of his room, his swag dangling from his hand. He set it down, took out his tobacco tin, and began to make a cigarette.

—Well, he said, looking around and breathing the morning. She's a great sort of day to be starting off, eh?

—Yes, I agreed miserably.

Father came over and spread himself, large and loose-jointed, at the foot of the porch steps.

—Well, it's no go with the car, Tui. I'm sorry.

—She's right, Tui said. Don't worry.

There was a silence.

—She a nice girl? Father asked suddenly, twisting his head to look up at Tui.

—Girl? Tui said.

—Don't you think we can guess? Father said, smiling.

—There's no girl, Tui said quietly.

—We can guess.

—No, Tui repeated. There's no girl.

—Then why you going?

—It's just time to be pulling out, Tui said. Time to be moving on.

Father rose stiffly. He looked at Tui.

—But the money you been saving up. Aren't you going to get married? I thought you might of been thinking about settling down on your own bit of land or something.

—No fear, Tui said.

—But what about the money?

—That's for me. To keep me going through the summer. And for things I want, like a rifle and stuff.

—And that . . . that's all you worked for?

—Sure thing, Tui said.

He tucked the cigarette in the corner of his mouth and deftly swung the swag up on his shoulder.

—Well, I guess I better be starting off.

But he didn't move. He and Father stood quite still, looking at each other. And I saw it wasn't just Father who didn't understand; Tui couldn't understand Father either. There were the two of them there, neither understanding the other, and I stood between, only knowing that of all the strange and terrible things in life the strangest and most terrible was that of two people not understanding each other. I knew that it was tremendously important that they should come to understanding, though I didn't know why and would never have been able to explain. I felt its importance and everything tangled inside me, things about Tui and Father, and somehow too about Mr Smith with his weak face and dead eyes, though I couldn't see what it had to do with him. I wanted to jump up and down between them, shouting words that would make them understand. But I knew no words, and was silent.

—Gosh, Tui said. I almost forgot.

He went back into his room and returned carrying two parcels. He handed one to Father, the other to me.

—Presents, he said.

Father's face looked queer as his thick fingers fumbled with the string and paper; his parcel was small, but mine was long and thin.

—A fishing rod, I guessed, grinning at Tui.

But he just smiled, not saying anything.

And it was. Then wrapping fell from Father's hands to reveal a combination spanner. The bright, brandnew steel glinted in the sunlight as he turned it over.

—You shouldn't of done this, he said, and his voice was as queer as his face. You shouldn't of—

—Forget it, Tui said.

—Thanks, Father said. But there wasn't no need—

—Well I better be starting off, Tui said, patting me on the head. You be able to have fun now, eh?

I nodded. My tongue was stuck dumb in a dry mouth.

—Oh yes, Tui said, taking an envelope from his pocket. I almost forgot this too. That's my sister's address. She usually knows where I am. If you have any troubles getting a new man you better tell her and maybe I can come and give you a hand for a while next year. O.K., eh?

—Thanks, Father said. That's real good of you.

He was not looking at Tui now. We followed him down to the gate. He shook hands and gave me another pat on the head. Then Father swung the gate shut while Tui walked away down the long white road. Dust puffed out under his shoes, leaving tiny settling clouds behind him.

Father leaned on the gate and I sat, my legs dangling, on the top rail. Tui's figure grew smaller with distance. Now and then he would turn to wave. Presently we heard his voice rising into the morning, the faint song receding. Then he was gone; his voice too. Father thumbed his hat back on his head and began to roll a cigarette.

—Well, he said.

The sun was reaching its full fire now, and the cool shadows of the trees splashed over us as we walked back up the driveway to the house, our feet husking over the parched grass. There was a soprano din of birds and cicadas, and whirring wing-flaps as we passed. A friendly fantail twittered round us, then wheeled away.

I expected Father to go directly to his brokendown engine and begin tinkering again. But instead he came to sit beside me on the steps of the porch. While I fingered my fishing rod, he sucked at his cigarette, puzzling and frowning.

Presently he rose jerkily to his feet. He picked up the spanner and envelope together, turning them over in his hand. Then he lifted his eyes.

—There's no one you can ever rely on, he said. Only yourself.

He spoke in the same way as I might repeat some school lesson; mechanically, without conviction. For the bewilderment had settled on him now, and he was saying the only thing he could find to say.

He looked down at the spanner and envelope again. Then, as though they foolishly contradicted him, he flung them away. The spanner fell with a dull sound to the baked earth; the envelope fluttered down limply, smothering in powdered clay.

—Only yourself, Father said.

Standing tall and straight above me, his brow puckered, his hands curled into tight fists, he considered what he had said. Then, breathing deeply and uncoiling, he moved loosely, almost shamefaced, to retrieve the spanner and envelope before he crossed the backyard to where the brokendown engine waited for him.

LOVE STORY

I

THE SUN burned in a glassy sky; the town under the hazy hills soaked up the summer heat. Mr Jackson lay belly-upwards on an unshaded part of the baked-brittle back lawn. The Saturday sports edition covered his face; his many-patched working trousers were rolled at the knees above milky flesh, and tight and swollen at the crotch; his undone shirt buttons revealed a thin tangle of hair on the sweaty chest which rose and fell with erratic grunts of sleep. He had been there since dinner; he had gone out of the house explaining he would do some gardening. Whatever his real intention had been, he had done no more than briefly survey the weedy ruin of the garden, sigh heavily, and settle himself comfortably on the lawn, taking the sports edition from his back pocket to make a cursory examination of the race results. But even that was half-hearted, and, drowsy, it was pleasant to let himself fall full-length on the lawn so that his heavy head rested on the parched, hay-smelling grass. He also found it pleasant to cover his face with the sports edition and swallow cool mouthfuls of shade. Just as he had probably not intended to touch the garden in the first place, he had probably not meant to doze, let alone sleep; for it was far too hot to sleep in the open sun. On the other hand, though, a walk back to the shade of the house would have demanded energy; and possibly too a return to work which he had in the first place sought to avoid.

The girl Gloria had no intention of waking him. She sat slim and relaxed in the deep sag of the yellow-and-blue deck chair. Her body was almost entirely bared to the sun; she wore only a brief red two-piece sunsuit which fitted trimly to the firm young shape of her body. Her skin, pink and tender, was now beginning

75

to sting; so she rose from the deck chair to walk back to the house. As she did, she glanced down at her father; and her small nose wrinkled.

The cool gloom of the house was edged with the crackling voice of the request-session announcer. Gloria stopped in the kitchen: flies sang above the unwashed dinner dishes, suicided against the speckled window. She turned on a tap, letting the first tepid flow of water splash over the ooze of gravy-fat on the sink-bottom and gargle down the plughole. When the water began to run cold, she filled a glass and drank quickly.

'Bring me a glass too, dear,' called her mother from the living-room.

Mrs Jackson had been listening to the radio since the meal, her body propped by cushions, her slippered feet folded comfortably on the end of the couch; she had smoked cigarette after cigarette, each lit from the butt of the last, and spilt ash dribbled down that part of her black dress which stretched tight over her bulky bosom. She was a large untidy woman with straggling black hair. Features which had once been not unattractive were effectively disguised with fat and age. Mrs Jackson's addiction to cigarettes at this particular time on Sunday was explained by the fact that she became sentimental while listening to music, and smoking helped calm and settle her. There was a warm glass of red wine on the table beside her and, next to it, several dog-eared women's magazines. These she thumbed through when the music did not appeal to her. She accepted the glass of water from her daughter, and sipped thinly.

'You're burning,' she observed, studying her daughter's firm flesh.

'I know,' the girl said sullenly.

'Hadn't you better put some cream on?'

'I was just going to. You don't have to tell me.'

'All right, dear. I was just saying—' What was she just saying? Mrs Jackson wondered. She couldn't remember. She was aware only of the cool disconcerting presence of her daughter; the sulky pretty face, high-cheekboned, tender-lipped; the dark hair and supple body. Mrs Jackson felt sad; she had been young and pretty herself once. What for? It was all gone to waste. 'What's your father doing?' she sighed. 'Or needn't I ask?'

'He's out there,' the girl said. Her gesture could have meant any one of a number of things; she turned away as if to leave the room.

'Gloria,' her mother said softly, reluctant to see the cause of her pleasant sadness depart.

'What?'

Mrs Jackson began uncertainly. 'I was just thinking—'

'Yes?' the girl said querulously.

Mrs Jackson found it difficult to explain; she abandoned the effort. 'It doesn't matter,' she said. But she still thought: a pretty girl like me, all gone to waste. 'You're looking lovely today, dear. The red suits you.'

Impatient, the girl made to move away again.

'Why don't you take a magazine and have a lie down, dear? There's a lovely story in this one.' But the girl would not accept the offered magazine. 'Is something the matter?'

'No,' the girl said shortly. 'Nothing.'

'You shouldn't have too much sun,' advised Mrs Jackson. 'Too much is bad for you. You don't want that lovely figure of yours to shrivel, do you now? Now, if I was a boy—'

'You're not a boy.'

'I was just saying if I was—'

But the girl went quickly out of the room, out of earshot. Mrs Jackson sighed, shook her head, adjusted the volume of the radio, which, she now suspected, was giving her a headache (or perhaps it was just the heat, or the wine). She flicked idly through the magazine which she had offered her daughter. The story had been a beautiful one, a love story, about a boy and girl who decided to spend a weekend in a lonely cottage together before they were actually married; but, at the last moment, as they set a fire in the grate to warm the cold cottage, they looked at each other guiltily and knew that it was, after all, a mistake, and that afterwards they would only remember it with a shame which would destroy the true happiness of marriage. So they kissed each other and, linking hands, went home again to their separate, celibate lives; an ending happy and wistful. Mrs Jackson saw herself in the story, young and fresh (like Gloria) and ready for the bridal bed; she saw also, in the light of the story, where her own mistake had been. Not once before marriage; but many times. She should never have let it happen. That was why, she was sure, she had never commanded proper respect from Mr Jackson; he knew quite well he was the last in the long line. Not even the last, for that matter; though there had, after all, only been one failure since marriage, and that with a fly-by-night traveller Mr Jackson knew nothing about. One of these days she would have to have a proper talk with Gloria; to make sure she made no mistakes. But she didn't seem able to talk to Gloria any more : such a self-willed, restless girl.

I must make myself a cup of tea soon, thought Mrs Jackson. Then I will feel better. Mrs Jackson had great faith in cups of tea; she had been making them all her life in an effort to feel better.

Gloria, meanwhile, was in her bedroom. It was a tiny room with one window, lace-curtained, which gave a partial view of the backyard where Mr Jackson still lay asleep in the sun. There was a faded grey carpet on the varnished floor, placed so she could lower her tender feet luxuriously on to it when she slid from the warm blankets on a cold morning. The remaining furnishings were functional; a narrow single bed, a light-blue chest of drawers, a kitchen chair, and a wardrobe with full-length mirror. On the chest of drawers, between the boxed collection of trinkets and the cosmetic set given her last birthday, stood a framed photograph of her sister. She had run away to the city with an engine-driver on the railways; and eventually married him. But the engine-driver worked late shifts and his wife still liked dances and parties, and there was a divorce, the reasons for which confused Gloria at the time. Gloria's sister still lived in the city; sometimes she wrote letters. The photograph was an old one, taken before she went to the city : plain, freckle-faced, with too-prominent teeth and a straight fringe of hair, smiling faintly with, perhaps, foreknowledge of the engine-driver, she looked down at Gloria every morning; and looked at her now, as the zip crackled under her hand and the sunsuit fell in two limp pieces to the floor. She admired herself naked in the full-length mirror, studying the white lines across breast and thighs which sharpened the new sun-colour of the rest of her body. Then she dressed in blue-flowered skirt and crisp white blouse. She touched lipstick lightly on her mouth, and she was ready. She pirouetted swiftly, the skirt snapping about her, slipped bobby-sox and sandals on her feet, and then went back through the living-room. Her mother was still on the couch.

'Going somewhere, dear?'

'Out for a while.'

'You look so nice,' her mother whispered. 'Is it a boy?'

'Don't be silly,' the girl cried. 'Can't I dress decent if I want to? I'm just going out for a bike-ride, if you want to know.'

'Where to?'

'I don't know. To Sheila's place, I expect.'

'Then you better watch out for Sheila's brothers,' Mrs Jackson said, trying to be friendly.

Gloria did not stay to answer. She had no real intention of going to see Sheila. She had no real intention of going anywhere. She only wanted to get out of the house. She wheeled her bicycle down to the front gate, hesitated, and then chose to ride in the direction of the shops. Houses slept in the hot Sunday. Here a lawnmower chattered, there a man clipped his hedge, there a woman read a book on a shady verandah. Everyone else seemed to be passing the time in satisfactory fashion.

They met on the corner after dinner every Sunday. It was a casual arrangement, made simply because they found it easier doing nothing together, rather than singly. Sunday was always a difficult day. Saturdays were never so bad : they played rugby for the Lions second-grade team on winter Saturdays; and recently a new club had organized cycle-racing on the recreation ground on summer Saturday afternoons. They all competed in the cycle-racing. At the beginning of summer, when the season was new, they had been enthusiastic about Sunday-afternoon practices. Use of the recreation ground was, of course, forbidden Sundays; so they conducted races for themselves over country roads. But the roads were rough and stony, and the summer had turned dusty and hot; and the novelty had gone.

Lately, on Sunday afternoons, they remained more and more within the town. Sometimes still they made sporadic attacks on country roads, following parties of cycling girls who usually remained aloof. Mostly they stayed together in the town, arguing about what to do. That was how they were now, an untidy collection of bicycles and boys in the shade of a shop verandah. The long flat main street, shimmering with heat, was white and empty.

'Well,' Harry said. 'What d'you reckon?' Harry was the eldest, and the leader. Tall and lanky, with thin blotchy face, he was very pale in complexion and had stiff black hair shiny with brilliantine and slicked straight with a comb. He took a damp-ended cigarette from his mouth and jetted smoke; he examined the cigarette with mild interest, then looked from face to face.

'Who, then?' Mick said. Small and wiry, aggressive-faced, Mick was the only one ever to ridicule Harry's ideas.

'Hell,' Harry said. 'Anyone.'

'Who?' Mick persisted.

'There you are,' Harry said, pointing. 'There's a nice piece for you.'

They looked. The approaching girl was white and distant at the end of the street.

'Christ,' Mick said. 'Gloria Jackson? She's only a kid.'

'Old enough,' Harry said.

'Who are you trying to kid?' Mick snorted.

'Would she be game, though?' someone asked.

'They're all game,' Harry announced confidently.

'And so who's going to ask her?' Mick said with sarcasm. 'You?'

'All of us,' Harry smirked. 'That's fair enough, isn't it?'

'You'd have no show,' Mick said, dissociating himself from the idea.

The girl halted a little way down the street to look in a shop window. They watched her.

'Well, then,' Harry said. 'One of us can ask her.'

'Who?' Mick said.

'You seem to know her pretty well,' Harry said.

'You're doing all the talk.'

'Someone's got to think of things,' Harry said, unruffled.

'The one who thinks of them ought to do them.'

'What's all the argument about?' Harry demanded. 'Hell, it's only a matter of asking if she'd like to come along with us for rides Sunday afternoons.'

'I know what you mean,' Mick said.

Terry snickered. Terry, thinner, paler, shorter, was almost a three-quarter size version of Harry. But they were not brothers.

'Don't tell me,' Harry said to Mick, 'that we're going to get all fancy about it? You want us all to write her pretty little notes on blue paper asking her what about it?'

Terry snickered again, nudging a silent member of the group. Gosh, Harry was a card.

It was almost time for afternoon tea: his mother was working in the kitchen. Ralph went outside, wheeled his bicycle from the back shed, and began to pump the tyres firm.

'You going somewhere, sonny?' his mother called.

'I thought I might just have a practice run,' he said.

'Practice run?'

'For the Saturday afternoon racing. And the Easter sports too. I need to practise.'

Mrs White came to the back door, wiping floury hands on her apron. 'You know best,' she said. 'I still can't say I'm very keen on all this business. But now you've joined this club, you might as well do the best you can, I expect. As long—' Mrs White found it necessary to take a deep breath here '—as long as you don't start hanging round with some of those others, that Harry Williams boy and his crowd.'

'No,' he said, pumping till the muscles of his arms began to hurt. 'I'm just going for a run by myself.'

'I certainly hope so. Mrs McIntyre was telling me only the other day that it's only a matter of time before those boys land themselves in trouble. It isn't healthy the way they go hanging round the place all the time, whistling at girls and goodness knows what else. I'd hate to think of you getting like that. You won't, will you?'

'No.'

'I'd hate people to think I was letting you get mixed up with that crowd. It's bad enough what they think now, with you joining that club. I've raised you decently, and I like people to see that. I know I've brought you up in the way your father would have liked.'

Ralph said nothing. He was shining the chipped blue paint-work of his bicycle with a kerosened cloth. It was a heavy-frame sports model, not a real racer, not like the flash feather-weight bicycles from the city the others in the club owned, with thin wheels and delicate frames. But he had stripped brakes and mudguards, turned the handlebars down, and bought a cheap second-hand racing seat; these things, together with the shiny new toeclips on the pedals, almost gave the impression that it was a real racing model.

'I hope you remember your father in whatever you do,' Mrs White said. 'He may have had his faults but he was a good man. You do remember him, don't you?'

'I always do,' he said.

'And what else must you remember?' she asked.

'That my mother loves me,' he said.

'Good boy. You're a good boy to your mother.'

Stooping, Ralph clipped the ends of his trousers.

'You won't stay for afternoon tea, sonny?' she appealed. 'I was going to make you some scones.'

He hesitated. 'I won't be long,' he promised. 'I'll just ride a little way and then come back again.'

Mrs White smiled, smoothing back a wisp of hair; she looked very tired. 'I'll be waiting for you, sonny,' she said.

'I won't be long,' he repeated.

She watched, the smile growing faint on her face, as he wheeled the bicycle down to the gate, swung up into the saddle with an inexpert flourish, and then rode out of sight. Frowning now, she turned inside slowly, wondering, with a small twinge of fear, if she had done right in allowing him the bike-racing.

A pity she hadn't suggested he play cricket instead; if he had to mix with other young people, cricket was nice and quiet, and more respectable. But the year before, when he asked, she told him she thought cricket, like the rugby she also denied him, too dangerous; that hard little ball flying through the air all the time, bruising people and breaking their teeth. And then this summer, when he came pleading for the bike-racing, his face eager and shining, she did not have the time to think the thing out properly. Otherwise she might have remembered the cricket, and suggested it. She had been confused : she had seen only the possibility of conflict. She detected in him a spark of rebellion, a spark which might ignite a flare of anger with one more denial. She gave the permission far too easily, she thought now; and, giving it, something had slipped from her.

I could have mentioned the cricket, she told herself accusingly. I wish I had mentioned the cricket.

Ralph's crouched shadow rode alongside him over the white road; then swung out and away as he turned into the main street. The tyres hummed and, as he completed the turn, the shadow returned small under him again. Already his leg-muscles ached, his heart hammered in his heaving chest, his breath rasped his throat. He fought to keep the handlebars steady, strove not to jerk the smooth running of the chain; he seemed to be going faster than ever before. Perhaps if he reached this speed on a Saturday afternoon he could win a race. He needed more practice. It was only practice that made you fast; made you a champion. One day he might even be as fast as Mick Parker; Mick won all the junior races. The road ahead was a fuzzy white, becoming distinct only under his front wheel. His body was taut, exhilarated and almost exhausted, as he urged the slim metal frame over the speeding earth.

There was a flash of blue and white at the edge of his vision; his name was called. Still travelling at speed, he looked up, looked around behind him, and saw Gloria Jackson dismounted from her bicycle in front of a shop window. She waved, smiling. He waved back, an awkward movement that almost lost him his balance, and made the bicycle lurch. As he regained control he wondered if she meant him to stop and talk with her; he wondered if he should turn back. But he was only playing with the thought; for he knew he would not. He hardly knew her really, though he had seen her often at school and around the town afterwards : it was too painful to face those big enquiring eyes. Still, he wished he could stop.

He was well down the main street now. His name was called

again, this time by several voices. He saw the group on the corner: Harry Williams and Mick Parker and others from the club. Even while he checked his turning pedals, his mother's face insinuated itself: he remembered what she said. But there was no harm in being friendly. After all, he raced with them Saturdays; he couldn't very well ride past them Sundays. They were not like Gloria Jackson whom he could ignore because she was a girl. He liked the casual way they called his name: as though he belonged.

As though he belonged.

He tasted the thought carefully, liking it. He turned back to the group on the corner. He stopped before them and swung off the saddle, his body beginning to tremble and drip sweat from the effort of the ride.

'You was going pretty good,' Harry said. 'We was watching you all the way down the street.'

'Going to clean up them Easter sports aren't you, Ralph?' Terry said, winking hugely at the others. 'Eh?'

There were one or two laughs: Terry decided the joke was good for some more. 'Ralph's the coming champeen,' he declared. He was right; there were one or two more laughs, though from the same people. Mick did not smile.

Ralph grinned uncertainly. Mick slapped his shoulder in friendly fashion. 'You was going well,' Mick assured him. 'So don't you take no notice.' Ralph smiled gratefully, confusedly, at Mick. He liked Mick; he was always nice. He looked sour, but he wasn't so bad when you knew him.

'Look,' Harry said. 'Here she comes now.'

Gloria was riding towards them, on the other side of the street. Her long legs wheedled the slack chain slowly; her dark hair fell loose over her shoulders; her gaze was fixed somewhere ahead.

They called her name. She gave them a remote, mild smile and continued along the street.

'Playing hard to get,' Harry sniffed. 'That's all.' He paused. 'Wait a sec—what's she doing now?'

They watched. She turned across the road, dismounted, and leaned her bicycle against the verandah-post outside the milk-bar. Then she went into the milk-bar.

'Now's our chance,' Harry announced.

'You go right ahead and do your stuff,' Mick said. He was tired of Harry; he often wondered why he hung round with them Sunday afternoons. But there was nothing else to do; and there was always the hope something might happen. 'Go on. Go right ahead,' Mick urged.

'Hell no,' Harry said. 'We'll all go.'

'I thought so,' said Mick. 'You're all talk. You're scared.'

Harry disregarded Mick; he turned to Ralph. 'You want to be in this too?' he asked.

'In what?'

'We're going to ask Gloria if she'll come for rides with us Sunday afternoons,' Harry said, using certain lewd emphasis.

Terry sniggered : it was like a danger signal.

'I don't think I'd better,' Ralph said quickly.

'Frightened?' Harry said.

Ralph didn't reply.

'Mummy's little baby,' Terry needled.

'Leave him alone,' Mick said. 'He doesn't have to if he doesn't want to.' Ralph looked weak and pathetic; Mick felt sorry for him. 'You do whatever you like. And if Terry doesn't shut up then I'll crack his nose in.'

Ralph didn't look at Mick. He stood blinking bleakly in the bright sunlight. He didn't belong any more.

'Well,' Harry said. 'We're not going to stand here talking about the price of fish all day, are we?'

'I didn't know you called it fish,' Terry giggled.

'You got a one-track mind,' Mick told Terry. 'A dirt track.'

'Who said we was worried about a price anyhow?' Harry said.

'All free,' Terry said, grinning as he inserted a cigarette between pale lips. 'Eh?'

They rode off towards the milk-bar and Gloria Jackson. Mick went with them. He felt oddly ashamed of himself : not so much for leaving Ralph by himself, as for letting Ralph see him go with the others.

Ralph watched them roll down the street, park their bicycles, and file into the milk-bar. Then he pedalled home slowly.

2

There was faint applause from the thin scatter of spectators as the leaders in the junior race flashed across the finish-line: Mick first, then Harry and a bunch, Terry and another bunch, and Ralph trailing. The impetus of the final sprint carried them well around the track. Uncrouching, straightening, back-pedalling, they unravelled gaudy colours as they cycled slowly across the green field to the pavilion.

Ralph rode apart from the others. Head down, breath still sobbing, he watched his front wheel husking over dry grass. Some distance from the pavilion, away from the spectators and other riders, he propped his cycle against a wire fence. He lay flat on the ground, trying to contain the fluttering of his body. Presently calmer, he sat up, unbuckled his headgear, and hung it on the handlebars. New riders began to circle the track before the last senior race of the afternoon.

Then he saw Gloria. Detaching herself from the spectators, she moved into a group of junior riders. Mick, Harry and Terry were there; and some of the others who met on the corner on Sunday afternoons. They were still arguing about their race. Mick, after congratulations, was proud-faced.

A whistle shrilled, a pistol banged, and the senior race began. Headgeared, taut-faced, the riders leapt from their saddles, jerking pedals, making speed, zipping past where Ralph sat alone.

But he did not see the senior race. He watched Gloria.

Her dark head was only just visible above a wall of masculine shoulders; a wall reinforced by a tangle of cycles flat on the ground. She bounced with excitement as the senior race ended; then the boys circled about her.

As he rode home, along the main street, he saw their cycles, with Gloria's at the centre, parked outside the milk-bar. He wondered if he should follow them inside; but he rode home, after all.

Next day, Sunday, he excused himself soon after dinner.

'Where are you going now?' Mrs White said.

'To practise. I told you last Sunday I need to practise a lot.'

'Sounds a lot of fuss and bother over nothing.'

'It's not,' he defended. 'I've got to practise.'

He saw her temper. He already knew the next question.

'You sure you're keeping away from that Williams boy and his crowd?' she asked.

'Of course I am.'

'I wish you'd chosen something else,' she said. 'Cricket or something.'

'You wouldn't let me play cricket,' he reminded her.

'You were younger then,' she said. 'It'd be different if you asked me now.'

'Anyhow,' he said, 'I'm not very keen on cricket.'

Mrs White relented. 'You won't be away long, will you? Promise?'

'I promise.'

'And what must you remember?'

'That my mother loves me,' he said, tiredly.

Ralph did not practise. He rode first past Gloria's house, but glimpsed only the deck chair empty in the backyard. Tar oozed and bubbled along the hot streets. He rode along the main street. The boys were not in their usual place on the corner. He idled his cycle past the milk-bar; there was only one customer inside.

They had gone.

Yet still he hoped he might come upon them, as if by accident and not design; and that they might again invite him along with them, with Gloria. He spent the afternoon riding roads which spoked out from the town, but did not see them. Towards evening he turned, at last, for home.

At about the same time, from another direction, they came riding into the town. The boys were crouched over their underslung handlebars : only the girl rode upright, shoulders squared, long-legged and proud, hair damp and twisted.

At the end of her street, while neighbours chinked curtains, they said polite goodnights to her. They left her riding towards the lighted windows of her home; and then travelled bunched into the main street. A string of blue sodium lamps illuminated the long bare street and its closed shops; a patch of yellow showed outside the open milk-bar. But they did not go there;

they dismounted, by general consent, on the strip of lawn opposite the post office. They lay on the grass. Above them, moths and mosquitoes whirred and battered uselessly against the pale suspended face of the town clock. The clock itself, towerless, fastened to a white post, was silent; its minute hand jerked soundlessly from numeral to numeral. They did not speak for a long time; they lit cigarettes and thought.

'Well,' Mick said.

'A bit of a dead loss,' Harry muttered.

No one denied it, or asked whose fault it had been. They had taken the road which spiralled thin and white above the town. After the long climb in the heat of afternoon, they descended, with whining wheels and a rush of cooling air, into a lonely part of country. Tar-seal gave way to a road of clay and pumice which wound through burned, dead-looking farmland and strips of bush; this road in turn dwindled to a stony track running beside a sunlit river and through a long gorge walled by sheer limestone. Gorse and blackberry fingered at them, catching in their clothes and chopping in the spokes. Then, with the track almost lost in fern and paspalum, they found a pool, a dark sparkling backwater curving out from the flow of the river and almost hidden by a tall stand of manuka; it was calm and clear, sandy-bottomed, and fringed with mossy rocks and green drooping fern. They lingered at the edge of it, excited by the discovery; and excited too, more mysteriously, by the mood of the day.

She left them without awkwardness, explaining she would find somewhere to change. After she had gone, stepping erect and serene into the grey and green concealment of the bush, her sandals crackering away over dry sticks, they were left looking at each other with faint embarrassed smiles. They were not quite sure what they should have expected her to do, even now; but she made everything seem entirely natural. Their smiles became foolish; lowering their eyes, they undressed quickly, scuffing out of shirts and shorts and underclothes. She called a warning; and then she stepped out of the bush, only a little self-conscious in her trim tight bathing suit. Again their eyes darted here and there in embarrassment.

Mick explored the pool for snags. There were none; so the other boys followed. They floundered clumsily, ducking, laughing, splashing, water glistening their pale bodies in the sunlight. She was poised at the edge of the pool; they clamoured for her to follow. For a while she seemed content to watch. But even when she lowered herself gently, timidly, into the pool, they still boasted and squabbled and fought, seeing who could remain underwater longest, who could win a race the short length of the pool. Always just at the periphery of the horseplay, she trod water with a remote, calm smile. Once or twice she allowed herself to be drawn into the frolic. Playfully someone would grab for the slender, rippling shape of her body; but she would anticipate it and slip swiftly and tantalizingly beyond reach.

Suddenly cold and shivering, they climbed from the pool, towelled themselves, and fell in a close circle about her; yet she, with her pink hairless body surrounded by scrawny limbs, seemed unconscious of holding court, seemed to consider herself merely one of them. Warmth seeped into their chilled flesh as cicadas crackled and chattering birds flitted through shadowy trees and the river made gentle splashing sounds.

Yet the silence seemed immense.

Harry told some jokes. But he was uncertain in telling them, they were only mildly funny, and soon it was quiet again. Each was stirred by the same impulse to reach out and touch her; each waited for another to make that first move. And so nothing happened, and the magic ebbed from the day.

The sun sank behind a high wall of the gorge, and cool shadow travelled across them : clearly the day was at an end. She excused herself softly and returned into the bush. Finally admitting that the right moment had gone now, and feeling better for the admission, they dressed and rode home with her; she was still in good spirits. They would meet again next Sunday.

Insects ticked against the clock. Sunday idlers clattered along the other side of the street. Mick flicked away a cigarette : it fell in a brilliant shower of sparks. 'I think I'll be getting home,' he said. And at last they dispersed.

3

Mrs White handed him his lunch-parcel. 'Oh yes,' she said. 'And in your lunch-hour could you go round to Hannah's and buy me some cottons. It'll save me making a special trip.' She described the kind she wanted. 'Anyhow,' she added, 'ask Gloria —what's her name?—of course, Jackson. Ask Gloria Jackson. You know her, don't you? Of course. What am I thinking about? You must have known her at school. Nice girl. Pretty. Rather bold, though. Probably the kind to get into trouble sooner or later. She always serves me. She'll know exactly the kind I want. Just ask her. That's a good boy. Goodbye now, sonny.' She kissed him. 'And what must you remember?'

That my mother loves me.

Miss Jones, the typist, racketed at her desk. Now and then, as she shifted in her seat, he glimpsed, with the lift of her red pleated skirt, the slender cool nylon curve of her leg.

Miss Jones was blonde and pretty; her fingers were long and clever, and an engagement ring flashed on her left hand.

That my mother loves me.

Miss Jones would marry Fred Saunders soon. Fred was a farmer's son, and first five-eighths in the Lions senior rugby team; he was good-looking, popular with the girls. A lot of girls wanted to be Mrs Fred Saunders in place of Miss Jones.

Miss Jones was a fine girl, a decent girl; she wasn't the kind of girl who suddenly hurried out of town to have a baby. Miss Jones was the kind of girl his mother liked.

She paused in her work, looked up, and caught his eye. 'You look all hot and bothered this morning,' she said. 'Something the matter?'

'Nothing,' he said weakly.

'It's the heat, I expect,' she said. 'It worries everyone this summer.' She smiled sweetly and chattered the keys again.

That my mother loves me.

His mother had chosen him the job in the bank. It offered security, she said; and if there was one thing you needed in this life it was security. He began at the bank after he passed his school certificate. Boys like Harry and Terry and Mick didn't wait till they passed school certificate : Harry delivered groceries, Mick worked in a garage, and Terry in the auction mart.

Gloria didn't wait either. She had left school six months before, as soon as she turned fifteen.

He felt the heat again.

Perhaps she would be out at lunch, leaving only withered old Miss Hannah to serve him. But what if she wasn't out at lunch?

'You sure you feel all right?' Miss Jones said suddenly. 'You don't look very well to me.'

He felt guilty : she had caught him watching her nyloned leg again. A fan whirred stale air in the silence. His body was burning.

'I'm all right,' he said. He bent over the papers on his desk, and felt released sweat trickle down his body.

After the sharp white glare of the main street, the shop was dim and musty. Vague, floating outlines became solid; and the dry wool-and-cotton smell prickled his nose. Gloria was smiling behind the counter. 'Hullo,' she said. 'How are you today?' She spoke in a light, cheerful voice. He found himself looking down at the brassière which she was folding deftly into a small parcel : then he was embarrassed. He raised his eyes and explained what he wanted.

'I saw you racing last Saturday,' she said, walking across to the cottons counter. He followed slowly.

'I didn't do very well,' he said.

'But you've only just started to race, haven't you? You can't expect to win straight off, can you? You haven't had as much experience as the other boys.'

'I'm not very good, though,' he said.

'That's just being silly,' she declared. She began to wrap the cottons he wanted. 'You could be as good as anyone if you wanted to.' She looked at him : her eyes were friendly. 'Do you go for rides Sunday afternoons?'

'Sometimes.' He nodded. 'By myself,' he added quickly.

'Why by yourself? Why don't you go with Harry and the others?'

'I like to go by myself,' he said.

She did not seem to disbelieve him; she handed him the small packet of cottons. 'That'll be two and six. I went out with them last Sunday. We had great fun.'

He knew suddenly that he was quivering, as if with fright; and his hands were sweating. He dropped his half-crown and picked it up : he couldn't look at her.

'We went up the Ohemai gorge,' she continued. 'Have you been up there?'

He shook his head; his mouth was quite dry.

'It's lovely there. Really lovely.'

'What did you do there?' he heard his own strange voice say. And he recognized that, even if only by accident, he had found the point : what *had* they done there?

'Oh,' she said, seeming unconcerned and entirely truthful. 'We had a swim in a beautiful little pool there, and sunbathed. You know.' The cash-register jangled : she handed him a receipt. 'You ought to come one Sunday. You'd enjoy it.'

'Yes,' he said, backing away from the counter and clutching his packet and receipt.

'You come,' she said softly, experimentally. 'I'd like you to.'

Gloria watched him as he fled the shop. Strange, the things she had discovered about herself this summer.

4

He wheeled his cycle off the road, through a patch of long grass, and hid it behind a ragged cluster of pungas. He lay beside it, in the ferny speckled shade, close to the dry heavy smell of the earth. He waited for perhaps a half hour.

Then he heard their voices as they pushed their cycles up the steep hill. Gloria's voice, light and circling; Harry's laugh, loud and braying; Terry's shrill echo, Mick's hard chuckle, and the bright mingling of at least three other male voices. They drifted past, up the road, leaving him with the oddly lonely sounds of cicadas and birds. He counted to a hundred. Then, hesitantly, another hundred; and he wheeled his cycle back to the road. Below, the white town shimmered in a tawny bowl of hills. He set his wheel in the opposite direction. Crisp chips spat from under his tyres as he pedalled with effort up the rest of the hill; then the road plunged down into open hilly country.

He was not long in catching them. They were riding slowly, spread wide across the road, with Gloria at the centre. He made it seem an accidental meeting.

'Fancy seeing you,' Gloria said.

'What d'you know?' Mick said. 'Getting in some practice?'

Mick and Gloria parted to let him slide into the slow-riding group. 'Just having a ride around,' he explained.

'Coming with us?' she said. 'We're going up the gorge.'

'Come on,' Mick said.

It was noticeable that Harry, Terry and the others did not make the invitation; they pedalled in silence.

'All right,' Ralph said, as if persuaded.

'You could have a swim too,' Mick said. 'You got your togs?'

'Yes,' Ralph said. 'I thought I might go for a swim myself.'

'Hell,' Harry said with sarcasm. 'Isn't that a coincidence?'

His pretence had, after all, been useless. Gloria smiled warmly at him, as if for consolation; she must have known from the first it was no accident.

The day was almost windless; heat gathered thickly in the gorge. They stood at the edge of the pool.

'It'll be good in there today,' Mick said. 'You bet it will.'

'I think I'll change now,' Gloria said. She went off into the bush with her bathing suit parcelled in a towel.

Harry had taken Terry to one side. They lit cigarettes and whispered. Harry laughed.

'What's all the talk about?' Mick demanded.

'Aha,' Harry said with mystery. 'We're just talking about who's going to be first.' He winked meaningfully at Mick, and made a sly nod in the direction of Ralph, who had his back turned.

'First?' Mick said. 'What are you talking about?'

Harry made another sly nod towards Ralph. 'First turn with her, silly,' he said. He jerked his thumb in the direction Gloria had taken.

'What?' Mick said. 'What are you—'

'We think Ralph should have first turn, eh?' Harry said,

attempting another wink before Ralph turned round to face them with bewilderment. 'He's the guest.'

'Lay off,' Mick said sharply.

'What's wrong?' Harry said with pretended hurt, and innocence. 'That's right, isn't it? The guest gets first turn.'

'Shut up,' Mick said.

'Look,' Harry said, ignoring Mick and turning to Ralph. 'We take turns, see. We can't all go at once, can we, eh?'

Ralph stood quite still. Mick's face was angry. Terry was giggling nervously. Someone laughed. Harry was still explaining. 'And you got to go first, see?' he finished.

'No,' Ralph said. 'Not me.'

'Leave him alone,' Mick said. 'Don't you take no notice, Ralph. He's trying to fool you.'

'Come on,' Harry said, beginning to bluster. 'We can't waste time. Don't you like being offered favours? Eh? You're a rotten sort. Go on. Go after her. All you need to do is go after her. You don't need to be told the rest, do you?'

'Perhaps mummy didn't tell him,' someone said.

'Go on,' Harry said, pushing Ralph. 'After her. Quick.'

'Stop it,' Mick shouted. 'Don't you take no notice, Ralph.' Mick jumped between Harry and Ralph: he seemed about to hit Harry. Terry and one of the other boys fell on him, dragging him away. 'Don't you take no notice,' he cried, fighting to free his pinioned arms.

But it was too late. Harry sent Ralph stumbling off into the bush, after Gloria.

Mick fought off the two boys. 'You sod,' he said to Harry, striking at him. The punch went wild and Harry hit him and he was pushed from behind. He fell heavily on rocks: the hot gorge sang around him. Harry laughed, and kicked him as he lay there.

'Why don't you go home? You want to spoil everything.'

'You sod,' Mick said. He rose painfully.

'Didn't you see?' Harry said with glee. 'Didn't you see? He really wanted to go after her.' He laughed. 'Yeah. He did.'

'Liar,' Mick said.

Harry was unconcerned. 'This'll be fun,' he announced confidently to the other boys. Mick was finished; Harry was incontestably their leader again.

'Your kind of fun,' Mick said. 'Not mine.'

'Yeah,' Harry said, still delighted. 'He really wanted to go.'

Mick ran from them. Holding his hurting ribs, he crashed through bush to the track. He retrieved his cycle and rode down the gorge: slowly, wondering if what Harry said was true.

Dry fern crackled under his feet. 'Gloria,' he called.

'I'm over here,' she answered, soft and surprised.

She had gone to change further from the pool than he thought. He found her in a small clearing. Though she had not altogether fastened her bathing suit, this did not seem to trouble her. The zip rasped; a thin strip of white flesh, paler than the rest of her body, was hidden. Her clothes were tumbled in a bright heap on a log. She was smiling.

'Ralph?' she said. 'What do you want?'

He didn't say anything; he didn't look at her.

'Is something wrong? I heard someone shouting.'

He was still silent.

'You sure nothing's wrong?'

'Yes,' he said at last.

'Did you just come to pay me a visit then?' she asked, still smiling. 'That was nice of you.' She was twisting her towel in her hands, as if it was wet and needed to be wrung: but the towel was quite dry. She was uncertain, perplexed. 'I like visitors,' she added in a voice without conviction.

'They said—' he began. 'I mean, Harry said—'

'What did they say?'

He told her. At first she seemed amused. Then she bit her lip and frowned. He looked at the ground.

'It's all lies,' she said. 'What they told you is all lies. Nothing happened like that last Sunday. Or ever.' She paused: he didn't look up. 'What's wrong? You didn't believe them, did you?'

He had to look up now; but he looked beyond her face, and saw a flimsy white butterfly flutter daintily across the huge blue sky. 'No,' he said guiltily. 'I didn't believe them.'

'You sure?'

'Yes.'

She bundled her clothes quickly. Then she took his arm. 'Come on,' she said. 'We'll show them.'

'Where you going?' he said.

'We'll go somewhere else,' she said impatiently, tugging at him.

'What about the others?'

'We won't worry about them any more. Come on.'

'What about our bikes?'

'We'll get them later on. Come on. Stop arguing.'

He followed her up the gorge. There was no track, and they picked their way through thickening bush tangled with supple-jack. Eventually they came to another pool. It was smaller than the other, and shallower. It was very calm; a thin line of rocks dammed it from the turbulence of the river. The bush and sky were mirrored and, at the centre, where it was sandy, the water was clear and without reflection, and trickles of yellowy sunlight played.

'Isn't it lovely?' she said. 'It's far enough away. They won't find us here.' She paused, and looked into his face. 'What's wrong?'

'I forgot my togs. I left them at the other place.'

'Never mind. You can swim in your shorts, can't you? After-wards you can take them off and let them dry. You can cover yourself up with a towel. Don't worry—I won't look. Come on. I bet it's beautiful.'

She dropped her clothes and towel and shed her sandals. Her body flew lightly, arching and straightening in a neat dive: there was a quick explosion of water, and spray hit his face. She rose spluttering, hair swimming. 'Come on,' she urged. 'It's won-derful.' He stripped shirt and sandals and followed.

They emerged quickly, shivering, at the sound of the calling voices. First the voices would call her name, and then almost as an afterthought, they would call his; but mostly it was Gloria's name.

Their bare wet feet splashed over dry grass. Placing her finger over her lips, she took his hand and drew him down into the concealment of a small cave of fern. They lay there quietly, grass and sticks prickling their bodies.

The voices, angry now, grew louder, then fainter.

The tension left them. She rolled on her side and looked at

him gravely. His hand still lay curled like a small, frightened animal in her hand. Her long body was dappled with coins of light; a fringe of fern-shadow, stirred by her movement, danced gently over her secretive face. She wriggled, restless and kittenish.

The voices had gone.

'Funny Ralph,' she laughed suddenly, jumping out of the fern. 'Quick. Let's have another swim.'

They were close together on the grass, their bodies browning in the drenching rich light, talking in quiet voices in the vast silence of the gorge. And in what seemed a very little while, the sun coppered the top of the gorge and shadow crept across the river.

Hand in hand, they made their way downstream to the second pool. The others had gone: within the semi-circle of twisted manuka, it was empty and forlorn. On the abandoned bank above the pool silver-foil glinted among crumpled chocolate-papers and cigarette-packets. His towel and swimsuit had been flung into the water: they still floated, though almost sinking, some distance out from the bank. He forked them in with a long stick, and together they wrung most of the water out.

'Aren't they terrible?' she said. 'I never knew people could be so nasty.'

They walked out to the track. But their cycles were gone. They searched, found some wheel-tracks, and finally located them hidden behind flax-bushes. The air had been let out of the tyres.

'Why are people ever born to do nasty things like that?' Gloria said, almost tearfully. 'I don't know.' Her eyes shone with a hard brilliance. 'I don't know why they're born.'

He carried the cycles out to the track and pumped the tyres hard again. Then they began the ride home. Shadow almost entirely covered the gorge now: the bush had turned a gloomy green colour, and only the tops of the tallest trees were lemoned with sunlight.

They had not ridden far, not more than three hundred yards, when they heard voices sharp in the silence, and feet smacking through brittle undergrowth.

Five boys ran out to block their way and drag them from their cycles. They held him and forced Gloria to the edge of the track. He fought at their hands, and kicked and bit. Gloria screamed. A fist clubbed each side of his head, then crashed into his face and chopped down on the back of his neck; he fell to the track, and rocks bit into his back. Two of them sat on him, one on his stomach, one on the side of his head. There were three of them with Gloria. He couldn't see what they were doing to her. But she was still screaming.

And then they went suddenly, the five, moving quickly, their legs jerking their cycles away.

They were left several yards apart. Ralph crawled slowly to Gloria. She was crying more quietly now; mostly the sobs merged in a single long moaning sound. He cradled her head and untangled the hair from her face.

'Gloria,' he said through swollen lips.

Mick, after he left the boys, did not ride back to town. He swam in a stretch of river further down the gorge. He found strange exhilaration in fighting against the swift, swirling currents. He would not surrender to them and let them take him downstream; instead his arms and legs flailed the fast water as he tried to swim upstream. He made, however, little progress; and finally he dragged himself from the water to fall on the bank limp and tired, and curiously at peace with himself. Tumbled in the racing water, his mind and body seemed emptied of hurt.

Birds sang around him as he rested in the sunlight. He thought, as he often did, of his single visit to the city: of the crowded stadium and the silky interweaving colours of the riders flashing around the long banked floodlit oval of concrete. That part of his memory always talked bright things to his tired mind. One day soon, not far away now, he would go to the city and find a job; and ride the floodlit track. He would do well: everyone seemed agreed on that. They said it was remarkable how a boy with so little competition on a rough grass track in a country town could develop so quickly and record such good times. He would, they predicted, be a champion. There, already, was his victory: his triumph over Harry and the others; so he did not care what they said, or how they treated him. They would never ride the floodlit track.

The thoughts pleased him. He drowsed; and suddenly it was late afternoon, and a lonely bellbird sang up the river. His mind was hot and confused, though his body was cool; he splashed water over his face and dressed. He looked with disbelief at the whirlpooled, tricky part of the river in which he had swum; and was bewildered at his own lunacy. He could easily have been ripped by a snag or knocked unconscious by a rock and drowned. His exhilaration and challenge of the river seemed, now, entirely stupid.

He found his way back to the track and his cycle. Then he heard the panicky voices and saw Harry and Terry and the others whirring down on him. They seemed to be running away from something; he did not know, then, that they were only fleeing from themselves. And he leapt out across the track to stop them.

'What's wrong?' he shouted.

'Get out of the way.'

He jumped quickly to one side to avoid being run down. And they shot past, leaving him alone.

He pedalled back up the gorge. He was not long in coming to them. The two walked together slowly, Ralph's arm supporting Gloria; with their free hands on either side, they pushed their cycles. Gloria's clothes were dirtied; she was crying, and tripping. Ralph's face was bloody, and his shirt torn.

Mick dismounted and approached. He relieved them of their awkward cycles : he pushed them along behind the walking pair. He found manoeuvring three cycles difficult at first; with two on one side, and one on the other, he felt off balance and clumsy. And Ralph and Gloria walked so slowly it was difficult to keep them upright anyway.

5

The mayor was a little gnome-like man; withered skin was stretched tight over a thin skull mounted with patchy grey hair. With short-sighted squint, he peered across his desk at the senior-sergeant.

'And the girl?' he said softly.

'Four months under the age of consent. Three months gone.'

'The family?'

'Ordinary enough. Mother's a bit scatty. Used to be quite a girl in her day, so they tell me. The old man's supposed to be henpecked, but I wouldn't know about that. Works at the lime-works, on the furnaces. Decent enough chap. Plays the race-horses in a quiet way and drinks a bit on the side. But not enough to cause any trouble.'

'Ah yes,' the mayor said. 'Yes. It shows you, doesn't it? The most ordinary of families. Yes.'

The senior-sergeant remained silent, apparently waiting for the mayor to elaborate on this remark. But the mayor did not elaborate; so he coughed and murmured agreement. He was old too; a silver-haired old man with tired face. Once, younger, he had achieved a certain reputation with a vigorous attempt to enforce the liquor laws in a lawless part of the country; his career in that part of country was brief and perilous, terminated by his transfer to a quieter rural district.

'No option but to lay the charges, I suppose?'

'No option. Not when the girl's pregnant, you see. And the mother's complaint.'

'It'll mean unpleasantness, of course,' the mayor said, frown-ing wisely, tapping his pencil slowly on the desk.

'Unpleasantness? Yes, I expect you could call it that. Par-ticularly in view of the White boy.'

'White boy?'

'Ralph White. Mother's a widow. Done her best to bring him up well, by all accounts. Father was killed in the war. El Alamein. Jack White. Carpenter for Evans' Construction, if I remember right.'

'Yes, yes. Of course.' The mayor was still frowning.

'Surprising, really. Of course we haven't got anything like the full story yet. The girl didn't name anyone. When the mother complained she told us the girl had been connected with some of the bike-racing boys.'

'That was it, was it?' The mayor, his interest taken now, leaned attentively across the desk. 'The bike-racing crowd, eh? I've seen them around, all right. Hanging round street corners. An unhealthy element.' The mayor fell silent, considering un-healthy, hairy-legged boys.

'Of course it was easy to work from there,' the senior-sergeant continued professionally. 'What we do know now, for certain, is that a gang of them started taking her out with them Sunday afternoons. Practice rides for the Saturday races. Practices, all right.'

The mayor smiled faintly at the quip.

'But just how many are mixed up in the affair it's hard to say. They all started taking her up the Ohemai gorge at the beginning. Then, from what I can make out, there must have been some kind of row between the boys. Anyhow, after the first couple of Sundays, there was just this boy Ralph White and another boy, Mick Parker, tagging along with her. Parker's an interesting case. Never had any trouble with him before. Works in Butterfield's garage. Quite a promising young rider too. You might remember you presented him with a big silver cup at the Easter sports. Won it against outside competition. Doesn't care much about anything except bike-racing, from what I hear. Seems—or seemed—a good enough boy. His father—you might know him, old Bluey Parker, always turns up for the Anzac day parades—was mustard-gassed in the first war. Bit of an alcoholic. The boy more or less supports both his parents.'

'So you think it's just the two of them?' the mayor said. 'Just this boy Parker and this boy White. That right?'

'I'm pretty sure that's right.'

'Well,' said the mayor, sighing. 'That doesn't sound so bad, after all. The way I first heard the story was that there might be up to a dozen or more boys involved. I don't mind telling you, I was worried. It's bad for the town. You know what I mean?'

'I said I'm pretty sure. Not absolutely sure. You see, on one hand there's the Williams boy. Harry Williams—you know, Sam Williams' kid. A real tall streak, covered in pimples. Always been a larrikin, though we've never been able to blame him for any actual trouble. Mind you, we've had our suspicions. But suspicions never proved anything. Never had much of a chance after his mother cleared out. Sam never worries about any of his kids. Always let them roam the streets till all hours. Well anyway this boy said they never had anything to do with the girl, he and his cobbers.'

'You think that's true?'

'More or less. Because it's Parker and White who've been seeing most of her. No doubt about that. But on the other hand Parker says Williams is telling lies. Parker says he and White have got nothing to do with the girl being pregnant. He rambled on with a long involved story about how the Williams boy and his crowd knocked the girl and the boy White about one day out at the gorge. And about how they—he and White, that is—were supposed to have invented a story of an accident to protect the girl, and so on. I couldn't make head or tail of what he said, myself. It didn't make sense. It seemed to me he was just trying to push all the blame on the Williams boy for what he and White had done.'

'And what about the White boy? What does he say?'

'He didn't say anything. That's what makes me pretty sure. He just kept his mouth shut. Very nervous boy. Listened to all I had to say and wouldn't answer anything. Almost as if he expected it. Queer, really. Couldn't get anything out of him, not even yes or no. And then, just as I was going, he opened his mouth and asked me what would happen to the girl.'

'What will happen to her, by the way?'

'That's for the Child Welfare to decide. She'll probably be taken away somewhere for a while. Best thing, in her condition.'

'Unpleasant,' said the mayor.

'Complicated,' said the senior-sergeant. 'But I expect we'll have it all sorted out by the time we go to court. When the girl knows who we've collared, she might come out with the truth. Or enough truth to help us, if you know what I mean. No one ever really tells the truth. I learnt that a long time ago.'

'Yes,' said the mayor. 'Complicated.' He paused, flicking fastidiously at some dust on his desk. 'It'll be, well, unpleasant for the parents, Senior.'

The senior-sergeant shrugged: it seemed, that sudden jolt of muscles, a profound gesture of patience. 'I saw Mrs White this afternoon. Soon as I tried to discuss the thing with her, she blocked her ears and ordered me out of the house. Then she broke down and asked me to tell her everything. Almost as if she was expecting it too. It was all very painful.'

'Yes,' said the mayor, catching eagerly at the new word. 'Painful.' He made a small whistling sound as he coughed. 'I don't envy you your job, Senior.'

There was silence in the dim office. A fly spiralled down from the ceiling, walked with unconcern across the mayoral blotter, and rose to the ceiling again. The senior-sergeant climbed from his chair. 'Better be getting along,' he said.

Awoken from thought, the mayor also rose. 'Yes, well, yes I really do appreciate your coming here this afternoon to acquaint me with the facts, Senior. You're a busy man. All this really isn't in my sphere, of course. I just felt it would be a help for me to know the facts; not morbid curiosity, you understand. You know how quickly wild rumours get around this town, and in my position—'

'I understand.'

'There's just one thing, though. This club—'

'Club?'

'The club that organizes the bike-racing.'

'Yes. Rather unfortunate for them.'

But the mayor didn't seem to be listening; he looked through some papers in the wire basket on his desk. 'Yes. The whole thing's bad for the town. That's my concern, of course. Now, let me see. Ah, yes, the agenda for the next borough council meeting. Here we are. Now I suppose you know that this club leases the recreation ground from us for the bike-racing. It's an annual thing, on the agenda for the next meeting. I think that possibly, after this, we may have to, well, reconsider—'

'I'm sorry. I don't understand,' murmured the senior-sergeant.

'It seems perfectly clear to me, Senior, after all you've told me. They represent an unhealthy element.'

The senior-sergeant shook his head. 'Well, of course I wouldn't know about that. You've got your job and I've got mine.'

The mayor looked up from his agenda, frowning. 'That's true, Senior. And you needn't worry. I'll be giving this a great deal of thought. A great deal. It's a bad business for the town.'

'No doubt about that,' replied the senior-sergeant, moving for the door.

'A painful business,' said the mayor. 'Unpleasant.'

6

That night Mick worked late at the garage, finishing an urgent job. He was impatient to leave; he needed to see Ralph, and talk to him. He was more concerned with Ralph than Gloria. After all, Gloria could more easily look after herself. They should, he thought, after that day at the gorge, have told the truth; and not invented the story of a cycling accident. Now no one would believe it. At the time it seemed simple enough; and necessary, to protect not only Gloria but Ralph too. Mick had never touched Gloria; and that was the truth. And Ralph?

He could not, he knew suddenly, answer for Ralph.

In the thickening autumn night, a sickle of moon faint in a black cloudy sky, he worked frantically to finish the job in his square box of light at the back of the garage. Tools spilled over the oily concrete around him; his face and hands and hair were smeared with grease. He was a small baggy figure in his soiled khaki overalls; his fingers were nimble, and his face was sharp and bad-tempered.

Then, still working in haste, the job unfinished, he heard the news. The news spread quickly that night.

He left the job unfinished, the tools spilled over the concrete. He shed his overalls. He fetched his cycle and began to ride.

He did not know where to ride. He circled about, like a trapped animal, in the main street. Then, as if to pick up the trail, he rode to Gloria's house. A black police car gleamed outside. The old house was patched with lighted windows, and voices came faintly. He did not listen. He rode past the house, the lighted windows, the gleaming police car.

He still did not know where to ride. Of all the roads he might choose, of all the roads the three of them had ridden in the fading summer; of all the roads just two were riding now.

But he rode. He did not find them.

Towards morning, considering, for no reason, that they might not, after all, have headed for the city and that they might, for no reason, have returned to the place where it began, and that they might be hidden somewhere near, he found himself alone in the silent gorge with the sound of a morepork and the sound of the wind. He dismounted, and let the cycle crash to the side of the track. He cupped his hands around his mouth, against the wind, and began to call their names.

But the wind snapped at his voice, tricked the names into separate, then mingling echoes. Thin, mingling echoes back and forward in the empty gorge.

When he stopped calling, he fell forward, into long grass. The sky was starless, the sickle-moon hidden; and the gorge dark. He closed his eyes, rolled on his stomach and blocked his ears against the singing wind.

Mrs Jackson lit herself another cigarette. The people had gone now. Mr Jackson had fallen asleep on the kitchen couch. All the lights in the house were still burning. It was as if there had been a party; and the party was over.

What a performance, Mrs Jackson thought tiredly. She slumped into a chair, blowing smoke.

I will make myself a cup of tea soon, she thought. Then I will feel better.

No lights burned in the White house. When the senior-sergeant called to see Mrs White he found the place black in the night. After he had knocked several times on the door, a light snapped on above his head and Mrs White looked out. Her face was crumpled and her eyes were bloodshot.

'What do you want?' she demanded. 'Him? He's not here. He's gone.'

She slammed the door and the light went out. The senior-sergeant made his way down a dark path to the front gate. He had all the information he wanted; he had only come to check that the boy had gone with the girl. He remembered, a long time ago, when young and fresh-faced in constable's uniform, watching a court for the first time; in an interval the detective-sergeant who was prosecuting had spoken to him patronisingly. He, the recipient of wise words, was flattered. If there was one thing that got everyone in trouble, said this detective-sergeant, it was one thing; and the old detective-sergeant, before the raw young constable, made a strange gesture with a stiffened arm.

The senior-sergeant went to organize the search parties. They would probably not get very far. That kind never got very far.

7

When Ralph returned from work that evening, Mrs White met him in the kitchen. Her lips were thin and tight and very pale. A harsh sound burst from her throat; and, choking and wordless, she began to strike him. She struck downwards, on the top of his head, on his shoulders; so that presently he was beaten to the floor. It was over then; and Mrs White collapsed across him, still hitting weakly, and sobbing.

He picked himself up and left the kitchen. Outside, a sharp breeze spun gaudy leaves about his feet as he wheeled his cycle down to the front gate and swung up into the saddle, not looking back.

Near the Jackson house he left his cycle, crawled through a hedge, and crouched behind a small shrub. In the falling blue dusk he waited until her window yellowed with light. Then he moved softly and swiftly across the lawn and tapped almost soundlessly on the window. Curtains rustled apart and Gloria looked out, bewildered and frightened, and then smiling. She seemed to understand perfectly, for she slipped on a coat, slid out the window, and fell into his arms. He led her across the lawn, under the hedge, to where he had rested the cycle.

She sat on the bar, her legs dangling. The pedals turned, the chain rasped, and they wobbled out into the road.

They avoided the main street and its bright sodium lamps, evening-walkers and picture-goers. They took dim back-streets, past timber yards and railway sidings, and rode safely clear of the town. Behind them, under the massing clouds and sickle-moon, the lights of the town grew like brilliant distant stars in an inverted sky. The cycle pumped forward steadily, the chain whirring, the wheels bumping, the spokes hissing, the lamp jiggling, the feeble light dancing over the white road and dusty drooping fern and gorse; over the white road moving slowly beneath them, and not the road ahead, long and dark and climbing.

Cloud Riders

THE PAUA GATHERERS

I

AFTER DINNER, after that third and worst argument of the day, he vanished behind a slamming door.

The crisp pretty black-haired girl found small things to lose the hurt. She chattered dishes through soapy water and whisked a broom over ash-strewn floor-matting. When at length the condition of the flat satisfied her, she felt calmer, more in control of herself. She went to a couch, relaxed on cushions and lit a cigarette; and raised her eyes slowly to see the closed door.

She could wait now, smoking, reading and listening to the low steady talk of the clock on the mantelpiece. Or she could walk somewhere. After all, it was Sunday, the day lonely people idled through city streets. Eyes, bleak and flickering, would watch from shabby doorways as her heels ticked through the streets; ticked her past lifeless window displays and aimless people and turned her eventually for home. But when she returned the door would still be closed against her, and the silence heavy.

A small hysteria rose: she felt trapped in this room, this flat, this city. She jerked to her feet and snapped on the radio. A solo saxophone, thin and sad, jazzed into the grey afternoon.

There was a sound of protest from his room. Her fingers, reaching quickly for the switch, strangled the saxophone. She lit another cigarette, looked in the mirror, removed a fleck of tobacco from her lip, took up a book, riffled pages and placed it down again. She stubbed out her cigarette in the polished iridescent bowl of a paua-shell ashtray and walked to the window.

The city lay below, the houses strewn around the harbour and heaped crazily up the flanks of hills; the scene was grey and dead in the flat winter light. Her first view from here had been different, on a bright warm summer day with cool breezes stirring along the narrow wooden streets. They stood at the window together, seeing the dappled buildings under the smoky blue heat-haze, the dark harbour shimmering beneath straw-coloured hills, the slender white yacht-blades cutting calm water. In a rare mood of enthusiasm for the discovered flat, the new city, Tim took her arm, his eyes lighting.

The girl stood at the window alone. She imagined how he would be now : tense while the slim point of his brush discovered line, finicked with colour. And she, in this room, waited confused, uncertain, unable to settle, only knowing that summer had gone; that it was winter, and she was alone. And she couldn't have complained, or even begun to explain to him. 'There are books,' he would say with a vaguely irritated gesture, indicating the titles cramped along the shelves. 'You can read, can't you? Other people find something to do with themselves, don't they?'

Other people found something to do with themselves. She could only remember.

There were two escapes.

Auckland, with its neon nights and rain fresh on the streets, was an escape from that lazy small town where white streets curled among green willows. She had gone there, to university, on a scholarship.

The coffee-shop, with its urgent young people in unfashionably fashionable dress, was an escape from that suddenly-dismal university world of clatter-tongued undergraduates.

Sandy had analysed her; Sandy the radical, who sometimes took her off to his wild proletarian parties in slummy Freeman's Bay, where kegs flowed and fights flared. 'You see, Ann,' he said. 'You don't belong to that, any more than I do. You come from working-class people, like most of us; and that's your trouble, you see, you're far too serious. You want ideas; they don't. You want ideas, to make something of yourself. They want an education, to make money.'

Ian, desperately earnest, trying to atone for his past on a small-town newspaper by writing obscure and erotic verse, told her more bluntly, 'You're sincere. If you want to get on in this world, forget it.'

There were the candlelit parties, with flung mattresses and blasting radiograms, in poky Grafton rooms; and the people from the shadows. Joe, who wrote morbid sketches about rapes and suicides until the day he took a job in an advertising agency and then slashed his wrists seriously enough to be taken to a mental hospital; Alex the actor, disillusioned and homosexual, who wept after the only time he tried to make love to her, and told her about his mother.

They came to the room she took in the city after she left the student hostel. Came hungry for food, thirsty for coffee; depressed, for sympathy. If they came alone, she allowed mild loveplay, smiled and turned them out; if they came together, she entertained them, laughed with them, and after the last coffee saw them down the stairs and locked her door before retiring. Sometimes, as she edged between the sheets, she heard returning feet come hesitant up the stairs, a knock on the door, the rattling chain; and then the feet slowly down the stairs again. She stirred then, hot and afraid between the cool sheets, her face crushed into the pillow; sometimes in imagination she built again the green town, the willows fingering the river, the tui in the flax, her small dangling feet scribbling the sunlit water.

Tim loomed suddenly into memory; so suddenly that she only recalled in quick flashes, like fragments of an old film, his enthusiasms, silences, hates and tenderness. But printed sharply was that morning awakening in his room, the warmth of him beside her, the raw light seeping beneath the ragged blind, the puddled saucers and streaked brushes, the scatter of paintings with harsh shouts of colour, the deserted easel, their clothes limply mingled on the chair beside the bed.

It was an awakening, after the scalding hurt, the lonely cry in the night, to the questions. To Tim the questions could only be a joke. 'Like all the rest,' he said. 'You all like to look free and easy. But deep down you're inhibited as hell. Full of phony middleclass ideals. But it wouldn't really be much fun going to bed with the Bible, would it now?' He couldn't understand. It wasn't what she meant at all; it was a thing she couldn't explain.

She couldn't explain a father's knobbled hands, a mother's shy expectation.

And when Tim announced from the heat of despair that he was leaving Auckland, shedding the old skin and the old way, the old life and the old people, the questions gathered like the unanswered letters from home. Only a lie, deftly told, could explain the move south, deserting university, abandoning the scholarship; the plunge down country to the new city, to the bitter present with Tim's desire to grow free and clean from the past, his voice raised always in anger.

And to defeat. Soon it would be over; in one week or another, on one day or another, the express, gathering speed, would racket north; over simply, a new fine fall of dust settling to overlay the dulled colour of the past. No longer would she come to him quietly, waking him gently to life. No doubt he would adapt with time, freeze into new solitariness.

She didn't mean to argue, didn't mean to hurt. But the questions, twisting inside her, strangled out the words she didn't mean; words to taunt and torment his failure while she stood to one side, like an apathetic stranger. It was as if day by day, piece by piece, they were determined to shred even the memory of those tenderly discovered times for which she would always only be grateful.

There was a knock on the door. She awakened to the present, to the wind murmuring the curtains, the stub of cigarette burning her fingers. The knock, repeated heavily as she went to the door, disturbed her, set the hurt quivering again.

Ted stood on the step; she was glad it was Ted. He was Tim's only real friend, a rolling stone who moved about the country from season to season, beachcombing with Maoris in Northland, sheelite-mining in the Alps, cutting tourist tracks at Milford sounds. Lately he had been living in the city; he was their only regular visitor.

He grinned from his black-bearded face and, duffle-coated, a small canvas bag swinging from a shoulder, he slouched in the door. 'And how are the kids today?' he said cheerfully, in his soft Irish voice.

She tried to smile in the particular way she always smiled at Ted. But quite suddenly she was blinking back tears.

He slipped his arm about her and helped her into a chair. 'There,' he said. 'What's all the trouble now?'

'Nothing, really,' she said. 'Nothing, Ted. You just caught me at the wrong moment. That's all.'

'There now,' Ted said. He dabbed lightly at her eyes with a red handkerchief. His face gentle, he stooped over her, one arm still about her comfortingly. 'Better?'

'Yes, Ted. Better.'

'The old man locked away again?' he said. He sat down, crossed his legs, and began to fill his pipe. Ted never seemed to worry about anything for long; she liked him for it. He was a comfortable person; he always put her at ease. She liked Ted to keep her company.

'Yes,' she said. 'He's busy.'

'What's the masterpiece now?'

She shrugged, wondering if Tim had been listening behind his closed door, and felt a dead weight of tiredness.

Ted looked at her curiously; and changed the subject. 'Well,' he said, slapping his knee. 'What do you say to a meal of pauas tonight?'

'Wonderful.'

He looked at his watch. 'Low tide's at four. I better get weaving. It's an hour out to the beach from here.'

She hesitated. 'Would I be a nuisance if I came?' she said quietly. 'I'd love to get out—'

'Fine,' he said. 'I hoped you'd come.'

'Then why didn't you ask me in the first place?'

'Because I like people to please themselves.'

She heard the quick slap of Tim's sandalled feet; his door sprang open. He emerged smiling, cool and tall in his paint-smeared black sweater; already the front of it was patchy grey with spilt tobacco-ash.

'How's the boy?' he asked Ted.

'Just fine.'

'Going somewhere?'

'After pauas. And Ann has just decided she'd like to come along with me.' Ted seemed oddly apologetic.

Leaning in his door, Tim lit a cigarette. 'Good idea,' he said casually. 'But it's a hell of an afternoon to go after them, isn't it?'

Ted shrugged. 'Maybe they'll taste better today.'

Tim laughed shortly: she sensed a strange tension between them. She hurried into the bedroom and returned zipping a windbreaker.

'You have to go right away?' Tim said.

'Why?' Ted said. 'You want to come too?'

Tim shook his head. 'I'd like to,' he said.

'Then why not?'

'Too much to keep me busy.'

'Give it a rest. It's time you got out of that room.'

Tim looked doubtful. 'I'll see how I go,' he said. 'I might just follow you out to the beach.'

'Right,' Ted said. 'We might see you.'

The tram jolted towards the beach. Ted, remembering the tears, wondered whether today was after all the best time to speak to Ann. Perhaps not; it would really be taking unfair advantage. And anyway he was not sure yet that he would be able to say what he wanted. He would have to coax the words from himself little by little, not suddenly. She might not understand; she might turn away, her face twisting against him.

Yet today he had her alone, clear of the flat, even if only for a short while. It might be his only chance.

The tears had surprised him. They could mean that everything was ending after all; that all he had to do was wait. But then it might be too late, and she suddenly gone. And then the words, still unspoken, might fade from his mind. Perhaps better to say them now, while they were fresh and full in their meaning. But first he would have to be sure of the words, sure of the time.

There was no sign now of the tears. Her face, nipped by the wind, glowed; twists of dark hair tangled from under her yellow head-scarf. She darted glimpses of the passing suburbs through the dusty tram window; and, talking to him, her quick hands gestured.

Curious, she and Tim. Yet what kind of girl should he have expected for Tim? And which Tim?

The first one he still remembered clearly. They met in Auckland—Auckland, that squat impassive city sprawled casually over a green South Pacific isthmus—not long after he arrived in the country; in the dust and dag-stink of a woolstore. New to the city, a refugee from an austere and lonely childhood on a depressed backblocks farm, that first one had been shy and timid. It was an achievement, after the small beginnings of friendship, to persuade Tim to show the work which so quietly obsessed him.

Tim took him home: by rattling tram and then by foot through side streets, lit by sunset, where lilac shadow played on the grotesque-faced old wooden houses: down a narrow path, tangled with weed, around a sagging ruin that had once been a sly-grog shop and brothel and now, raddled with decay, supported a dozen Maori families: and then through a rusted corrugated fence and into a small shed where a weak bulb hung from the slanting tin roof showed Tim fumbling beneath an old iron bed. He displayed his drawings carefully, explaining cautiously that he had no training. And beneath the crudeness, the childish crayon, leapt a groping talent and a passion to understand which informed the features of his people—the crab-faced landlady, the fat boozy watersider, the black-bonneted salvationist, the passionless old coal-heaver—with a rare and wry compassion.

He helped Tim, encouraged him, found him a better place to live and work, loaned him money for paint and brushes, sketchbooks and canvas; and introduced him to others who might help. And when he was satisfied he could do no more, that Tim had all he needed, he went deer-culling for a year.

And then he found the second one. More assured, Tim moved with confidence in a new circle of friends and, influenced by them, sought after new things: the dazzled gold of a sunlit autumn park, the involuted whorls and stylised figures of Polynesian motifs. They met more as equals now.

On Saturdays, under dark walls hung with yellowed pictures of forgotten racehorses and boxers, they drank together in a small waterfront pub where they rang glasses on the bar and joked with their friends—Josef, the Dalmatian fisherman; Harry, the retired burglar; Andrew, the disillusioned evangelist turned alcoholic. For Tim they were friends only now; no longer subjects. His subjects, tangled with theory and technique, were after the fashion of his other friends. Ted argued with him, argued through nights at arty parties, ragged and lunatic, when mornings found them with soured minds. But at least they could agree then: no, they didn't belong, not to this; and they returned to the pub, to Josef, Harry and Andrew.

Then there was the third. The grown-tall Tim, almost a stranger, who had shaken off all friends, not only the simpering hangers-on, the corduroy theoreticians, but even too the friends of the waterfront pub (because there was only his work, his paintings which exploded in blocks of violent colour knifed with heavy lines). Yet somehow Ted broke across the cool distance which separated them, and they found their way back to friendship.

Finally, after a long spell out of cities, Ted discovered Tim gone from Auckland; there was the story of the girl who had left with him.

'A skinny little bitch,' Hans, an effete continental poseur, had told him. 'Absolutely characterless and uncreative. Out to suck him dry. You see.'

'She might do him good,' Bridget said hopefully, examining her long cigarette holder with interest, when Ted went to her flat.

'You think so?' he said, while wondering if Bridget was remembering her own affair with Tim; she had been Tim's first woman.

'She's only a child, really. But you never know, do you?' Bridget's plucked, pencilled eyebrows arched with question. 'She might be just what he needs. There's something gone wrong with him somewhere, hasn't there, Ted? Inside him, I mean. When I remember that time you first brought him up to see me—' She made a small gesture of despair. 'I don't know. Do you?'

Ted spent the night with Bridget; slept with her because it was expected of him. And in that same bed in which Tim had once been initiated into the rite and mystery of sex he found no more than he knew he would find: afterwards, his inner despair.

Once, younger, he knew everything with certainty; now he knew nothing. Once he had run barefoot over rain-silvered cobbles through the Dublin mist; once scrambled brilliantly up the ladder of learning away from the ritual, priested religion of his father. And then, though nothing was changed, everything was changed : he had wandered too far off the track, was lost in the forest of his own uncertainty, seeking a single thing that was not ephemeral, seeking a single thing of value, and discovering no way back, no ladder to descend, no silver path unwinding back through the mist.

But he had found something in his friendship with Tim.

In the morning, dressing-gowned and showing her age, Bridget demanded, 'Well? Why don't you stop talking about him? Go down to Wellington and see him—or them, rather. See what it's all about.'

He knew suddenly that Tim meant something to Bridget too. Out of a lurid confusion of husbands and lovers, she still fed on his memory. Perhaps she had conjured from Tim's awkward young body some unexpected degree of tenderness; or perhaps, like himself, she simply found meaning. She always seemed so young when she had Tim, showing him off, arranging exhibitions, selling his work. And she seemed at first to accept his violent departure with the same grace as she had accepted him into her bed. ('After all,' she said to Ted when it was over, 'he'll always be a very lonely person. Won't he?' But for just a moment her over-anxious voice cracked, her poise was gone, and she seemed, after all, only another forsaken woman.)

She looked at him sharply over the breakfast coffee. 'Well? Why don't you go?'

'All right,' he said. 'I'll go.'

'Don't think it's because I want you to go, Ted,' she said. 'Because I don't. I like to have you here. But you know what I mean, don't you? It'd be interesting to know what he—'

'I know,' Ted said.

'And remember,' she added, 'if you want to come back, you're welcome here. Any time. And, whenever you want it, I can always arrange a job on the magazine for you. Any time.'

'I know that too,' he said.

So he travelled to Wellington and found the flat high above the city; found Tim more strangely aloof than ever; and found the girl Ann. She was vivid and birdlike among the brightly covered old furniture, the yellow cushions, the checkered sisal floor-matting, the walls hung with French prints. (Tim wouldn't allow Ann to hang his own work. He had—so she told Ted— offered contradictory excuses, saying first that it would be vanity, and then that he was working on new things not ready to be seen yet. But whatever the real reason the unhung paintings accumulated steadily in his room, always closed from sight.)

After the greetings, the drinks, the restrained reunion with Tim, he said, 'Maybe I'll stick around one or two weeks. Find a place to live and pick up a job on the wharf.'

One or two weeks—he had been in the city three months now. Why? Tim had said, far too simply, 'This is Ann.'

Seeing her loneliness and Tim's neglect, he felt at once sorry and angry. He soon saw she needed his company; he took her to concerts and films, and helped her through the long winter evenings, reading to her, listening to music with her.

When, at last, he came to an understanding of himself, and remembered his loyalty to Tim as a friend, he tried to keep away from the flat.

But it was no use. Tim, surprisingly hurt, demanded to know why he stayed away; and Ann missed him through long friend-less weekends and evenings. It was no use: if he really wanted to remain loyal to Tim, he could have left the city then; instead he used the excuse that Ann needed him to cover his different need for her. And there was the second excuse, that if he waited, waited long enough, there perhaps need be no disloyalty.

If he waited. But the waiting had grown too long now, the Wellington winter too cold, the warm open country of the north too attractive. He could escape from this dilemma as he had escaped all others; find peace with rugged men who asked no questions and posed no problems. Who worked hard and drank hard; and accepted him.

For what had he to offer any woman? Nothing; nothing beyond his own restlessness and uncertainty. He was in no posi-tion to ask anything of anyone. He was not even sure what he did want of Ann. Only that it was something more than that one thing he had ever asked of any woman; something more than those fumbled couplings without residue of warmth and affection.

If only he could find the words he wanted, if only she would not turn from him, then perhaps he would be able to resolve himself; and know.

The tram banged to a stop. 'Here we are,' Ted said. They swung down from the footboard.

The suburb was sunk in peninsula hills at the end of the harbour. They climbed clear of the houses and a road led them down through a deep cutting to the open sea. Then the beach, winter-bleak and deserted, spread in a grey sweep below them. The sucked-out tide left straggling reefs of black rock. Dark cloud smothered the sun; gusty wind riffled dull lights from the sluggish breakers.

They took a thin path which ledged down to the beach. The coarse sand rasped underfoot as they picked their way across tide-swirls of driftwood and weed.

With the sharp wind prickling her face, she turned to Ted, laughing. 'Know something?'

'What?'

'Who cares if we don't find pauas?'

'Me. I like them.'

'And I just like getting out, getting away—' She stopped, suddenly aware she had said too much. 'I like that smell of the sea,' she added lamely.

'Who doesn't?' he asked, grinning easily.

She was surprised at her own calm. Ted was a relaxing friend; he always seemed to understand perfectly.

He helped her over the rocks, his hand brown and sure around her slender pale wrist. Then, seeking the grey-shelled pauas, they peered into shallow green rock-pools and into crevices where the sea still rose and boiled.

2

Suddenly he realized they had been gone half an hour. And he still had not finished what he wanted to finish. Perhaps it was no use trying. He spent too much time here, too much time in this cramped room fighting with himself until he lost all sense of time. He should get out, look around, let everything fall into place again.

But there never seemed the time. The work, urgent and unfinished, was always there. It would be too easy to lose his grip. There were enough distractions already.

Yet he was sorry now for what had happened. Her voice, flicking coldly at his frustration, stung out the bitter words he didn't mean. And when he regretted those words found too easily, he could not find new ones, gentle ones, to replace them and reassure her; it was like scrabbling on the sandy bottom of a dry well.

He couldn't blame her for anything. She followed her own logic; he followed his. That was what he tried to explain, haltingly, the only time they ever discussed marriage; but she read a wrong meaning into his words and turned away, hurt and tearful, from his clumsy mouthings. It seemed impossible to express himself clearly anywhere but here, where he could only build, geometric and hard, the ugly accumulating symbols of defeat. That was all there seemed left to express now.

For too long he had lost himself among other people. That was why he had come to this new city, to find himself again. But he had found nothing, nothing but his own sickness, because people still confused him; made him unable to see things cool and clear as he had once seen them.

He needed to be alone, free of her. For her good and his.

Without thinking, he had slipped into a coat.

Then why lie to himself? If he really wanted to be free, why follow them? He knew Ted too well not to know what was happening, not to know why Ted had stayed in the city so long. On Saturday afternoons, when they drank together, their desultory conversation and bleak pauses only reminded him of other conversations, other places, when their cascading words splashed bright free patterns of argument; when they laughed at themselves, at each other, and felt no hurt.

Then Ted could have her, he told himself.

Why couldn't he say that and believe it? Perhaps it was only selfishness that prevented it, only that he didn't like losing the animal comfort, the prepared bed and spread table. If there was more, more to be lost, then he could not consider that. There was only the fact he had to be free.

So why follow them? he asked himself. The dead faces and wooden seats in the jerking tram gave no answer.

At the terminus he stepped out into the clean bite of sea air. He began to walk briskly through the suburb. Then he slowed, seeing suddenly the neat homes in the Sunday quiet, the gaunt interlace of skeleton trees against the sky, two boys racketing a trolley, a squall of small girls with tumbling curls and dangling dolls, an old woman forking a grey flower plot to rich chocolate. How long had it been, he wondered, since he took notice? He was seeing things freshly, excitingly, as if for the first time. He didn't get out enough; that was the trouble.

He climbed above the houses and into the cutting, frowning, bewildered at himself. Turning walls of yellow clay opened to reveal the beach, the surf ribboning along the long margin of sand. He saw, presently, the two distant figures moving about on a stubble of rock.

He paused, thoughtful; then he stepped down from the roadway, where they might have seen him. Screening himself behind patchy scrub, he slid down the bank by degrees, nearer to the beach. A little way above it, he sat on a projection of rock, his feet resting comfortably on an upward curve of clay.

Their voices were faint: from where he sat he saw them framed by limp fern and lifeless broom.

Gulls circled noisily above them as they searched.

'His real trouble,' Ted was saying, 'is that what he's doing is abstracting himself from life. He's got the fool idea into his head that he has to get clear of it to look at it properly. But he's not even interested in real things any more. Just in himself. You know how his work's got. Ideas about ideas. All calculated and precise. No rough edges, nothing left unsaid, no mystery. It's all cold and hard'—Ted tapped his head—'all intellect. No instinct, no warmth. No fire in the guts. All cold and dead.'

'Yes,' she said, and then fell silent.

'I'm boring you.'

'No, Ted. Not at all.' She raised her eyes above the sea to the wheeling, crying gulls. 'Ted,' she said quietly. 'Do you think he loves me?'

The sea sucked at the rocks.

Ted, head down, avoided her eyes. Like a woman, he thought. Always it had to come down to the personal level.

'Do you think he can?' she said.

Ted shrugged, watching the confused weed tangle up in the swell. 'Don't ask me,' he said.

'Be honest. Forget you're his best friend.'

'He's too abstracted,' Ted said. 'He can't go outside himself.'

'What does that mean?'

'What I say. I'm beginning to wonder if he's still in the race.'

'What race?' she asked, bewildered.

'The human race.' He smiled wryly.

'But I mean, it doesn't have to be like that—not always, does it?' Because, she thought, Tim was not like that, not always. But that was something impossible to explain. Sometimes out of torment she had gone to him, a wild savaging animal strange to herself, and loosed him from despair, torn him from his cage, reared him on a lance of fire; and discovered him all at once as helpless and defenceless as a child.

'We're not doing much good here,' Ted said. 'Best to move on a bit. The tide'll beat us if we don't find something soon.'

Light was seeping from the afternoon; and the pleasant feeling had left her. Talking had only confused her. And built a strangeness between Ted and herself.

'I wish I could do something to help,' Ted said, reaching out to lift her over a broken shoulder of rock.

'Thanks, Ted. But there's nothing.' Of course there was nothing; why persist? But it was one thing to be logical; another thing to leave Tim.

Ted rolled his trousers and waded into new crevices. She stayed above him, pointing to where she thought she saw the colour of the shells among the surging weed. Then he would feel underwater, knife in hand, for the pauas. He found some small ones. 'They'll do,' he said. 'If we don't find more.'

Presently he straightened, hands on hips, the sea washing

about his knees. 'The tide's coming in pretty fast,' he observed
in a flat voice.

'Is something worrying you?' she said.

'Me?' He laughed, without conviction.

'Something is worrying you, isn't it?'

He didn't answer; she watched him climb slowly from the sea.

3

He was building it carefully now. Their two figures in the
foreground; and behind them the brooding sky, the thin light
flickering the sea, a demented dance of spray over black rock, a
flight of pale gulls balancing the dull white of a far-off fishing
launch. The emphasis strong, their colour rich against the leaden
day.

Ted, stooped, would be gathering the shells into his canvas
bag, his back curved, the blue tartan shirt falling loosely about
his waist, his brown corduroys lifting above his pale bare ankles,
the black of his hair flowing to the stub of his beard; the pipe
jutting, the face absorbed and serious. The face was difficult,
elusive; he had drawn it before. Strange to remember those old
drawings. They were of another life, another time.

And Ann? Standing, looking down at Ted, arched slightly,
the head-scarf fallen loose and yellow about her neck, the open
green windbreaker snapped by the wind, revealing the red
sweater beneath, the gentle line of the small breasts. The slender
hips tugged by the swirled fawn skirt. The hair cascading about
the face. The face retreated, half-hidden.

Why not? The thought surprised him: it was a long time
since he tried anything like that. It could be interesting. He had
no paper, no sketchbook; he began to draw on the back of a
cardboard tobacco-packet, shaping the image with a pencil stub
before the outline left his mind. Presently, with an odd feeling of
satisfaction, he looked up to see that they had moved further
along the beach. Their voices were lost altogether now. In a
moment he would go down to join them.

He thought he might speak to Ann then. Instead, scrambling
awkwardly from the sea, he dried himself and pushed the shells

into his bag. She said nothing; she merely watched him curiously. Too conscious of her, his thick fingers fumbled clumsily with the bag. He closed it, slung it on his shoulder, and suggested they walk a little way along the beach to see if more pauas could be rescued from the rising tide. He did not look at her.

'Tim didn't turn up, after all,' he said. Why should he feel guilty? He had said nothing, betrayed no friendship.

'Did you really expect him to?' Ann said.

He shook his head, his eyes still distant from her face. 'I don't know. I had a feeling he might.'

'Has that been worrying you?'

'Why should it worry me?' He discovered an irritation in his voice.

'It has been worrying you, though. Hasn't it?'

'It would've done him good to get out,' he said irrelevantly. 'He never gets out. Cooped up in that room all the time.'

She was silent. The sea hissed under the darkening sky. Cold spray spat in her face.

Suddenly he swung about to look at her; his face was agitated. 'All right,' he said. 'So you know. You needn't be so damn smug about it.'

She looked bewildered, hurt. 'What?'

And then he saw, and was sorry; she had not seen, nor even remotely guessed.

'What is it? What have I done?' Her words scrambled away in the wind. But she knew. And now she had to admit this defeat too.

She felt chilled and tired. Perhaps, in that cold cynical part of him, Tim had even calculated on this. Ted's voice was quiet; she could scarcely hear it above the sound of the sea.

'I'm sorry,' he said. 'I just wanted to have a talk with you this afternoon. It doesn't matter about what. It doesn't matter now.' How did you ever talk about it, anyway? he thought savagely. Stupid to think he could. It was like slicing yourself open.

He looked at her.

'Getting dark,' he said. 'Shall we get moving?'

He jumped lightly across a gap in the rocks, then waited to catch her. 'All right?' he said, observing her curiously.

'All right,' she said. If all defeat was admitted, she thought with sudden fright, she was entirely free, entirely alone. She looked to Ted for reassurance and he smiled weakly. She shivered. 'All right,' she repeated.

She jumped. Her feet slipped on greasy rock; a sob leapt unexpected from her throat and tears stung her eyes. But Ted's arms caught her before she fell. He swung her up to him, and planted her down firmly. She clung to him; he did not push her away.

'It's all right,' she said, recovering.

He did not release her. His hand slid gently down her loose hair and then, with sudden urgency, lifted her face. He was warm against her, and gentle; his lips tasted faintly of tobacco.

Then he let her go.

'I'm sorry,' he said brokenly. 'I forgot myself. It's just that—' He raised his arms in appeal, then let them fall helplessly. 'I'm sorry.' He turned away and she caught at his arm, despairingly.

He saw them come together, the two distant figures in the fading light, to become motionless, silhouetted singly on the dark rocks against the light lines of surf. Presently, still the one silhouette, they moved along the beach, becoming indistinct against the darkened sand. Then they were lost to sight behind a finger of land. He scrambled down the bank, to the beach, trying to catch sight of them again. Sand slid under his feet; he stumbled and pitched forward. He rose and ran down the beach, the sea hammering in his ears. But behind the land-finger he saw only a small grove of pines and a derelict boat-shed, weathered white and almost luminous in the falling dusk. He stopped running. Breathing heavily, he looked towards the shed. Then, with surprise, he looked down to see that one hand had fisted tightly around sand. He opened the hand and let the grains dribble out between his fingers. Then he turned stiffly and walked away.

4

The wind, creaking through the pines, slapped the broken boards of the shed. He could hear the waves beating over the rocks, sighing up the sand.

Her white face was lost, her body withdrawn into the darkness.

'I expect we'd better go now,' he said. His voice sounded faint to himself.

A match scratched, and a yellow glare flickered her face as she lit a cigarette. She offered him one. He shook his head and turned his smarting eyes away.

'Ted,' she said quietly.

'Yes?' He turned and watched the glowing tip of her cigarette. 'What?'

'I'm sorry,' she said presently.

'For what?'

'For—' He heard a sharp intake of breath. 'It doesn't matter,' she said finally.

'For what?' he repeated limply. He raised himself slowly on an elbow. 'Go on. Tell me.'

'You've got to understand,' she said.

'What?'

'That—' She hesitated.

'That it doesn't mean anything?' he said. 'Because I know that already.'

He slumped back to the floor, turned his face deliberately into a chill draught of air. Then he had killed it; killed everything. Tim too. There was nothing to be done now; nothing except to turn his back on the deaths. And begin again.

Ten years ago, five years even, that would have been easier to tell himself. What he needed now was not so much escape as refuge. Somewhere where he need not think or struggle, where he could cocoon himself snugly with trivia and sink cushioned into the wreckage of civilization, eluding the only too palpably fleshed people strung to his questions.

'I'm sorry,' she said. 'It's my fault.'

'Your fault. My fault. Tim's fault. And nobody's fault.' He saw now she would cling to Tim no matter how thin the chance, and he could only wonder why. 'We can go now,' he added presently, but he made no move.

'Yes,' she agreed. She was perfectly calm. The cold of the night still tingled her warm flesh; the smoke whispered cool in her dry mouth. She felt purged, solitary, no longer afraid. She could be independent too, even if only of love.

She reached gently for Ted's hand and found it in the darkness. 'Yes,' she said. 'We can go now.'

From his room he listened to them enter the flat. The light tap of Ann's heels, the scuff of Ted's heavy shoes. He heard them talking quietly in the kitchen as they prepared the meal, hammering soft the paua-steaks.

He concentrated again. Glancing at the crude notes on the tobacco-packet, he worked quickly, building it on sketchpaper with thick vivid strokes of black pencil. Then he was lost. The figures jutted angular, the sea lurched against agonized rocks. He would have to fight away bitterness to see the two, cool and clear, in the sullen day.

And ask himself no questions. Questions had to wait. They could only turn self-accusation into self-hate.

From the kitchen he heard the hiss of gas, the pop of flame. Presently the rich smell of the frying steaks seeped into the room. He heard the pit-pitting of percolating coffee, the low mingling of their voices.

He began another. It was better; the stiffness, the harshness, was gone. A calm, a profound quiet, flowed from its centre. Important that he work carefully so not to lose it. Important that he understand.

She called his name.

He held the drawing to the light. It was rough and awkward still. And curiously incoherent; as if in an hour he had forgotten everything. And yet she rose out of it, arched and supple, and alive. Perhaps, with the brush, he could find the colour of meaning.

She called his name again.

As he set the drawing down and turned away, he discovered, with surprise, that anger had left him.

Ted had built a fire : the resinous pinewood crackled volleys of yellow sparks. They sat before it, eating the pauas.

Summoning cheerfulness, he congratulated them on the meal,

tried to joke with them. Ted only smiled weakly, avoiding his eyes; Ann stayed quiet and aloof. So presently he fell silent too.

Ann rustled through the silence as she cleared the dishes and poured the coffee. When she finished she sat cross-legged on the floor between them. She was wearing slacks now, and black sweater, and looked trim and neat and boyish. Ribbons of tobacco smoke began to curl about the warm, quiet room.

'Working on anything interesting?' Ted said finally.

'Something quite interesting.'

'New?'

'Really new.'

'Good.' His response, like his questions, flat and mechanical, Ted said nothing more.

Tim began to feel desperate. If only they would act naturally, as though nothing had happened; instead they sat in that guilty silence which made him suspect that he was giving himself away. Running a hand abstractedly through his hair, he tried to conjure up a subject for conversation.

Then he saw they were both looking at him.

At least not at him. At the grains of grey sand which showered from his disturbed hair.

He affected, very deliberately, not to notice. And he rose and walked across the room very slowly and switched on the radio and waited for music to end the silence.

5

Ted stood at the door. His pipe fixed between his teeth, he gave his full attention to fastening his duffle-coat. 'I meant to tell you earlier,' he said. 'I think I'll be pushing off this week.'

'Pushing off?' Tim said. 'What's all the hurry?'

'No hurry. I've just been thinking lately it's time to push off north again. It'll be warmer.'

There was a pause. Tim looked at Ted.

'You don't really have to go, you know,' he said.

Ted lowered his eyes and fidgeted with the top fastening of the coat. 'I've been here long enough. Time to be moving on again.'

'I wish you didn't have to. I'll certainly—I mean, we'll both certainly miss you.' Tim was aware of Ann standing beside them; and of the thing unspoken. He couldn't say what he wanted to say: he felt trapped, hopeless. 'You'll see us again before you go, won't you?'

'I'll try,' Ted said. 'But I'll probably be busy. Packing and things, you know. And I might just push off tomorrow, or the day after.' Ted thrust out his hand suddenly. 'So here's just in case.'

The handshake was brief and austere. Ted's eyes looked retreated, dead. Tim wished there was some way to reassure him; but there was no way.

'We'll be seeing you down here again, won't we?'

'Sure thing,' Ted said, without conviction.

He opened the door. Thunder slammed beyond the hills and brief lightning made the horizon vivid. New rain began to spatter through the darkness.

'Anyway I'll be able to get in touch with you?' Tim thought at last to say.

'Through Bridget, probably.'

'Bridget?'

'Why not? She's still a good friend of mine. And a good friend of yours once too—or do you forget people so easily?'

'I know that. But I mean—' He looked at Ted searchingly. 'Staying with her?'

'For a while, probably. She seems rather on her own now.' Ted shrugged. 'Besides, she promised me a job on her magazine. Any time I wanted it.'

'And you want it now?'

'I didn't say I wanted it. I just said it was a job.'

'But you used to say that was one kind of thing you'd never—'

'I used to say I'd never do a lot of things.'

Through the open door they looked out upon the wind and rain, the growing storm, from an island of light and warmth.

'I'd better go,' Ted said.

Ann spoke at last. 'Goodbye, Ted,' she said quietly.

'Goodbye.' Ted raised a hand in salute. 'Be seeing you both sometime.'

They watched his back retreat into the rain and dark, heard the dwindling sound of his footsteps. The front gate clicked shut.

Tim closed the door. Ann switched off the radio and turned to face him. They were alone now. The fire crackled and rain hissed on the windows.

His mouth was dry, without words. It was, he saw now, too late for Ted; too late for Ann.

'I'll sleep on the couch tonight,' she said simply.

He turned away, without hope.

'Whatever you like.' He needed to escape. But her voice checked him as he went towards his room.

'And I'm sorry,' she said.

'For what?' he said, swinging sharply.

'For everything. For you.'

'I don't want sympathy,' he snapped. And more quietly, in tired voice, he added, 'I expect you'll be going too.'

'Yes, oddly enough. Are you surprised?'

'Not really. With Ted?'

'No. I'm not going after Ted. You heard what he said.'

'Then where?' he said, perplexed.

'Home.'

'Home? Back to your people?'

'Back to my people. I still happen to love them, you see.'

There was a silence. Blue lightning flickered the windows, blinking the electric light. Thunder crashed. He looked at her bleakly and formed the words with effort.

'I'll marry you. If that's what you want.' He tried to smile.

'But don't you see?' she cried. 'That doesn't matter. I thought it did too. But it never mattered, really. It was what you wanted that mattered. And you never knew.'

So she had won at last, she thought; but she found no victory, only a bitter taste. Seeing her slip away he made this final gesture fumbled and frozen; frozen because it could only ever be a gesture, because it would print itself in her mind along with this memory of him broken and pathetic, defeated and alone. A memory, she knew already with despair, that could only haunt her through listless days and restless nights. But, after all, didn't he possess now what he always wanted? Now he had shed every-

one, rejecting them and turning their lives askew, he should at
least have been happy, free and alone.

In a moment of weakness she wished she could comfort him.
But it would have been no use.

'How long will you be at home?' he said. 'For long?'

'For long? I don't know. It depends.'

'On what?'

She did not hesitate now. 'On you,' she said.

'On me?' His stomach lurched.

'It has to depend on you. You see?'

Outside, the first violence of the storm was spent; there was a
pause of quiet wind-rustlings, and then fresh rain began to rattle
the windows.

'I see,' he said. He was limp; and sweating foolishly. He
should have been glad. But he could feel nothing yet, and there
seemed nothing left to say.

'You have the bed,' he told her finally. 'I'll take the couch. I
expect I'll be working till late.'

'Shouldn't you get some sleep? You look awfully tired.'

He shook his head. 'I've got something to finish.'

'To finish? At this time of night?'

'To start, then. Whatever you like to call it.'

He turned awkwardly into his door.

'Tim,' she called.

'What?'

'Nothing,' she said, changing her mind. 'Forget it.'

'Nothing?'

'A lot of things, really. But nothing I can tell you.' She
paused. 'Can I make you some coffee?'

'That'd be fine. Thanks.'

'Have you much to do?'

'Quite a lot, really.'

He swung his door shut and she raised her eyes slowly, with
a kind of dull dread, to see it close against her for the second
time that day. Suddenly remembering Ted, she made a small
choked cry, too low to be heard, and darted to the window. But
there was only the rain; the rain needling the glass, bleeding the
bright image of the night city.

PLAY THE FIFE LOWLY

1

SHE RAN, her legs jerking steadily forward, her feet striking cold echoes from the moonlit streets. Quick swallows of air rasped her throat and stung her lungs; her coat slapped back and forward, as though trying to impede her progress. She still called his name. Once she thought she heard an answer; once a distant voice in faint, mocking song.

But there were only deserted corners where the wind sidled through rustling papers, and empty streets leading to more empty streets: and these lined with the same decayed shops and secretive houses, quiet and shadowed in the milky night.

She paused and, in the moment the echo of her own footsteps died, she heard the other feet ringing behind her. She began to run again, faster now.

2

Helen was afraid of following feet. She did not consider it, even now, an altogether unreasonable fear, like a small child's cringing horror of the dark. She had known it since that night when, tired of seeing all the other girls in the flat rustle prettily away with their sleek boy friends, she decided to forsake her usual Saturday evening by the fireside, and walk by herself.

It had been pleasant at first: her heels clipping over the gleaming pavements, carrying her through the rain-cooled darkness, past the quivering spears of blue and red on the night sea. And there was the shabby wharfside milk-bar where, from a rainbow juke-box, a thin masculine voice wheedled for the return of lost love. Sipping her milk-skinned coffee, she watched the Saturday-night drifters : sad, shuffling old men; middle-aged women with dusty furs and shapeless hats; sallow young men with pin-stripe suits, nicotine-yellowed fingers and tragic faces. She felt an affinity with them : she was like them, she told herself, one of the strays of the unfriendly city. The idea, new and vivid, came warmly to chasten her loneliness. Only afterward, walking home again past the shimmer of water, did the mood shatter : a figure lurched out of shadow, a bottle smashed and a slurred voice called. She began to run : unsteady feet hammered behind her. Once she fell, shredding her stockings and skinning her knees. But she was on her feet quickly, running again, not stopping until she slammed the door of the flat and leaned limply against it, listening, waiting for the footsteps that never quite came.

Sometimes, waking from a dream of smothering, she thought she heard the feet again : it was almost as if the quick, ringing footfalls were always there, somewhere just behind her, always ready to burst into earshot. She remembered them more calmly at other times: on the Saturday nights, in the first numb moments in the suddenly-quiet flat, when the truth of her own solitariness came swiftly to her. Then she would put down her book, silence the radio, hesitantly approach the mirror, remove her glasses, and tell herself : I am twenty-five, not pretty, and will never be married.

But those were Saturday nights before Gerald. Not that she could regard Gerald as more than a casual friend, a Saturday friend. He was mild, pleasant, courteous, but hard to take seriously. And when she realized finally that for some unaccountable reason she had aroused his deeper interest—now that the first strain of friendship was gone, and they could laugh more easily with each other—she was not sure what she should feel : she was aware only of a curious mingling of pleasure and regret. Pleasure, she supposed, firstly: that was only natural. Then regret, foreseeing already his eventual turning away from her polite rebuff.

Yet she was no longer sure, now, she could once again face

the nights in the flat alone; the nights when not even books or music could seduce the truth.

And tonight, in the restaurant, as Gerald leaned intimately across the table, fingering his engraved cigarette case and exhaling smoke smoothly, she decided there was no real reason why she should not, after all, marry him. As she half-listened to his murmured confidences, she avoided his clear, expressionless eyes and, turning her head slightly, studied his reflection in the dazzled wall-mirror : he was even handsome, she supposed, in his clean boyish way; she had never considered his attractiveness a great deal. In his neat suit, starched shirt and college tie, he always seemed so much younger than herself, though they were the same age. She glanced at her own reflection only briefly, meeting the weak eyes spaced too far apart, seeing with renewed distaste the cramped, plain features, the dowdy straight black hair cropped short from desperation, and the modest neckline of her new yellow frock. By all the rules she should be glad to marry Gerald. Unless, perhaps, there was somewhere a forgotten provision for love; a clause inserted by some romantic who would also have pictured courtship as wild, stormy and utterly novelettish while conjuring up elaborate images of fevered caresses and crumpled frocks; who would never have seen it as this, so quiet and tepid that it had been difficult for her to recognize it as courtship. But, after all, Gerald could be likeable enough : she would have to be content with that.

And then, leaving the restaurant, he spoilt her mood of acceptance : he spoke curtly to the girl behind the cash-register about a noisy drunk the girl had allowed to enter the place. He was needlessly unpleasant, and it brought back all she had tried to forget : his ridiculously pompous mannerisms, his lifeless and self-opinionated monologues about himself, his friends, his prospects, when she could only listen in silence, trying in panic to find something that might link them through shared conversation. She would fail even to build that necessary illusion; and see the lie as absurd and futile.

She recognized his mood as they drove to the party : he sat stiffly silent behind the wheel, his impassive face flickered by light; and she knew he was examining a new approach, calculating her response. She was almost certainly in for another serious talk. In his delightfully subtle fashion he had even prepared the way, at dinner, by telling her about his new promotion at the office.

The street into which the car turned was broad and prosperous, with large white homes set back among orderly tangles of dark greenery. Street-lamps, obscured by trees, sprinkled winking lights over the car bonnet.

Gerald slid the car to rest, silenced the engine.

'Well,' he said, speaking for the first time in minutes. 'Here we are.' He paused, fumbling through his pockets for cigarettes. She waited, tightening her coat about her neck, stiffening slowly.

'You know . . .' he began, inserting a cigarette in his mouth.

'Yes?'

'It ought to be quite fun tonight,' he added lamely. His fingers fidgeted with his lighter : the sudden flare lit his tense face forcing a smile.

'Any particular reason?' She felt calmer : he surely wouldn't attempt to say anything now; his moment had escaped him.

'A bit of a joke, really,' he said, tilting back his head to exhale smoke. 'But Tom Anderson's been invited.'

'Tom Anderson?'

'You must have heard us talk about him.'

'Was he the one—'

'—the one that went all arty after college. Really went off the deep end. Everyone knew he'd come a flop. He did, all right. Hit the booze and got T.B. and God knows what else. Trailing round with all types. I hadn't heard anything about him for years. Mike met him accidentally in the street. Thought it might be a bit of fun to invite him along tonight. But I don't know whether it's such a good idea. You can't tell, with some of these people.'

'Wasn't he your particular friend?' Helen said, feeling her way back through the memory of grey conversations; to the rare places, here and there, where her interest had been lit.

'Just a friend,' he corrected quickly. 'That was all.' His tone dismissing the subject, he settled back in the seat; self-consciously he slid his arm around her. He seemed about to make another attempt at serious talk.

'Tell me more,' she said evasively.

'About what?'

'About this Tom Anderson—and what he's like.'

'He's not really all that interesting.' He drew her towards him. 'You're much more interesting.' His hand felt clumsily at her face, tilting it upwards. 'Helen,' he began.

'But you still haven't told me—' she protested.

'I wish I hadn't mentioned him,' he said petulantly, jerking back into his part of the seat. He shot open his door. 'Come on. Let's go inside.'

A beam broadening across his lumpy face, a glass wedged in a huge fist, Mike met them at the door and led them inside. Guests were beginning to swarm through the large comfortable rooms; momentarily garish under the sharp lights, they grouped and re-grouped, manufacturing brittle conversation. Almost all the boys, like Mike, were friends of Gerald from college days; to Helen they all seemed to possess the same clean features, meticulous grooming and tricks of speech, as if they had all been designed to the same neutral pattern. She often had difficulty remembering names, telling them apart. Only Mike was distinctive : heavy and shapeless, lumbering and loud-voiced, but always the leader, the one who had held them together since college.

At the bar, as Mike poured drinks, she looked about, fore-seeing the nature of the evening ahead. First, tipsy but not yet drunken, they would conjure names and events from the past to hide lapses in conversation : 'I say, did you hear about Hamish?' 'They tell me Robin . . .' 'You remember that time?' 'I always laugh when I think back . . .' Later, as alcohol took greater effect, they would return from rumour and reverie to the present; to back-slapping, name-calling, boasting and rowdy frolic pursued with vast seriousness, as though they desperately wanted, now the first novelty of adult life had worn thin, to escape from themselves and recapture the lost variety and vitality of their schooldays. The girls present—the limpid girl friends and affectionate fiancées—would appear mildly shocked at first :

it was almost necessary they show some measure of disapproval, as if this only made the ritual more wholly delightful. But later, naturally, they would join with the boys in feverish dancing, stamping conga-lines and suggestive games. And at the end, the antic scrambles subsiding, there would be illness and upsets, tears and flushing toilets, and frantic petting on the verandah, in the bedrooms, and in car back-seats.

In another room a radiogram pulsed a dance-beat : through a doorway Helen could see several couples scraping listlessly around the floor.

'Well,' Mike said, handing out their drinks. 'Anderson hasn't arrived yet.'

Gerald frowned. 'I'm rather hoping he doesn't.'

'Why?' Mike demanded, regarding Gerald shrewdly. 'Don't you want to see your old cobber?'

'It's not that,' Gerald said quickly, beginning to stammer. 'I mean—well, it's just that . . .'

'What?' Mike said, cocking his head to one side. 'Just that what?'

Helen, perplexed, saw faint colour show in Gerald's face. 'Anderson's—well, all right,' he continued to stammer. 'But, I mean—inviting him here . . .' He faltered, surrendered to the sudden silence and, lowering his eyes, began to sip his beer.

Mike laughed hoarsely. 'Gerry,' he said, 'you know something? You're getting stuffy in your old age.' He slapped Gerald roughly on the back. 'And you want to know something else? I should've thought you'd only be too glad to see your old friend Tom. You're the chief reason I asked him along tonight. That's a fact.'

Helen felt irritated : they were talking round the subject, sharing something, leaving her outside. Mike seemed determined only to hint, and Gerald to remain reticent.

'What's so terrible about this chap anyway?' she said.

'Ask Gerry,' Mike said with a malicious grin. 'He was Gerry's friend.'

'For God's sake,' Gerald said sharply. 'Can't we just forget about him?'

The situation was suddenly uncomfortable and disturbing. Mike's head was still cocked slyly and Gerald's eyes were downcast. And it all seemed so ridiculous: Helen was finally relieved to see Sylvia, Mike's fiancée, swaying towards them. Sylvia always had a certain awkward serenity, even when she had been drinking heavily; tall and cool in blue, her blonde hair frothed about her fine sunburned features, she came to stand before them on unsteady feet, smiling warmly at Helen. Helen had always liked Sylvia; she was the only one of the girls in the crowd to whom she could talk for long.

'I bet I don't need three guesses to know what you're talking about,' she declared tipsily; her large glass of iced gin slopped and chinked in her hand. 'My God, Helen did you ever see anything like it? You know something? I think this chap's only a rumour.'

'You're only a rumour,' Mike said with sarcasm. 'And a pretty vague one at that.'

Sylvia frowned dully, slow to discern the bite in his voice. 'Don't you talk to me like that,' she snapped finally.

Mike, mildly amused, shrugged and turned his back on her. 'By the way, Gerry,' he said, 'did you hear about Tony?'

Sylvia touched Helen's arm. 'Let's get out of here,' she said. 'It stinks.'

She followed Sylvia from the room. Near the door they passed a thick group conversing loudly.

'I always said Anderson—'

'—but, really, the way all these so-called talented people think they own the world.'

'My God,' Sylvia said as they moved down a quiet passage to the rear of the house. 'You wouldn't read about it. Talk about animals picking on one with a broken leg.'

'Are you and Mike having trouble?' Helen asked quietly, as Sylvia led her into a bedroom.

'Trouble?' Sylvia crowed. 'Give the girl first prize for the understatement of the year.'

Standing before a mirror Sylvia plucked out hairpins and began to brush and pat her hair into shape. Presently she turned to look at Helen, her eyes sharp, her voice sibilant.

'Listen, sweet, you're pretty broadminded. You want to know what my big trouble really is?'

'If you want to tell me.'

'When Mike finally got me to bed it hurt his hothouse feelings when he found out I already knew the routine. His poor pride, you know. Thought he was going to be the conquering hero. Instead he turns out the lamest runner in the race. Now he's busy finding excuses not to get married. Funny, isn't it?'

Sylvia jabbed the hairpins back into place. 'I think it's absolutely hilarious,' she went on. 'Because the funniest thing is I don't even want to marry the randy clot anyhow. Stupid, isn't it?"

Helen didn't answer.

'Well—isn't it?' Sylvia demanded.

'I'm sorry it's gone wrong,' Helen said softly.

'Gone wrong?' Sylvia laughed without mirth. 'If I had any sense left I'd get out while the going was good. That's really the stupid part. But there comes a time when it's now or never. For me it's now—or else. I can't afford a reputation. And I ask you —who'd give me one quicker than sweet little Michael with his damn big voice?' Sylvia turned from the mirror. 'Well, pet, and what about your trouble? How's dear Gerry? Still getting frightfully serious?'

'Yes. Still serious.'

'A stayer, isn't he? When d'you think he'll get sick of it?'

'I haven't the faintest idea.'

'Don't tell me you're weakening?'

Helen shrugged. 'Hadn't we better go back?'

'In a moment, petal,' Sylvia said, clicking open her purse. 'Just a wee daub of warpaint for a weary old warhorse.' She inclined towards the mirror, half-stooping and peering intently at her reflected face as she worked the lipstick. 'Funny,' she murmured. 'But I had an idea he'd get you sooner or later.'

'What do you mean?' Helen said.

'What I say,' Sylvia said primly: satisfied now, she replaced the lipstick and clipped shut the purse. 'Anyway, just how ridiculous can we get? I ask you.'

'What's ridiculous?' Helen said sharply.

'Everything.' Sylvia threw her arms wide. 'Every damn thing. Here's me fighting like hell to get married when I don't want to get married. And there you are fighting like hell not to get married when you really want to get married. If that's not ridiculous, what is?'

Sylvia glanced finally into the mirror; she pinched and smoothed her frock down her slender figure. 'Do I look all right now? My God—my knees still feel weak. You know what time I started tippling today? Eleven this morning. Had to—to face up to him tonight. Ought to feel weak, poor things, shouldn't they?'

Helen didn't answer; she was listening to a dull explosion of voices from the front of the house.

'What's that?' said Sylvia, bewildered. Then, elated, she added, 'Don't tell me. This character must have actually arrived. We'd better have a look. Before they pick the meat off him.'

As they moved to the door together, she caught at Helen. 'Look, darling, before I forget. Perhaps I was shooting off my mouth too much just now. But you won't say anything to anyone, will you?'

'Of course not.'

Sylvia squeezed Helen's hand gratefully. 'I didn't really imagine you would. It's just that I'm in a big enough mess now without—' She stopped, frowning. 'Do you ever feel all kind of cramped up and suffocated? Well, that's what I feel like now. All cramped up and—' She paused again. 'What's the use? I don't know.'

She jerked Helen through the door. 'Come on. Let's have a look. It's all free.'

The commotion had shifted from the front door to one of the rooms; it had begun to subside. When they pushed into the room they found attention centred on a strangely various group. There were four Maoris, two boys and their girl friends, young and bewildered in the alien atmosphere. The boys wore gaudy-flowered inner-and-outer shirts and had guitars strung round their necks; the girls were slim and neat in flounced, warm-coloured skirts and pastel blouses, and they stood close to the boys, as if for protection. With them was a delicate youth with thin feminine features; he wore a yellow turtle sweater, and curls of fair hair tufted from beneath a black beret. He was surveying the room with apparent unconcern. If he had been the only other one with the Maoris, Helen would have mistaken him for Tom Anderson : he seemed more the fragile male she had pictured. She hadn't expected the tall dishevelled figure which dominated the odd group : red hair flared above a squarishly attractive face set on jutting broad shoulders; the whole figure had an immense solidity about it, challenging as it stood now, legs wide and feet planted firmly. Clothes did not mould to it : they clung limply and fell away; his unbuttoned wool tartan shirt peeled from the chest to reveal crinkled red hairs on milky flesh; his soiled corduroys were hitched askew, and a flap of the shirt hung out; bare feet were sandalled loosely.

Speaking loudly, ignoring Mike, he hustled his friends into seats. Then he slapped Mike on the shoulder.

'Give drink,' he commanded. 'And we give music.'

Mike stared foolishly, seeming to hesitate between hostility and obedience : he paused indecisively, then went to the bar. 'What do you all want?' he said from the silence, summoning coolness into his voice. 'There's gin and vodka and scotch and—'

'Forget it. Beer.'

Small noises, the chatter of bottles on glasses, the stiff rustle of frocks, the click and flare of lighters, threaded with thin conversation at last began to ease out the silence.

Helen was suddenly aware of Gerald standing beside her. 'Serves Mike right,' he said. 'He should have known there'd be trouble.'

'What trouble?' Helen said. 'There's no trouble.'

'No trouble?' Gerald laughed shortly. 'You're a bit innocent, aren't you?'

Sylvia, who had been listening, turned on Gerald. 'What exactly did you expect him to do? Come creeping in on hands and knees? Or did you just want him to stand up against a wall so you could throw darts at him?'

'I was talking to Helen—if you don't mind,' Gerald said stiffly.

'All right,' Sylvia said. 'Don't get shirty.'

Helen moved away.

'What d'you think you're doing now?' Gerald demanded, lunging after her. He was curiously flushed and panicky.

'I thought I might help Mike with their drinks. Someone could be polite after all.'

Their exchange of words, quite suddenly, had become an incident. People stared; and from the other side of the room, she realized with cold shock, Tom Anderson regarded them with amusement. She broke free of Gerald and went to the bar.

'Can I help?' she asked Mike.

He raised blank eyes; sweat beaded thickly over his upper lip. 'Oh—yes, thanks,' he said. 'Thanks. Thanks a lot. What a mess this is. What a mess. What would you do?'

She didn't answer: it was the only time she had seen Mike discomforted at one of his own parties, and for some reason she was rather beginning to enjoy it.

Gathering up the filled glasses on a tray, she moved slowly across the room. Tom Anderson stood protectively before his friends; he intercepted her.

'Thank you, ma'm,' he said with mock grace, receiving the tray. 'Damn kind of you.' His eyes, lit with a strange mixture of insolence and friendliness, were keen and compelling.

'And who do you belong to?' he said. 'Gerry?'

'To no one,' she said swiftly, turning away; and her ticking heels carried her hot face back across the room.

Gerald was engaged in intense debate with Mike at the bar. He ignored her, but she overheard him say, 'After all, Mike, it's only a question of squeezing them out, isn't it?' Near them a large group talked in animated staccato. 'What a hide, though—' 'Those tar-babies and that fellow in the sweater—if you ask me . . .'

'Well,' said Sylvia, coming to stand beside Helen. 'There's only one thing for it. Get tight and watch the fun. Like a gin?'

Unabsorbed, isolated, they sat in an alcove, a recessed window seat; the Maoris occupied the seat, the fair delicate young man was arranged languidly on the floor, and Tom Anderson squatted on his haunches, waving an empty beer glass as he conducted the Maoris' singing. The fair young man sang fitfully, when he knew the words, but most of the time he spent gazing about the room with liquid, shallow eyes. Around them the party continued in a weak attempt to heal over the inflamed wound : voices were raised unnaturally high, glasses chinked, people eddied brief silhouettes back and forward against the raddled colour of the group in the alcove. It could almost be considered a normal party now, Helen thought : almost, except that only the newcomers appeared to be enjoying it. In the rest of the room there was just a grave determination to continue and to not acknowledge the disaster; and the guitars and pleasant Maori voices, circling bright and contrary, made the scene absurd.

'What's wrong with your boy friend?' Sylvia said. 'He's a cat on hot bricks.' Helen looked towards the bar and saw Gerald still talking earnestly to Mike.

Someone carried the radiogram in from another room in an effort to drown the singing. Then, just as music began to thunder from it, the fair young man, who had apparently developed a dislike for a rather elegant girl sitting near him, said something insulting to her. As if they had been waiting for precisely that moment, Gerald and Mike sprang across the room to where the fiancé of the elegant girl now stood threateningly above the fair young man. Trying to pacify everyone, Tom Anderson moved into the argument. The radiogram roared unchecked, smothering the clamour of voices : the six of them, the five boys and the girl, postured and grimaced like dumb characters in intricate tableau.

'It's getting really good,' Sylvia said, teetering on excited feet.

By the time the volume of the radiogram was lowered, Tom Anderson had somehow managed to calm the trouble. The sudden gathering dispersed, with warnings and meaningful gestures.

'Pity,' Sylvia murmured with a click of the tongue. 'I was just beginning to enjoy it.'

With a new rush of music, several couples began to spin about the floor. The group in the alcove did not attempt to sing again. After persuading the Maoris to join in the dancing, Tom Anderson spoke softly to the fair young man, who had sulkily taken a place in a shadowed corner of the window seat. The only response was a violent headshake. Then, ignoring the young man, he took up a guitar and began to idle his fingers over the strings while looking out over the room. He saw Helen : he winked broadly, grinning, as if they shared some secret, and raised his glass to her : she jerked her eyes away.

'Well,' Sylvia said drily. 'Don't tell me you've made a hit.'

Gerald came towards Helen. 'Dance?' he said, almost apologetically. She slipped into the crook of his arm and let him slide her away.

Over his shoulder, as they danced, she watched Mike approach Sylvia and say something. Sylvia hesitated, bracing herself, and then she hissed a reply. Mike backed away as though stung.

'I'm terribly sorry things have gone wrong,' Gerald was saying. 'Everything's gone wrong tonight.'

She could, she supposed, have replied that on the contrary she was enjoying the evening; but the sarcasm, even if it were lost on him, would have been pointless and cruel.

'Let's try and make up for it,' he went on, as though he had learned the phrase by heart from book or film : spoken in his unbending way, it sounded faintly ridiculous.

Sylvia's blue frock flashed towards the alcove. Helen's view was obscured for a moment, and then she saw Sylvia dancing with Tom Anderson.

Gerald stiffened. 'Do you see that?' he said.

'What?'

'Sylvia.'

'I know,' she said calmly.

'The sooner Mike wakes up to her the better. I've been trying to make him see.'

'See what?'

'See she'll only mess him up.'

'What's wrong with Sylvia?'

'Ask yourself. Look at her tonight. Drinking like a fish.'

'Have you ever thought Mike might be the reason why?'

'Look here,' he said sharply. 'Mike's my friend. I'd like you to remember that.'

'Then I wish you'd remember that Sylvia's my friend,' Helen said in a small, even voice.

'Please yourself.'

There was a pause.

'And there's just one thing I'd like you to tell me,' she said.

'What's that?'

'Why are you so afraid of Tom Anderson?'

'Who said I was afraid of him?'

'In that case you're putting on a marvellous act.'

'Look,' he said with irritation. 'Can't we just quietly forget about him? He'll be gone soon, anyhow.'

'Why?'

'Because we just got him to promise to clear himself and his menagerie out of here soon—that's why.'

Helen was silent. She was quite certain what she had to do, now. There was only the one question to ask.

'Dear old Gerry's girl friend, eh?' Tom said. They were dancing: they moved lightly, swiftly, through the turning colours: blues and reds, golds and crimsons, flickered confused patterns before her eyes. His voice was low in her ear. 'Friend, is it—or fiancée?'

'Friend.'

'Well, well. And when shall it be fiancée?'

'I don't know—that it will.'

'He's asked, I suppose.'

'Yes. He's asked.'

'Well,' he said with his friendly smile. 'Dear old Gerry.'

Close, his face quickly lost its crude strength: cheekbones formed gaunt ridges in the thin white flesh, and in the eyes, retreated down dark sockets, there were webs of redness. He regarded her quizzically.

'Would you tell me something?' she said.

'Anything you like. A pleasure.'

'Why is he so afraid of you?'

'Who?—Gerry?' he asked, with affected surprise. 'Is he afraid of me?'

'You've seen him tonight.'

'Well,' he said, with a slight lift of the eyebrows. 'I'd never have guessed.'

'You were good friends at college, weren't you?'

'Excellent friends.'

'Then why does he hate you now?'

'Perhaps,' he suggested, 'he's just forgotten—that we were friends.'

'He hasn't forgotten—you know that.'

'Well, then—I can't understand it. Can you?' He smiled again, as if the whole thing were charmingly inexplicable.

'But you do really understand.'

'Do I?'

'Tell me what you and he were like at college.'

'Well,' he said, pausing briefly. 'He used to keep me company when I wandered about the countryside with my sketchbook. He was never much of an artist himself, as I remember; not that I ever was either, come to think of it. Also he used to produce poetry of a rather badly written variety; a pastime in which I encouraged him, since there might have been something there. That satisfy you?'

He paused for breath: smoky air wheezed in his throat. 'Or perhaps there's something else you want to know?' he said.

'And Mike?'

'Ah, yes. There was Mike. The big bad philistine in the background. All rather a good setting for a melodrama, don't you think?' His breath wheezed again, and he added, 'You could say the first act ended when I was expelled. Mike informed on me, of course. Liquor on college premises—it wasn't at all the thing. Nor girls over the college wall.'

'And why did Mike inform?'

'Well, let's be fair, shall we, and say that perhaps he wasn't a patron of the arts and would have preferred me to give my full attention to rugby, a game at which I sometimes excelled. Not a puritan, mind. Not Mike—I never did find out where he got his own liquor from.'

'And what about Gerald?'

'Yes—alas, poor innocent Gerald. Betwixt and between.'

'And which act would this be?'

'The last,' he said, glancing about the room. 'If tonight's any indication. How would you put the sub-title? After the passing of several long years . . .'

He appeared, suddenly, to have dismissed the subject.

The dance was faster now. Walls jazzed fleetingly, faces twitched in and out of focus, points of light blinked. He swept her around, not roughly as she had expected, but like a fragile thing. There was an electric gentleness in his fingers. She was out of breath suddenly, leaning against him, his stubbled chin prickling her cheek: she could smell his sweating male warmth.

'Enough?' he said softly.

'Yes.'

'Then let's have a drink.' He steered her towards the alcove. 'You will drink with us, won't you?'

'Of course. Why not?'

'I'd hate to get you into trouble with Gerry.' Strangely, he seemed to mean it.

'It's too late for that.' She frowned, biting her lip, for the moment unsure of herself. Gerald had left the room some time before. But why should she worry, even if she did hurt him? Would Gerald have been as concerned for her feelings?

But that was no answer: she knew that. There was no answer. Only her smile and Tom's laugh.

'You haven't met Derek yet,' Tom said as he led her into the alcove. 'Helen, Derek. Derek, Helen.'

The fair young man didn't rise from his seat; he raised cool eyes briefly, his face still pouting. 'How do you do?' he said in a light disinterested voice.

'Derek plays the violin,' Tom said. 'He's really most enchanting when he plays the violin. Now Helen here is extremely interested in things, Derek. You should get on well with her. Interested in things like—ah, yes, poetry. Extremely interested in poetry. Isn't it pleasant to meet someone like that, Derek?'

Derek didn't look up again.

'Excuse him, won't you?' Tom said, as though apologizing for a child.

The cough came without preliminary: one moment he was smiling at her; the next he was doubled up with the sudden violence of it. And then, as quickly recovered, he smiled again with unchanged assurance. 'We'll drink, shall we?' he said.

Serving himself, he fetched new drinks from the bar. 'And now,' he said, 'perhaps we could toast something? What do you suggest?'

'To—' She hesitated. 'To poetry. Badly written.' Their glasses touched with light sound.

'And to all the rest that never got written,' he added quietly, without emphasis.

She looked at him quickly, expecting to see in his eyes, perhaps, some wistful trick of light to betray his smile. If there was something there, she was too late to see it; the eyes blinked, and the lids rose on lustreless pupils, circled by the same red webs.

She realized, for the first time, that he was drunk, though his manner and speech did not show it. He tilted back his head and drank with a flourish, his neck-muscles rippling. It was a gesture of defiance.

'Tell me something,' he said as he wiped his mouth with the back of his hand. 'Do you really think you'll marry Gerry? Or shouldn't I ask?'

'You shouldn't ask,' she said lamely. The question made her remember Sylvia. She looked about and saw that Sylvia too had vanished from the room. Perhaps to be ill.

'Who are you looking for?' Tom said. 'Gerry?'

'Sylvia.'

'Sylvia? Ah, yes, Mike's fiancée. She danced very nicely.'

'I really think I should find her,' Helen apologized.

'It's all right—if you want to go,' he said, touching her arm lightly.

'How do you mean?'

'I mean it's all right if you want to go. You don't have to make an excuse.'

'But I'm not making an excuse. I'm just worried about—'

'In any case,' he observed, 'you'll notice everyone else seems to be leaving us.'

She saw the room beginning to empty: the radiogram had just been disconnected and was being carried through to another room. Apparently they had decided to isolate the unwanted guests altogether.

The Maoris returned to the alcove; their brown skins were shiny with sweat from the dancing. They were anxious and tense.

'I think we better go now,' one of the boys said, showing white teeth.

'Nonsense,' Tom said. 'Let's make more music.'

'I think we better go,' the boy persisted.

'More music,' Tom insisted. '*Kapai te* music.' He began to talk quickly and persuasively.

'Really, Tom,' Derek appealed in his thin, affected voice. 'Don't you think all this has gone far enough?'

'Everyone sit down,' Tom commanded. 'We're just getting started.' He turned to Helen. 'Aren't we, Helen? You will stay, won't you?'

And his eyes, hinting again, seemed to add : after all, there is no real need to say anything; we understand each other, don't we, you and I?

'I'll stay,' she said faintly.

'Really, I think—' Derek began to protest.

'Shut up,' Tom said mildly.

He drew up a chair for Helen and sat himself on the arm. The Maoris crowded back into the window seat, and Derek slipped unwillingly to the floor.

Everyone else had left the room, but at that moment Gerald returned to stand at the door.

'Helen,' he said quietly.

There was a silence. Sylvia wobbled into the doorway to stand behind Gerald.

'Helen,' he repeated sharply.

He stood only a few yards away, at the other end of the misty room. But it seemed a much greater distance; a distance across which words would never carry, never reach him. There was no way to answer.

She shook her head. He stared with disbelief, then turned away.

There was the sound of Sylvia's high, brittle laugh; Mike came and Sylvia allowed herself to be led away, still laughing. The door slammed and there was silence.

Tom touched her arm lightly, gratefully; but she did not look at him. The guitars began to strum.

It was after midnight : out in the passage goodbyes were said as another group of guests departed.

From other rooms came the subdued sounds of the dying party : a drowsy twilight, settling over the rest of the house, had infected even those in the quarantine room, for weakening voices had fallen away to leave Tom Anderson to pluck sad, reflective notes from a borrowed guitar and sing alone.

The lights had long before been turned out. The moon chinked slanting silver through the curtains; pale, half-lit features emerged from the dark. They listened in silence : he had passed, now, from the robust and bawdy song; and his solitary voice, mellow and haunting, found the sentimental ballad.

> *When I walked out in the streets of Laredo*
> *When I walked out in Laredo one day*
> *I spied a young cowboy all wrapped in white linen*
> *Wrapped in white linen as cold as the clay*

For one moment it seemed the song would break off altogether; she felt the body beside her arch and quiver as his voice cracked and his fingers faltered discords. But this time he smothered the cough quickly with a balled handkerchief. He paused for voice : from the silence she reached out a hand, awkward and hesitant. His fingers responded gently to her touch before they shifted to the silent strings and discovered the tune again.

> *'I see by your outfit that you are a cowboy'*
> *These words he did say as I boldly stepped by*
> *'Come sit down beside me and hear my sad story*
> *I'm shot in the breast and know I must—*

Suddenly she was aware of something new and disquieting. Moving her eyes slightly she met Derek's steady unblinking stare; moonlight and thin shadow met on his face, intensifying the high-boned sharpness of his features. His eyes, small and faintly gleaming, continued to regard her with contempt and distaste : she looked away quickly, trying to check her sudden trembling. For one moment she was afraid she might cry out.

It was once in the saddle I used to go dashing

The door sprang open: an oblong of yellow light leapt across the floor. Mike entered the room and, peering uncertainly into the dark, sought Helen out.

First down to Rosie's and then to the cardhouse

Mike spoke quickly, slurring his words. 'Sylvia—she needs you. Says she won't talk to anyone else. I can't do anything with her. She's squiffy as hell. I can't—' He caught at her arm in dumb appeal. 'She won't talk to anyone but you. You might be able to do something with her.'

Get six tall cowboys to carry my coffin

'Please,' Mike said. 'Please.'

Six purty maidens to sing me a song

She realized, as she rose and left with Mike, that she needed suddenly to escape the room, the eyes, the song, the singer. But, insistent and mocking, the voice followed them as they moved down the passage, their feet striking dull sounds from the carpet.

O beat the drum slowly and play the fife lowly

'You leave me,' she said to Mike over-loudly. 'I'll look after her.' The voice, fading, pursued her still: it seemed to have acquired another dimension now, so that she glimpsed beneath the bright surface of defiance another, darker level.

When I walked out in the streets of Laredo

She slammed the door. She leaned against it, her hot cheek pressed to the cold panel, until she was recovered. Then she turned to face the bedroom.

Washed in pale green light, the room had a heavy, enclosed smell; faint streamers of smoke lingered towards the ceiling, and on the table beside the bed stood a depleted bottle of gin and two large glasses, one overturned in its own puddle. The bed looked crumpled, slept-in: Sylvia's frock, a splash of blue on the sheen of the red bedcover, twisted up towards her thighs to reveal long nyloned legs and a transparent white underslip. She lay face down, one brown arm crooked out from the body, the hand clenching and unclenching a corner of the bedcover. Hair tented her face in a tangle of blonde.

'Get out,' she said, jerking convulsively. 'Get out you bastard.'

'It's only me,' Helen said quietly. She went to the bed.

Fingering back her hair, Sylvia raised her face. The skin was puffed and tired, the make-up smudged by tears; the lips, still a faint red, were like a thin scar, and the eyes were watering and bleak. 'I'm sorry,' she murmured. Her breath caught in her throat; she smiled, crookedly. 'I'm sorry,' she said again.

'Are you all right?' Helen said.

'I'm all right.' Sylvia tried to smile again. 'There's only one thing wrong with me. I've been starting to think too damn much.' She looked at Helen through drying eyes. 'Do you think sometimes.'

'Everyone thinks sometimes.'

'I mean thinking about things—about everything. About how you used to think once there were all kinds of beautiful things in the world. And how you find out it's only a dirty cheat, the things they put in music and poetry. Don't you ever think about that? Don't you?'

But she gave Helen no pause for reply.

'No? Well you're not educated then. You'll soon find out what a dirty cheat it is. There's no beautiful things. Just randy bastards and chemists' shops. You'll get educated.' A shudder rippled her body; her glazed eyes danced over Helen's face. 'Where's your Gerry, anyhow? What've you done with him?'

'He's somewhere. I don't know.'

'Poor old Gerry. You know something? He doesn't know quite what to make of you. He thinks he might be in on a win if he had an intelligent wife. But you only get him all balled up. What he really wants is a dumb decorative blonde like me.' She stopped a second. 'So you've been with them—with the others, all night?'

'Of course.'

Sylvia laughed. 'I knew you didn't understand.'

'What don't I understand?'

Sylvia's laugh rang again; it was edged with bitterness. 'Tom Anderson's not interested in you. He's only playing a little game with Gerry. Can't you see? He—' Her voice broke, and the laughter welled out in thin hysterical crackles. Helen tried to force her back to the pillow. The hysteria subsiding, they fought wordlessly, from anger and despair. Presently Sylvia lay limp and silent. Helen, trembling, drew back from the bed.

'I'm sorry,' Sylvia murmured. 'It's not true what I said. I didn't mean to say it—I don't know—' She sat up suddenly and pointed to the door. 'Go on. Before it's too late to try. Go back and find him.' She seemed to choke. 'And God help you. God help you both.'

Outside, there were voices: a door banged; someone laughed. Helen flung open the door and ran from the bedroom. Along the passage Gerald and Mike blocked her way.

'It's all right,' Gerald said. 'They've gone. We got rid of them.'

'Where did they go?' she said.

'They've gone,' Gerald repeated. 'Gone.'

'Sylvia,' Mike said, as Sylvia came stumbling along the passage. 'You should've stayed—'

'What do you think you're doing?' Gerald said to Helen.

'Can't you see?' she said. 'I'm putting on my coat.'

'You're not—my God, you poor fool.'

He caught at her shoulders. She tried to burst free, but he held tight, beginning to shake her. 'Can't you see—can't you . . .' The words bubbled frantically in his throat; his face quivered. She couldn't be angry: no longer certain of himself, he was bewildered, lost, pathetic, alone. She could only be sorry for him.

She almost wished she could have stayed so not to hurt him; but there was not even any question of choice now. Even if her flight or pursuit, whatever it was, in the end was only futile, then it was still something she had to do; a simple thing, like proving she was still herself.

Confused, struggling, the four of them were bunched in the narrow hallway. Sylvia's open hand smacked twice across Mike's face. Mike, recoiling, lurched heavily against Gerald, and Helen

broke free of him at last : she escaped through the front door into
a cool silent world laced with moonlight : trees, gardens, and then
streets, pale, empty and echoing.

3

Somewhere she had taken a wrong turning. She was, suddenly,
quite lost. The familiar part of the city was vanished behind her;
ahead it was new and strange. Sagging and weed-tangled, rickety
buildings conjured from nightmare lined the way; and the curtained eyes of unlit windows.

She ran still : she ran until the feet ringing behind her slowed
and a voice called her name. She leaned against a wooden wall
and waited until Sylvia, limping, came to stand beside her.

They looked at each other without words; their breathing
sobbed. A loose shop-awning flapped monotonously in the wind.
Sylvia moved nearer.

'I should have made you understand,' she said. 'It was no
good. That boy and—'

'But I knew,' Helen said.

'You knew? Then why—'

There was a pause.

Suddenly they were clinging together as though in fright. The
wind grieved through overhead wires : it slapped and rustled,
nipping them with cold. Sylvia lifted her head and tried to speak.

'No,' Helen whispered. 'Don't say anything at all.'

KNOCK ON YESTERDAY'S DOOR

I

Turning without hesitation into the remembered door, he escaped from the hot world where trams hammered down narrow valleys of old wooden buildings, where the dying sun left cooling veins of violet in the sky; inside the house, he paused at the place where the worn carpet began to track erratically up the thin stairway, and then his feet struck volleys of creaks from the old, warped wood; at the top of the stairs he took breath, smelling the cool mustiness which hung between the dark-papered walls, and then, stirred sharply by memory, he moved down the gloomy passage to the door of the end flat.

He heard, now, a woman's singing voice.

His knuckles hit three times on the varnished wood : inside the flat the voice dwindled, and was silent. Sandalled feet slapped towards the door; the lock unclicked and the door swung open a little way.

'Who is it?' Val said, peering into the gloom; her voice was tremulous, slight. 'Who—'

The open door let an angle of light fall into the passage : he moved into it. 'Only me,' he said. 'Roger. Remember?'

'Roger? But—' Her arms jerked in a small theatrical gesture. 'Roger,' she repeated softly, pleased now. 'Roger.'

There was an absurdly awkward moment. Then she swung the door wide.

'Come in, Roger,' she said in a slow, pleasant voice.

He moved past her, into the flat, gathering the faintest smell of perfume. And then he stood in the small living-room, embarrassed, out of place. Val always made him feel large and clumsy. She closed the door and turned her back on it; the snapping lock sounded final, irrevocable. He was boxed in with her; and there was no escape. She leaned back against the door, looking at him in astonishment still, as if refusing to credit his existence. He felt he should say something, but his confidence was gone already. He wished, suddenly, he had not come.

'So you've come back,' she said. 'After all this time.' The crisp voice conveyed nothing, yet the smile which quivered on the slim mouth seemed at least to say she was pleased to see him.

'It's a long time,' he said; the obvious statement sounded flat and inadequate.

'Yes,' she said. 'A long time.' She gave the words a different emphasis; gilded them with meaning significant and profound. She went lightly across the room and picked up a packet of cigarettes. 'Fag?' She offered the packet with a neat flourish.

He shook his head; he had been smoking too much. But he remembered to take matches from his pocket and light her cigarette. The small flame trembled at the end of his fingers, and he avoided looking at her. He had a slightly giddy feeling; liquor lay warm in his empty stomach.

Cool, assured, she rested against the table, slipping into her familiar stance, legs crossed and arms angled so that the cigarette remained conveniently near her mouth; her grey eyes, behind the twining streamers of smoke, regarded him with curiosity.

'Fancy,' she said. 'Roger. Back from the dead. Nobody's heard anything about you in a long time. Not since—'

'No,' he said quickly. 'I've never written letters.'

'I've often thought about you,' she said. 'Wondered how you were. It's silly, isn't it, when a person goes right out of your life, how you start imagining things? Quite unreal things.'

'For instance?'

'I imagined you might be settled somewhere by now. Married, probably. In a little, well-weeded garden of content.' She paused. 'You're not, though, are you?'

'No.'

'Not settled, not married, not in a little garden of content.' She sighed, smoke circling from her ovalled mouth. 'You disillusion me.'

'I'm sorry about that,' he said sullenly.

'Sensitive Roger,' she laughed. 'Poor old sensitive Roger. That's what Peter used to say.' She smiled, and added decisively, 'You haven't changed.'

'You aren't giving me much chance to prove anything else, are you?' he demanded, irritated. Still awkward in the centre of the room, he was aware of growing discomfort; his palms were sticky, and moist underclothing itched on his body. The heat of the day, in this cooling room, seemed suddenly more oppressive.

'For goodness sake, Roger,' she said with friendly sharpness. 'Loosen up. Relax. You look awful just standing there. Take off your coat and sit down.'

He obeyed.

'And stop looking like a startled rabbit. I'm not going to eat you.' Her tone was brisk. 'Now,' she said, offering the packet again. 'Will you have a cigarette this time? Come on.'

She lit it for him before he could light it himself; her hand was perfectly steady. Then she went across the room, rippling through oblongs of pale gold light, and opened a window. A breeze whispered the curtains. 'Feel better?' she asked.

'Cooler, anyway.'

'That's good. You'll stay to eat, won't you?'

'If it's not too much trouble. I mean, if you've got plenty.'

'Of course I've plenty. Don't be so stuffy.'

A side of the room was partitioned with a curtain. Inside stood an electric stove, a half-size refrigerator, a sinkbench, and shelves of crockery and food. She went there and, the burning cigarette dangling from a moistened lip, began to click switches and bang pots down on the stove. 'It'll just be some poisonous hash,' she said. 'But you won't mind, will you?'

He tried to smile. 'I always did like your hash, remember?'

'Did you?' Busy and distracted, smiling vaguely, she moved with precision about the stove. 'Well, haven't you anything to tell me?' She began to peel onions.

'About what?'

'About what?' she repeated, mimicking his voice. 'Good God, man. About yourself. Where've you been? What've you done?'

'I don't know.'

'That's delightfully obscure. You mean to say you haven't been conscious all this time?'

Her voice needled him, stung the liquor awake. 'What do you want to know about?' he demanded. 'The time I worked in a timber mill? The time I was a fisherman? Or the time I was an editor?' He was, he knew, boasting now; but he wanted to shock her out of her composure.

'It all sounds interesting,' she said. 'Tell me the lot.'

'I'll tell you about Jack,' he said. 'Jack was my cobber in the timber mill. Jack and I went on the bash every Saturday. In the first town out of the bush, twenty miles away. Drink all day and pay a visit to the local house at night. Nice girls. Every Saturday.'

'Sounds pleasant,' she murmured.

'What about Wally? I'm sure you'd love to know about Wally. The only difference is that Wally and I didn't get drunk regular. Only when the boat was tied up. And there wasn't a local house. So we picked the girls up around the wharf and lured them down to the boat and fed them gin. Easy, then. Free, too.'

'Lovely,' she said calmly. 'You've really been seeing life, haven't you?'

'And I'm sure you'd just love to hear about that little town oozing with butterfat money. Nice little place, lousy with prosperity. I bluffed my way into getting a job as editor of the local rag. Nice, comfortable job. I could still be there. If I hadn't started writing about the H-bomb instead of butterfat prices or rugby football. Not that I was fired for the editorials. Oh, no. The publisher, a nice greasy little sod, questioned my morals. Not my politics. You'd think I was infecting the town, the way he talked. I drank too much, he said. It was bad for the paper's reputation. And he didn't like me sleeping with the advertising manager's wife. I imagine he was hoping for a shot at her himself. He only made one mistake, though. I was tanked when he fired me. But I got the biggest fright when I hit him. I hadn't really hit anyone before, not like that. The funny thing is, I enjoyed it.'

His voice had become thin and ridiculous; he was being absurdly adolescent. Val was peeling the onions with a slow, meticulous motion of the hands.

'Sounds as if you've become a real alcoholic,' she observed mildly. 'There's some sherry on the mantelpiece. Sorry about the other thing, though.'

He sat silent: her serene voice calmed him, shamed him, brought him back to the room. It had not changed in two years: the warm colours of the old furniture Val had covered and painted, the pastel walls, the rattan-shaded lamps, the light-varnished record-player, the bright Dufy prints, the Knight-Turner drawing of Peter, the grease-mountained candle in the empty chianti bottle on the mantel, the half-filled decanter of sherry beside it; yet the whole effect of the room, perhaps because of Val's more conventional touches, was of veneered compromise with bohemia. And in one corner, in a niche formed among glutted bookshelves, stood Peter's desk. The appearance was almost of a shrine: the typewriter cased, papers and manuscripts in neat stacks, pens and pencils arranged in a rack, and the large clean paua-shell ashtray gleaming copper and purple colours: dustless, poignant, it was plain that Peter had long ago left the desk. For Peter, long hair tousled, shirt split down his chest, corduroys bagging, always worked in demented confusion, papers flooding the desk and slopping to the floor. Only Val could have supplied that tidiness; only Val, arranging and dusting through the weeks and months, salvaging a clean skeleton of order from the living flesh of chaos.

'No,' Val said softly. 'You haven't changed, Roger. You're still full of yourself.'

'And I suppose Peter wasn't,' he said bitterly.

'He could forget himself sometimes.'

'You've got to live with yourself all the time.'

'And with other people,' Val added quietly.

'Remember that Sartre play you acted in?' he said. 'The one Peter thought so decadent? *Hell is other people.*'

'Heaven, too.'

'What do you mean?'

'Heaven is other people too, Roger.'

'Charming thought, anyway,' he said. 'Please yourself.'

'One day,' Val said evenly, 'you might grow up. Meanwhile, do you want some sherry or not? Because I do.'

'I'm sorry,' he muttered. 'I forgot.' He fetched the decanter of sherry and poured two drinks. His hands were still unsteady; his forefingers were nearly black with nicotine stain. She left the stove and accepted her glass gracefully.

'Well,' she said, smiling. 'Here's to the return of the wanderer.' Their glasses touched lightly. He could smell the perfume again. 'Two years,' she said. 'And all that time you were running away.'

'If that's what you want to call it.'

'It's true, isn't it?' She paused. 'Didn't it work?'

He shrugged. Then he fell into a chair and looked at his sherry. 'No,' he said. 'It didn't work.'

'And why have you come back?'

'Why does anyone come back?'

'That, if I may say so, is begging the question.'

'All right. I was curious. That simple enough? I wanted to see how different things were.'

'Things are different here, anyway,' she said, going back to the stove. 'That's obvious.'

A savoury smell drifted from the cooking food. He felt the thin sherry ribboning down to his empty stomach. He had not eaten since he left the train. He brooded all day in pubs, hoping whisky might give him the courage to face her.

Why come back? Already, in this single day, that question to himself had become monotonous. He had begun to ask it when the express hissed along the platform yellowed in early morning sunlight. Why come back? Certainly not from curiosity. He had come back because he needed to come back. He needed to see if he had changed; for he was sure he had. Yet here, in the familiar room where he thought he might discover the new self, he found only the old self; or at least found himself slipping back into the skin of the old self, defensively truculent and cynical. This was not how he wanted it; this trite protection of words against Val. He wanted to be honest. But from the moment he entered the flat that intention seemed to have been foundering. He felt lost, and helpless.

He thought too that for the first time he might see himself clearly without Peter. This room, with all its associations, with

Val, should have been all that was needed to coax the emotion of loss. His restless, solitary life about the country had obscured the original emotion. Yet now, with the emptiness actual before him, the desk tidied and dustless, he felt nothing.

Perhaps they would talk of Peter presently.

But if he could not see himself, he could at least see Val. Lately she had become too shadowy in his mind, too lost behind Peter; now she was living and vivid, once more the girl he knew. Strangely, she did not seem lonely; she seemed to live with assurance beside the memory.

She came from behind the curtain, humming a gypsy tune and smiling as she emerged. 'Nearly ready,' she said, moving towards him, slipping an unlighted cigarette into her mouth.

He had always watched with pleasure the crisp, certain movement of her limbs: the quick, slender brown arms; the pert ankles and long legs; the firm thighs stirring behind a light skirt. Her head was erect on a delicate neck; her face, tanned a cool olive complexion, was high-boned and clear-fleshed, entirely undeceptive in expression. Her blonde hair was pony-tailed with a dangling blue ribbon and a cotton tartan shirt, shaped slightly by her breasts, fell loose below her waist, around the yellow skirt.

He had known her before Peter. But the two affairs could not have been more different: his own an end to agonized adolescence, the loss of his virginity (though not the loss of hers: that body seemed never to have been a stranger to love) on the creaking springs of the old metal-posted bed where he spent the restless nights of his student life; the other a cautious courtship with Peter, wise and adult, coaxing love and finding marriage. Then she was no longer the girl, Val, whose name awoke an alien tenderness in him, who thrilled with whispering limbs and husky voice as no one since had done. She was suddenly a stranger; his best friend's girl, his best friend's wife.

He lit her cigarette; her grey eyes surveyed him gravely. 'You know something?' she said. 'It's comfortable, having you around again.'

He remained silent and obscurely troubled. Her expression grew cheeky. 'There's only one thing, though,' she added.

'What's that?'

'I can't argue as well as Peter.'

'You don't do too badly.'

'Really? But you've no idea how much out of practice I am. I haven't heard a good argument since—well, for quite a long time.'

2

Peter always argued well.

At college there were heated collisions with teachers; he always seemed to get his own way, to win before teachers sheltered behind scholarly dignity. Peter, brash with the queer innocence of adolescence, accepted nothing; questioned everything. Teachers were warned about him, advised to avoid classroom controversy.

The college was a modern one, with new paint and fresh concrete, and large-windowed, bright classrooms; the headmaster a mild grey elderly man who vaguely approved of advanced educational theory. But Peter, for whom no theory made provision, entirely bewildered him; after a classroom disturbance, he often escorted Peter to his study and begged him to be reasonable. But for Peter reason lay not in quiet and acquiescence, but in the sound of his own voice stitching fact and opinion into an intricate lace of argument.

All through college he had been Peter's closest friend. They were together in school debate; together in the backline of the school rugby team. In their last year they jointly edited the college magazine; and together resigned from the magazine when publication of Peter's contributions was forbidden after a panicky staff conference. The headmaster saw, in an article on modern education and a piece of political satire on the atom bomb, anarchism flowering darkly in his shining new college. Roger also resigned as prefect; Peter, for some reason, had never been made a prefect. Roger's own contribution, a harmless schoolboy piece of nature verse, remained in the re-edited magazine; Peter, kind though rarely condescending, saw promise in it and advised him to write more. But because he saw what Peter left unspoken, saw through Peter's eyes the poem as facile and empty, he never wrote another.

Strange, then, that Peter's radicalism at university should have separated them. Roger's childhood, in which the depression talked grey memories, was working class and radical; Peter, like most students, was from the middle class. His father was a doctor of liberal opinion who was imprisoned and ill-treated as a conscientious objector in the first world war. Disillusioned with all political and moral remedy, he died while Peter was at university, a tubercular and prematurely frail old man who had long before purged his shame and self-respect to become an accepted member of society. On the other hand, Roger's father was once a militant union organizer. Though now a tired old man indistinguishable from a hundred other tired old men who weeded backyard suburban gardens on weekends, he still smoked a pipe with his old leftist cronies and mourned the lost revolution in the corner pub, and once a month presided over bleak meetings of his Labour Party branch. Roger had seen him once arrested for leading an illegal strike; and as a child had helped him deliver anti-war leaflets. Leaflets warning against the approach of a war about which Peter's father found it expedient to remain silent.

But the real difference between Peter and himself was not of class, not of fathers : the one who rebelled from idealism and the one who rebelled from necessity. The difference was of acceptance. Roger accepted with sympathy his father's defeat; Peter had only contempt for his father's surrender. He remembered not the young clear-faced medical student of yellowing photographs who was led away like a criminal and made a plaything of sadists, but the shrunken grey man trapped in a small-town surgery, sensitive to rumour and hurt, and burying belief beneath nihilism. And that man, whom he could not accept, he toppled easily, like a top-heavy monument. But had he paused before he overturned the monument, hesitated before he sent it shattering, he might have observed a small dull stain bleeding slowly from the hewn grey stone.

There was more too; Peter had still to feel the real pressure of the world. Roger knew it, had lived with it all his life. He remembered not just his handcuffed father, the leaflets which could be delivered only late at night, but his isolation as a child by the mocking children of the middle class; the schoolboy taunts about his father. He had learned, long before, not to go too far; to keep his distance, keep his silence.

So now, as if from instinct, he found himself keeping his distance from Peter. Seeking excuse, he discovered easy pose in cynicism. They would differ; he found allies in Koestler and Gide. 'All right,' Peter said. 'So Stalin isn't a Christ who walks on water. So what? Do you deny a religion because of the immorality of a priest?' Nevertheless, they remained good friends; he seemed to act as a point of return for Peter to argue his mind clear. And even if he accepted Peter's Communism and new sharp-talking friends only with reserve, they still saw each other often. After evening lectures at university they sometimes wandered talking through the city, through bright streets and dim lanes, and along the waterfront past ocean liners and fishing boats and glittering water.

At university he moved among a different set; a drifting common-room element, sporty and party-going. Sometimes there were the awkward, embarrassing questions : 'I say, aren't you a friend of that Peter what's-his-name, that Commo character? You are? I thought so. You're a Commo too, I suppose. What's that? You're not? Well, what do you know about that?' Peter was soon singled out for abuse by the right wing in the university; and for jest by the indolent common-room intellectuals. Communism in the 'fifties was an anachronism, a foolish survival from the 'thirties; the 'fifties knew better. Roger would argue this and other things with Peter. 'I take it, then,' Peter answered calmly, 'that you approve of the way things are now?'

'Don't be fatuous. Of course not.'

'Then what other alternative is there? If you're honest.'

And he could, with the guilty self-knowledge of surrender, privately half-way agree with the implicit criticism of himself; and then realize that in another way he was honest because, unlike Peter, he refused to abandon doubt. Doubt bred question; and a single question sprang a dozen answers. And doubt, with questions and answers, left him impotent.

Then he met Val. She was new to the university, from a provincial city, and excited by new ideas. She was already, untutored and raw, a considerable natural actress; he met her after a play, a drearily produced Ibsen piece in which her acting was the only thing of interest, at an after-show party which he and some of his friends gate-crashed. Giddy with alcohol, astonished at his own daring, he complimented her on her performance; and found her friendly. She was unlike the other bright-sweatered varsity girls, vivid as butterflies and brittle as chalk, whom he disliked; they had not yet infected her with their disease of sophistication. She was naïve and altogether impressionable; and he, for a time, must have impressed her. He only knew that by confiding in her he found relief from self-accusation, and his guilt at deserting Peter.

Inevitably, Val met Peter. He had seen no significance in their meeting; not even when, immediately afterwards, she questioned him about Peter; not even when their short fumbled undergraduate affair came to an end. He saw other reasons for the break, found the cause in his own inadequacy.

And perhaps because of that he felt no real grievance a month or two later when he learned Val had broken with her family and was living with Peter. They had, he learned, done their best to keep the affair hidden from him, for fear of hurting him. This in fact was successful. If he felt resentment at all, it was not against Peter for taking Val, but against Val for coming between himself and Peter. When Val turned twenty-one, she and Peter were married; Roger was best man. At that time Val managed to effect a reconciliation with her family; it lasted until Val's father, president of his city's Chamber of Commerce, discovered Peter's political affiliation.

Roger saw less of Peter. His degree uncompleted, Peter left university in despair and disgust with students and intellectuals after the collapse of the radical club he had organized there. It had early flourished under Peter's wild, erratic leadership; and then died when his efficient, cold-eyed party-lining friends began to take over behind scenes. The students in sympathy with Peter's initial loud rebellion soon drifted away. But Peter chose to blame the drifting students, and not his friends; and abandoned the university to conservatism.

First he applied unsuccessfully for admission to teachers' training college; then unsuccessfully for a post in a Government department. 'Security police everywhere,' he explained cheerfully to Roger. 'They must have a good dossier on me.' He took a job as unskilled labourer and became active in trade union politics. And now that Roger no longer saw Peter about the university, he had often to get news through Val, when he met her in a corridor. 'He's just the same,' she would say with a swift, deprecating gesture. 'Busy with his Party work nearly every night of the week. Did I tell you he's been elected president of his trade union? Oh, yes—and he's still trying to find time to write a novel.'

If he called around to the flat on a Sunday to see Peter, Val would of course be there, moving lightly about the room while they talked, singing softly as she dispensed coffee or cooked a meal. Marriage seemed to give Peter strength. He argued against Roger with supreme confidence. The world might, in Roger's eyes, be falling to pieces; but Peter, deftly sorting the pieces, would show dialectical pattern and shape where Roger could see only confusion; see hope where Roger could see only despair.

But something was wrong now; and Roger was troubled. Peter's words had always had an edge of glibness; with sincerity, it had not seemed so important. Now, for the first time, the easy-falling words became irritating. They were no longer questioning, gently exploratory words; they were words precisely ordered for defence and attack along a fixed front. Peter had discovered the answer. His arguments were formally perfect and clever; without heat, without passion.

Roger recognized, now, the secret faith he had kept that Peter was right and himself wrong; a faith nourished by despair. Now he saw his own half-genuine, half-sham reasoning as right and Peter's formulas as treacherous, he felt obscurely betrayed. All this time he had been wanting Peter to be right. He felt sick. Was it he who had changed, or Peter?

And so their arguments grew in violence.

Caught between Peter's glibness and the smugness of his other friends, he cried finally, 'Only one hope for us all. The bomb. And let it come quickly.'

And Peter turned away in disgust.

Val laid two thin bamboo mats on the dining-table; then arranged knives and forks for the meal. 'Remember the night when you and Peter had that big row?' she said. 'I didn't ever think we'd see you again.'

'You nearly didn't,' he said. 'It was almost a year, wasn't it?'

'A long time, anyway,' she said. 'Funny to remember.'

Finished with university, a useless degree after his name, he found himself suddenly aimless in a pointless world. After their final, seemingly irrevocable argument, he never saw Peter; and Val, now he had left university, only rarely. He did hear, through a remote connexion, that Peter's trade union had sent him to a peace congress at Vienna, and he had travelled back through the Soviet Union and China; the person who told him was most impressed by the fact that Peter had met Sartre, but knew little else.

He was tired of the people he knew, the parties where conversation circled gaudy and empty. He toyed briefly with the idea of joining the army to go to Korea; then rejected it, for no reason other than the probability of his own discomfort, and the possibility of his own death. He told himself there was no moral issue. He took a job on a newspaper. He told himself there was no issue there, either; that in fact his cynicism would be ideal since he would suffer no illusion about the nature of the glossy variants of truth he would be obliged to write.

'The bomb,' he would say, drunk and joking, in pubs, at parties. 'The redeemer of us all.'

So that, eventually, even his own drifting set of friends sickened of him. They saw him as someone with a mental quirk; a tiresome oddity. One or two predicted his suicide; they could almost have been right.

Loneliness became suffocating. Since Peter there had been no real friend; only loud-voiced drinking friends who successfully used the wisecrack as a shield against knowledge. And since Val no girl who appealed to him; only casual encounters, bed-mates for a night or a month, of a kind who left the taste of ashes in the cooling mouth.

One night, floundering friendless through the city after the pubs closed, he picked up, from a coffee-shop he frequented on occasion, a strange little pallid-faced girl with large red mouth and tight black sweater. Decked with huge black ear-rings, thick gold necklace and chunky metal belt, she looked as though fresh from an existentialist grotto. Her oddity appealed to him. Talking a mixture of affected English and bohemian jargon, she led him through a series of nightmare tableaus, vivid and violent, climaxed late at night in a brawl at a drunken party with a sly-faced and obscene pansy; anti-climaxed under an oak-tree in a park with the strange girl. He babbled foolishly to her, articulating a parody of tenderness; and then, in desperation, began to shout ill-assorted and unrelated fragments. Clever and sober, she eventually shrilled in his ear, 'Make up your mind. Who do you think I am? Molly Bloom or Joe Stalin?' And he pushed her, protesting, beneath him to no point other than to find impotence and vomit his despair under a starless sky.

3

'Why did you come back?' Val asked.

'That's twice you've asked me that.'

'The other time, I mean. Not this time.'

'The reason's probably no different, then.'

'From curiosity? Surely not.'

He hesitated. 'Because I needed to,' he said, conscious of telling her the truth for the first time that evening.

'And you needed to this time as well?'

'Yes,' he agreed.

She smiled then : the smile discovered dimples in her cheeks. 'Like to wash before the meal?' she said.

'Love to.'

In the bathroom he stripped to the waist and splashed cooling water over his hot sticky flesh. As he towelled himself, he thought of Val; and found, in thinking of her, a mellow, warm sensation.

He looked about him absently, seeing objects—limp nylons hanging to dry, face cream, hairpins, uncapped toothpaste, squares of white material tumbled in a corner, a streaked tin of talcum, safety pins—that his mind made no attempt to sort and classify; so that he might as well not have seen them at all.

When he turned back, it was to Peter, not to that hope or salvation that Peter might have offered. It was true that, like a disconsolate atheist returning to childhood religion, he sought a symbol; but the symbol was a human one.

When he went back to the flat again, after a year, it was as if there had been no year. Nothing seemed changed. Val's welcome was warm; and Peter, sliding his chair back from the untidy desk, rose slowly and gravely to his feet, hitched up his corduroys, and drew up another chair for Roger as though they were merely about to resume an argument discontinued the day before. He ran a large freckled hand through his hair and grinned slyly at Roger. There were quiet, warm minutes as Val fetched coffee, and then all three of them began to talk quickly. He saw immediately, with astonishment, that Peter was as glad to see him as he was to see Peter. He didn't attempt to account for this; it was enough to know that their friendship was not, after all, a one-way affair.

For he didn't observe Peter as in any way changed. He was still dazzled by the surface swagger, the angry brilliance. He wanted to find the old Peter; he found exactly what he wanted to find.

Certainly he knew Peter's life was changed. He had abandoned his labouring job and union position to return to university. He was studying law, living on his father's legacy and Val's slender earnings; and apparently making no attempt to disturb the quiet which had existed there since the collapse of his radical club. And he was no longer out at meetings almost every night of the week; but Roger accounted for this simply by the fact that Peter now seemed to be giving a good deal of his time to writing. Plainly Peter must have made the decision—or the Party made the decision for him—that he would be far more effective politically as an intellectual than as a worker.

He felt close to Peter again; Val no longer seemed to intrude. When they argued, Peter was less dogmatic, if no less optimistic. They often found agreement. Peter presented his writing for approval. The polemic for left-wing magazines was deftly written and skilfully argued. But Roger could feel no enthusiasm for the other literary work, a long novel and a sheaf of stories. The approach was mechanical, the plotting precise, the characters wooden. It was as though he had learned it all from a book on dialectical creativeness; nothing came to life. Roger hid his disappointment and escaped giving his real opinion.

Only once, in the six months that followed, did he find something disturbing. It was early on a summer evening : they had, all three, been on a beach picnic. They returned, pleasantly tired and salty and flushed with sun, and, after taking turns with the shower and eating a light meal together, they were working about the flat. Val ironed the weekend washing while he and Peter washed and dried a large accumulation of dishes. He liked slipping into the quiet domestic routine of the flat; it helped him feel he was in no way disturbing the life they led.

The windows were still sunlit and, beyond them, the pointed rooftops of the old wooden houses were sharp blue silhouettes. He was analysing, as he mopped dishes in hot soapy water, the virtues and failings of a mutual friend at university. Peter, tea-towel in hand, lazily ignored the undried dishes gathering on the sinkbench. Sitting legs astride a back-to-front chair, he listened to what Roger said; a fist propped his chin and his face was attentive. Beyond the curtain partition, Val sang as she ironed.

The friend Roger analysed was an ex-Catholic. And Roger observed, among this friend's failings, a contradictory attitude towards his old faith. Among Catholics he was bitterly anti-clerical : yet with non-Catholics, when religion was discussed, he took up a curiously defensive position for the church, and even argued in favour of certain things which he attacked in different company. It was, Roger said, an interesting manifestation of guilt.

Some sequence of thought took him to discussion of intolerance. The fish-eyes, the fanatics, were surely always the real danger. He used as example Peter's radical club at university. It had been successful only so long as it was loose and wild-hitting.

It died as soon as the fish-eyes, the dogmatists, arrived to squeeze it into ideological shape. Rigid form always pressured out the original idea. It was, he added, precisely the same in art as in politics : emphasis on form and technique often tended to turn content into a grey dead thing.

He watched his hands turning dishes through frothy water as he talked. Then, when it occurred to him that the conversation had become one-sided, he glanced sidelong at Peter, almost surreptitiously, and saw with shock the alteration of the features. It was as if, while he sat relaxed, a thin mask had slid up from Peter's face. The whole expression was pensive; flesh about the mouth seemed to quiver, and the eyes had a vacant staring quality. His fist was crushed between his chin and the top of the chair.

Roger looked away quickly, guiltily. His first reaction was that he had been boring Peter. 'You see what I mean, don't you?' he resumed hastily, without much regard for what he said. 'The laughing boys might make the revolution, but it's the fish-eyes who determine it in the end. Because apart from his trying to formalize ideals that can't be formalized or formularized, the real danger of the fish-eye, no matter what good intention or tradition he's sprung from, is that he has a supreme distaste for what people really are. Real humanists must take people as they are, not as they might conceivably be; accept man with all his imperfection; love men for their good not in spite of their bad, but because of their bad. Otherwise man, real man, is rejected. The fish-eye worships the man of tomorrow, the product of his revolution. For the imperfect man of today he has only contempt. Contempt enough to cheat, to twist, to lie for an end that becomes more and more questionable. The lie becomes its own oppression.'

His argument, in his haste to continue talking, carried him further than he thought : he was suddenly bewildered. Did he himself honestly care for imperfect man? If not, then he was burying the truth of his argument beneath dishonest garbage; and he had no right to lecture Peter who, after all, at least showed he cared. And surely that was the most important thing—to care.

Still bewildered at himself, he turned to Peter. 'Don't you think so?' he asked weakly.

The mask slid down again: Peter smiled and blinked. 'Absolutely, old chap,' he said. 'Absolutely.' He levered himself up from his chair. 'Don't worry yourself about him. He'll snap out of it. Some ex-Catholics are a bit funny like that.' Peter paused. 'What's wrong, old chap? You look a bit startled. Did I lose the thread of your argument somewhere?'

'No. Not really. I was just rambling on.'

'Sorry. I'm a bit absent-minded today.'

Roger was perplexed rather than hurt by the discovery that Peter hadn't been listening. Perplexed by the long silence, the pensive expression; it was not like Peter. He felt there must be some significance. But he did not pursue the feeling and attempt to translate it into thought. He wished, later, he had.

And he was still more concerned with where his own argument, unheard by Peter, had taken him. If it was important to care, it was also important to demonstrate that he cared. To act from choice, from positive act of will: to produce credentials to show he cared. But what choice, what act?

At that moment, there seemed only one possible.

For the first time in years, his own conflict at truce, he felt settled and whole. He and Peter seemed all the time to be finding greater agreement. Yet from embarrassment he delayed announcing to Peter that he intended to take a side, to involve himself: that, despite everything, he would join Peter in the Communist Party. Prompted by an obscure sense of the dramatic, he wanted to save the announcement for some crucial occasion, when its significance might become more meaningful. But that crucial occasion never came.

He called at the flat one afternoon and found Val alone. She had been weeping; her eyes were bleak. Guessing only a domestic quarrel, he pretended not to notice; and asked where Peter had gone.

'Christ knows,' she said bitterly. 'I thought he'd be with you somewhere.'

'Why me?'

'Why you?' she snapped. 'As if you didn't know.'

'Know what?'

'The wonderful act he's been putting on for your benefit. Since you're his only friend, the only one he can act for now. And you're making it no better. Oh, yes—you kid him along, get him going. I wish to hell you had to live with him.'

Numb and confused, he heard her out. Peter had been expelled from the Party six months before. The reason given was for gross breaches of Party discipline; the real reason that Peter refused to abandon freedom to disagree. Since his expulsion there had been a name-blackening campaign, in which even his morals were called into question, to discourage other dissenters. That was why Peter's life had quietened; he retreated in defeat, broken and hurt, and now only moved beyond the flat from necessity, to take Val out, or to go to lectures. Old political friends avoided him; and Roger was one of the few remaining visitors to the flat.

'I thought it might have done him good, having you here again,' Val said. 'I thought it might have got him outside himself. But all you've done is given him your own bloody sickness.'

'But look, Val,' he tried to explain. 'He almost recruited me to the—' But it was plainly no use; Val was too distraught to grasp his meaning.

'You act so terribly innocent. Stringing him along. Making it worse.'

It was no use trying to make her understand when he couldn't understand himself. He left her then; he had never seen the flat or Val again until tonight.

4

In the darkening room, meal finished and coffee-cups drained, they sat silent on the cushioned window seat. Outside, the city tangled necklaces of yellow light in the cool blue dusk. Traffic noises came faintly through the open window.

She stirred; her uncurling body made whispering sounds over the cushions. She leaned towards him, the glow of her cigarette briefly illumining her face; then, shadowy again, she said quietly, 'You see, I blamed myself first. It hurt too much; so I blamed you. But it wasn't either of us. Not anyone, really. And even if there was someone to blame, it wouldn't matter. Not now.' She

paused. 'So don't blame yourself. Or imagine that I blame you.
You weren't to blame.'

He wished he could believe that. For he had never questioned
the lunacy of those last two weeks.

He found Peter drunk and maudlin in a waterfront pub which
once Peter had often frequented with his leftist friends; where
once his figure, tall and compelling, stood among milling people
in animated conversation. Now, ignored by the same people, he
drank alone in a corner. The retrieved idealism which had separated him had turned already to sourness. He reviled Roger and
Val as well as his old friends; for no one could be excluded from
his bitterness and disillusion.

The act was over, the mask gone, the actor revealed perverse
and destructive. The symbol Roger had sought, and for a short
time seen, was punctured and collapsed; in its place flickered the
image of his own defeat.

Peter assured him he had left Val for good. He only laughed
when Roger suggested he return to her. 'What?' he demanded.
'And have her swallow me down in some little suburban swamp?
Get me bogged down with a house, a kid and a garden? No
thank you very much. Do you think she's different from any
other woman? Do you?'

Roger saw the unreason; but he also saw everything too
sharply. Peter, looking back, had seen the curve, the anger, the
rebellion, the shattered faith; already he could see himself comfortably married, studying law, slowly strangling in the mesh. For
six months he might have argued against Roger's pessimism and
strung a tenuous thread of hope through his writing; now the
arguments were gone, the thread snapped. That had only served
to keep him alive; when Peter began to surrender to the argument, and the writing to dry from its source, he had only to see
through the thin farce, look back to his father, and cascade the
avalanche. Now, floundering in the mesh, he hit out at Val: its
only palpable symbol.

Roger could have argued against the unfairness. Hadn't Val,
after all, been loyal, unquestioning in her own small form of
faith? The elemental faith, without gods or creeds, of one human

being in another. He could have argued against Peter; but he didn't. He let Peter smother Val with words of contempt. That was why he still blamed himself.

'I'm finished with this bar,' Peter announced. 'I know better ones. Coming?' And, of course, he followed. That was it : Peter was still the leader. The outline was still there; an outline as superficial as gross caricature. A leader with a single follower.

From one bar to another, from one city to another, always the same demented pursuit; the leader, the follower. Through the bars with concrete floors and cobwebbed windows, the bars with carpets and scenic windows, the parties with ranting bohemians and smashing windows, the awakenings in hotel-rooms with torn wallpaper and cracked mirrors; the leader, the follower.

And at the end of two weeks there was the small key waiting to be twisted in the ignition; the car ready to be stolen.

They had been at a party; and he missed Peter suddenly. He went outside just in time to see the headlights flare, the car lurch off into the night.

He ran after it, calling out, stumbling, falling, running again.

They were silent once more : he was conscious of her nearness to him. Her reflective face was lit softly by the lights beyond the window. She leaned forward, elbows on knees, hands linked loosely. An impulse moved him to want to reach out and touch her, as if that act would join their separate sadness. She must have sensed it, for before he could move she rose quickly and crossed the room. She clicked a switch and the room filled with pleasantly warm light. The windows became dark mirrors which caught Val's bright reflection as she moved to draw the curtains.

The mood of the darkened room was lost altogether now. Smiling and apologetic, she acknowledged the fact. 'You start brooding, sitting in the dark,' she said. She gathered dirty plates and carried them to the sinkbench. 'I must see how Peter is,' she added.

His stomach lurched. 'Peter?' he said faintly.

'He's been a bit feverish all day. The heat. I fed him and put him to bed before you came.' She went to the bedroom door.

A sick mind, he thought; a sick mind feeding on fantasy. She must have seen his expression; she drew back from the door. 'What's the matter?' she said. 'Didn't you know?'

Of course : the whole flat was different, Val was different. But he had still been seeing another flat, another Val. Even in the bathroom : the tumbled white squares, the streaked talcum, the safety pins; his eyes had declined to interpret their meaning. Then just what had he expected at that moment? Peter to come walking in the door?

5

The slewing skid-marks ran up a steep angle of road, over a grass verge, and stopped at the edge of a bank. The car, carried by its own momentum, must have hurtled some distance through emptiness : they found it, bashed and tangled, at the foot of a slanting power pole.

In the cold dazzle of headlamps they gathered about the flung figure with shredded clothes and torn face. A car sped away to fetch doctor and ambulance; but the haste, Roger saw, was pointless.

Peter opened his eyes, once, and saw him. Recognition came slowly. While engines hummed and brakes screeched and the growing crowd flickered the light, the years dwindled to minutes, and the minutes to seconds, and they looked at each other.

'Here it comes,' someone shouted.

Twin lights bloomed along the damp highway : the nearing ambulance trailed a thin ribbon of sound.

Peter stirred, the pain shocking his body and twisting his face. He smiled weakly and his dry lips moved. The siren grew louder. Roger knelt, turning his ear to the contorting mouth. But no words came.

The eyes shadowed and closed : he withdrew from the body in a slow, sighing motion. The sudden void was filled with the strange confusion of other voices, and the queer, fading whimper of the siren.

Their movement into the room awakened the child. It stirred, eyes blinking open, small hands clutching, pink lips releasing choked sounds. It had kicked in restless, fevered sleep, churning the miniature sheets and blankets in the cot.

'Hello,' Val said softly, taking up the child. 'Hello, Peter.'

The widening grey eyes focused sharp with recognition. Then, seeing Roger, the child buried his face in Val's neck.

'Doesn't like strangers,' Roger observed lamely.

'Fancy you not knowing,' Val said.

'It would never have occurred to me.'

'A year and four months,' she said.

'Then Peter—' he began, shocked. 'Then Peter knew?'

'I knew,' Val said. 'But Peter—' She shook her head. 'He never knew. At least I don't think so. I didn't want to tell him. Not right away. It would have been—well, just one more complication.' She paused; she was frowning now, and withdrawn. 'At least I think so. It would have been just one more thing to blame me for.' She paused again, uncertainly. 'I don't know. Perhaps he guessed I was pregnant. Perhaps that was the trouble. Then again, if I had told him, perhaps he wouldn't have gone. I've never been sure. God, I wish I knew. I've just never been sure.'

At that moment, holding the child tightly to herself, she looked forlorn, all confidence and assurance gone.

Quickly her expression changed; she smiled, and held the kicking child high for inspection. 'Don't you think he's a fine boy?' she said.

'Yes,' he said thickly. 'A fine boy.'

The child glimpsed Roger again, and began to cry. Val stroked his back soothingly. 'Peter doesn't think you look very friendly,' she said shrewdly. 'Why don't you say something nice to him?'

'Like what?'

'Like "Hello, Peter." '

Roger took the child's tiny bunched fist. 'Hello, Peter,' he said, feeling foolish. 'Hello, Peter.'

Then he saw or imagined the likeness. As it puckered painfully, the soft child's face was suddenly, grotesquely, that twisting face lit by flickered headlamps. He turned away quickly.

'What's wrong?' Val said.

'Nothing.'

He forced himself to look at the child again. The likeness was gone; he must only have imagined it. Small grey eyes now regarded him curiously, without fear. 'Hello, Peter,' he whispered. The child smiled uncertainly.

'I shan't be long,' Val said. 'I'll just settle him down for the night. You can go and make more coffee if you like.'

He went gratefully from the bedroom, made fresh coffee, sat on the window seat, and lit a cigarette. He was calm again; the scene in the bedroom seemed entirely ridiculous. Val was some time with the child. He could hear her crooning softly. He pictured her bent over the cot; even this close, it was something still too difficult to picture. Presently she backed out of the bedroom and closed the door quietly. 'He's all right now,' she said.

'Sorry I frightened him.'

'You?' Her eyebrows lifted; she seemed a little amused as she poured coffee and relaxed in a low chair. 'I thought for a moment it was the other way about.'

Her insight irritated him. 'Why should I be frightened of a baby?' he said.

She shrugged. 'You would know better than I.'

'What are you getting at?' he demanded. 'That I'm jealous?'

That was the point: he could see that. It might have been true, once. But it had not been true for a long time. And it was never less true than now. For he had come to understand and admire her. He saw the nature of her solitary struggle too clearly. Somehow he had to show her that he did understand. That what had turned him momentarily from the child was not jealousy, but something else altogether, something he might never be able to put in words.

'Partly,' Val said.

'Then I still don't see what you're getting at.'

'I'm not sure what I'm getting at, either,' she said. 'Except that, well ...'

'I'm listening,' he said. 'I'm waiting.'

'That we made love to each other,' she said quickly. 'Peter and I.'

He was suddenly angry. 'And what is that supposed to prove? That I'm not a pansy?'

Val rose, lit a cigarette, and stood with her back to the mantel-piece. 'I don't know. I don't know quite what it's supposed to prove. Except that it's something important. That—' She hesi-tated. "Well—that I knew him as something different, Roger. I imagine that's what I mean. I knew him as he was; and it was enough. Funnily enough—because I dragged him down to his animal level, I knew him as a human being. An ordinary, rather frightened human being. You see what I mean?'

'No,' he said stubbornly. 'I don't see.'

'Then I can't explain,' she said. 'I was stupid to think I could. I'm sorry.'

'Thanks for the dramatics, anyway,' he said bitterly; and then regretted saying it. For she was immediately hurt and angry; and he saw her, at that moment, as quite as lost as himself. They were contesting, now, their claim to the dead. It was absurd, and yet there was no stopping. Absurd because he was beaten before he began; absurd because he already recognized her rightness. Absurd because, while he could be honest with himself, he could not yet be honest with her. And here they were, two lost human beings, scrabbling at dust.

'I'm sorry,' he added. 'I didn't mean that. But you seem to think I have illusions about him.'

'Haven't you?' she said in a voice strangely calm.

'No,' he said. 'I'm not trying to build him up into anything.'

'No?' she said coolly.

Her complacency angered him again; he discovered himself suddenly on his feet, shouting. 'No. Not me. It's not me who's trying to make him into something. It's not me who's got illusions. But I'll tell you who has.' He strode across the room to the desk. 'So he's dead. Dead. Dead two years. I come here and what do I find? His desk all decked out as if it was sacred. Saint Peter worked here, in case anyone doesn't know. Saint bloody Peter. And you try to tell me I've got illusions.' He stood over the desk, riffling papers, flicking open folders of manuscript. He recognized, now, that by hurting her he was trying to purge himself of hurt. 'He was just a failure. Just another failure. That's all. Like his father. Like my father. Like me. Like millions of failures. Do you think all his soap-box ranting ever made an ounce of difference to the world? Do you think he ever wrote a line worth two-pence?' He pointed to the scrambled papers. 'Do you think any of it mattered?'

But even as he said it, as he sank down in a chair, he knew he was wrong. Of course it mattered. Of course.

'Have you quite finished?' she said evenly.

'Yes,' he said. 'I'm finished.' He had succeeded only in hurting himself. He saw now what Val meant. His own special kind of illusion sprang from disillusion; he had wanted Peter to be a failure, and no more than that. Then there were no implications to disturb him.

He had, then, not even been honest with himself, though he had all the time been sure he told himself no lie. What did he tell Peter that summer evening two years ago? The lie could become its own oppression.

Val was still silent.

'I'm sorry,' he said. 'You should tell me to get out.'

'You see,' she said slowly. 'It doesn't matter. That's what I've been trying to tell you.'

'What doesn't matter?'

'That he was a failure.'

'Then you—' He looked at her foolishly.

'Of course he was. If you like to look at it that way. But it doesn't matter.' She paused. 'I remember reading somewhere, I don't recall where, that there is no such thing as success. There are only different kinds of failure. Well, his was a very simple kind.'

Roger was on his feet again, walking about the room. He stopped before the drawing of Peter framed above the desk. The strong, square face; the lazy curve of hair along the forehead; the soft eyes. There was something in it he hadn't seen before; some hint of tenderness, of weakness, where he had only seen hardness of feature. Yet it made the whole picture.

'But it's not important at all,' Val said. 'The important thing is that he tried.'

He turned from the drawing. 'That he what?'

'That he tried.'

He was sweating again, and trembling. He walked stiffly back to the window seat. Then he sat down limply. She was right; she was always right. She had to spell it out for him.

'Some people never try,' she added softly.

6

He was not long in leaving. Val suggested more to eat and drink. He thanked her and apologized: it had been a long, tiring day. Val said she understood.

She accompanied him down to the street. They stood together in the mild starlit evening.

'What are you going to do now?' she said.

He shrugged. 'I'm not sure. After I've found a place to live, well—'

She regarded him critically. 'Yes?'

'I've a lot of things to think about. A lot of reading to do. Perhaps even some writing. If I can begin seeing things clearly enough.' In a way, he found himself thinking, Peter had been lucky; he hadn't seen his dream turn nightmare on tank-trodden barricades. But it was still important to care.

'I hope you do,' she said simply. 'I think you will.'

'Thanks.' He smiled wryly. 'Then you think there's hope for me yet?' He laughed before she could answer. 'And what about you?'

'Peter keeps me busy. When he gets older I'll go back part-time to my social welfare job. I'm hoping to do a play soon, too. It'll be good having people around me again. There won't be time to be lonely.'

'I can't imagine you lonely.'

'Nor can I,' she said, laughing lightly. 'At least I don't want to imagine it.' She paused. 'It's been good seeing you, Roger. You will come again, won't you?'

'Of course.' He had been waiting for her to ask.

'And if you're wanting somewhere quiet, books to read, a type-writer to use—and a desk—you know where to come, don't you?'

'Thanks. It's kind of you.'

'They've been waiting a long time for you, Roger.'

Words, now, seemed entirely inadequate. 'Val,' he began.

Impulsively, he reached out and touched the bare brown flesh of her arm; then, as quickly, he withdrew his hand.

'Yes?'

He shook his head. 'It doesn't matter.' There would be plenty of time to find what he wanted to say : plenty of time.

'You quite sure?' Her face lifted; the eyes were frank and appraising. Small blonde lights glittered in her hair; most of her face was in shadow.

'I'm sorry we argued,' he said. 'I hope—' He broke off, shaking his head again.

'So do I hope,' she whispered quickly.

Her lips darted moist and cool against his cheek; and she was gone. She ran into the house : he heard her feet creak up the stairs.

He stood for a moment on the footpath. He did not feel at all tired now. He would not take a tram; he would walk back to his hotel, along the waterfront, past the fishing boats rocking dark on the slapping water, the ocean liners tangled with light. He wanted the feeling of moving of his own volition; he wanted, tonight, to hear the sound of his own feet hitting through places bright and dark; he wanted to see twisting streets unwind, to see his solitary shadow race before his moving feet.

A young couple rose out of the evening, dawdling slowly past him, laughing softly and mysteriously in the summer darkness.

He began to walk quickly.

In the Blind Canyon

MARIA

HE FIRST saw Eleanor, after so many years, in Soho one summer afternoon. She was half-concealed in a doorway, a sketchbook held awkwardly before her; her face had that concentrated, almost tormented expression he had once known so well. She had a pencil fixed between her teeth and was industriously rubbing away with her little finger at something he could not see. When he cried her name, she started and her eyes widened with fright. Then, as if seeing him were the most perfectly predictable thing in the world, she took the pencil from her mouth, smiled quickly and held up a finger for silence. He slipped into the doorway beside her. 'What are you doing here?' he said. She held up the finger again. 'Please,' she whispered urgently, and ignored him. Looking over her shoulder and raising his eyes from the vivid black lines of the drawing, he saw from her viewpoint, through two dusty distorting sheets of plate-glass, the small scene a little way along the opposite side of the street. In front of a short stretch of brick wall spattered with torn posters, three girls smoked and ambled along sunlit pavement. Their figures were long-shadowed in the late afternoon; their cigarettes curled arabesques of smoke in the still, sultry air. It was a lifeless day and passers-by were infrequent; a car snarled sluggishly around a nearby corner; a cash-register rang from an espresso bar along the street. And the girls paraded hopefully. Their beat was confined at one end by an alley; at the other by a line of cascading garbage cans.

'Good old Eleanor,' he said. 'You haven't gone abstract yet, I see. Still the good social realist.'

'Shut up,' she said. 'Just for a moment.'

Idling lazily in the sunlight, the girls re-arranged themselves. One, a short plump creature in tight red frock, called amiably to someone across the street, whispered something behind her hand to her companions, and burst into shrill laughter. Eleanor turned the page of her sketchbook and began a fresh drawing. He could see she had done several.

'Wouldn't it be more convenient if you sat in a car, or something?' he said. 'It might be more comfortable.'

'Please be practical,' she hissed, 'and shut up.' Her pencil snapped back and forward over the new page. He observed that she noted a scene in an impressively neat fashion. Her style had always been as precise and tidy as her mind.

One of the girls reclined against the wall, her knee jutting forward, as she looked in her handbag for cigarettes. She was tall, long-legged, and remarkably well figured; she had long black hair and a darkish complexion. She wore a blue suit with a split skirt that flashed white petticoat as she jiggled in her handbag.

'The tall one's new,' he said. 'I haven't seen her before.'

'You know a lot,' she said. She turned to a new page.

'Aren't you sick of it yet?' he said.

'You don't have to wait for me.'

'I don't think it's very healthy for girls to stand alone in doorways here. Had any pick-ups yet?'

'Lots,' she said briskly, and went on drawing.

'What the hell is all this anyway?' he demanded. 'Is this all you can find in the old world? Garbage cans and tarts?'

'Oh God,' she said. She banged the sketchbook shut. 'What's the use?' She glared at him. 'Well, you might at least be decent enough to take me to coffee—now you've spoiled everything.'

They came out of the doorway. 'And you,' he said, 'might at least say how pleased you are to see me.'

'All right. How pleased I am to see you.'

'Fine. That's settled anyway. How are you keeping? How long have you been over here?'

'I'm keeping well, thank you. And I've been here just two months.'

'I wish at least you'd *act* pleased to see me.'

'Oh,' she said. 'But I am.'

'Act interested, I mean.'

'I'll try.'

'Now,' he said. 'Let's begin at the beginning. I expect you won a scholarship or something.'

'It's or something. Let's wait till coffee. I'm parched.'

Eleanor, he thought. Sweet, prim Eleanor. He hadn't seen her for three, four, nearly five years. She was unchanged, still the quaint old-fashioned Methodist girl from a lush Taranaki dairy farm who walked briskly into art school out of a bright Auckland summer morning.

'How's everyone at home?' he asked, over coffee. 'Tell me all the news.'

'The country's bankrupt,' she said, 'but apart from that things are fine.'

'For example,' he said. 'How's Ed?'

'Ed? Well, Ed went into advertising, you know. He was a great success. He bought a big car and crashed it. Now he's in a wheelchair for the rest of his life.'

'Well, that's an encouraging start.'

'You want to go down the list? Well, there's Eric. Remember Eric? The pale little nervous boy with the tic who painted awful nudes? Well, he was in a mental hospital two years. Now he's fine; he's given up art and gone Polynesian, up in Northland among the mangroves somewhere. Then who else do you know? Well, there's Norm. You know, the quiet one, did ghastly abstracts. He found out he was colour-blind; and got married. And Peter? Yes, of course you must have known Peter. Well, Peter gave up painting and began writing a novel. He gave up the novel and began writing short stories. He gave up short stories for poetry. And he gave up poetry for the development of an entirely new literary form. He worked on that two years and then went into business. Now who else? Oh, yes—Robin. Robin announced there was no possibility of a native art being created in New Zealand, became dreadfully homosexual, and got arrested last year for forging cheques.'

'Enough,' he said. 'You haven't mentioned the girls yet.'

'Well, there's Sheila. Sheila had two abortions and married a racehorse trainer. Marjorie went teaching among the Maoris; haven't heard of her in years. Beverley had a fling at documentary films in Wellington. Susie married a Catholic and has three babies now. Barbie became the mistress of that terrible little poet creature on the North Shore, pined for love when he dropped her, and got TB. Sarah's very successful as a dress designer and Evelyn's absolutely magnificent as a gossip columnist. Now who else?'

'There's yourself. You seem to have survived the storm anyway. Right?'

'After a fashion.'

'You look as pure and virginal as ever.'

'Thank you. You always say the sweetest things.' Once, long ago, she would have blushed. As she had in the days when, drab and timid and a butt for jokes, she came to their gaudy student parties. That, he thought, at least was different.

'Now can I have my turn? What happened to you after you came over here on that scholarship?'

'Quite simple, really. I lost interest.'

'And stayed here?'

'And stayed here.'

'I think it's disgusting,' she said. 'Really disgusting. All that money gone to waste. And what do you do now?'

'As little as I can. Sometimes I work in a gallery.'

'And don't you want to go back?'

'To that dump? Never.'

'You know,' she said accusingly, 'I suspect you've become a rootless cosmopolitan.'

'Probably,' he said, lighting a cigarette.

'I'd be ashamed to admit it.'

'But you are not the one admitting it, my dear.'

'After a while you all talk alike, look alike. You all want to be so, so individualistic, and you're the most regimented crowd I've ever seen in my life. Walk through Greenwich Village, along the Left Bank, through Soho—and what do you find?'

'Us,' he said. 'The rootless cosmopolitans.'

'You know,' she said. 'I don't think I like you.'

'I don't mind, so long as you pay for the coffee.'

'You make a religion of art, and when art turns empty, what have you got?'

'Rootless cosmopolitanism, as you say, my dear.'

'You've got no values. Nothing.'

'All right. So you don't like me.'

'I'm sure I don't. Now, shall we go?'

They walked back along the street. There was only one girl, the tall dark one, left in front of the wall. 'She's very pretty,' Eleanor said. 'I can't understand it. Why does she do it?'

'Shall I ask her? I'll say the lady wants to know.'

'Don't be ridiculous.'

'I'm serious.'

'You dare make a fool of me and I'll—'

But he crossed the street jauntily, hands in pockets, and began to talk to the girl. Eleanor paused uncertainly, hot and flushed, on the other side. He talked to the girl for a while. Then he walked back.

'Why don't you come and meet her?' he said. 'Her name's Maria and she comes from Spain. Came here to work for an uncle who runs a café. But he was not a nice man. Now, as you see, she is independent of him—more or less.' He took her arm. 'Come and meet her.'

'Really, I don't—'

He steered her across the street. 'You always want to observe the wicked world from a distance,' he said. 'Now be brave. Meet it face to face.'

'I hate you. I—'

'This is Maria,' he said.

The tall girl smiled down at Eleanor.

'Go on, you old puritan,' he said. 'Be polite. Say something.'

Eleanor stood blinking in the sunlight. And the tall girl still smiled.

One idle day, some two weeks later, he took a bus out to Notting Hill Gate, to the address Eleanor had left with him. He was some time finding the place; it was an old house just off Portobello Road. She lived up two flights of creaking stairs.

'Hello,' he said, when she opened the door. 'Just wondering if you'd like to see a little more low life.'

Her room, facing the sunlit street, was large and bright. It was neat and tidy, everything in place. Eleanor was dressed, in businesslike fashion, in slacks and paint-smeared check shirt.

'You're low life enough for me,' she said. 'Thank you.'

'Well,' he said, 'if you're working, don't mind me. I'll just make myself at home anyway.' He fell into a chair.

'I can see that.' She went to the gas-ring in the corner. 'I expect you want some coffee.'

'The hospitality overwhelms me.'

'Why can't you talk like a normal person? Behave like a normal person?' She lit the gas and filled the percolator. 'The strange thing is I thought you were rather fun, once. I used to like you.'

'I must say you always showed it marvellously.' He rose and walked about the room. 'Mind if I look?' He nodded towards some drawings and water-colours arranged in a dustless corner.

'I don't doubt you'll look anyway. But go ahead.'

'You're improving,' he said presently. 'I always thought you took yourself too seriously to get anywhere. You worked so hard. Had an exhibition yet?'

'In Wellington. Just before I left.'

'Sell anything?'

'Two pictures.'

'Quite. Another prophet without honour departs.'

'Not at all. You see, I don't happen to see the need for forever carrying a chip on one's shoulder about one's country. And using it as an excuse for doing nothing. Like some people.'

'Well hell,' he said. 'You dear old patriotic philistine.' He paused. 'Hey, what's this?' He held up a drawing of a woman's head: it was sharp, austere, high-featured, rather striking.

'Don't you remember? That's the girl we met. Maria. I ran into her again.'

'Just by chance?' he said.

'Of course,' she said. 'Just by chance.'

'Really,' he said. 'Amazing.'

'We took coffee together.'

'And she sat for you?'

'Yes.'

'How wonderfully fortuitous. And did you try to save her soul?'

'Why do you have to give such an excellent impression of being an imbecile?'

'You surprise me.'

'As a matter of fact, I found her rather a pleasant girl. Isn't *simpático* what you say?'

'Only rather unfortunate in the choice of profession.'

'It seems to me, for all your talk, that you are the one who wants to erect barriers.'

'So naturally you'll invite her here for coffee one day?'

'Naturally.'

'My God,' he said.

'As a matter of fact, she wanted to see the drawing when it was finished.'

'They'd love to hear about this at home, wouldn't they?' He dropped back into his chair and laughed. 'Dear me. It's too rich to be true.'

'I think you are deliberately misunderstanding me. Her life is her own business. I'm not trying to change it.'

'Oh no,' he said. 'Of course not. Nothing could be further from your mind.'

She poured the coffee. 'Do you take sugar?' she asked, coldly.

When he next called, on a Sunday afternoon three weeks or a month afterwards, he found Maria curled like a large lazy cat on the couch. 'Surprise, surprise,' he said. *'Buenas tardes.'*

She sat up uneasily, her large ear-rings swinging, and looked to Eleanor for reassurance.

'You're worse than a bad penny,' Eleanor said. She turned to Maria, smiling. 'You remember him, don't you?'

'Yes,' Maria said. 'I remember.'

'Well, seeing how you've come all the way up the stairs, you might as well stay for a bit,' Eleanor said.

'Such a relaxing atmosphere, I'm sure.'

He sat down. There was a silence as Eleanor fetched coffee.

'You are of New Zealand, also?' Maria said at last, tentatively.

'Unfortunately,' he said.

'Please?' she said, puzzled.

'Yes,' he said loudly. 'I am.'

'Oh,' she said. 'Eleanor tells me much of New Zealand. It is interesting country, no?'

'No,' he said.

'Please?'

'Not very interesting.'

'But it is of much beauty. Eleanor tells me of its beauty.'

'Really?'

She sat in distinct discomfort now, her hands fidgeting in her lap. Eleanor slipped between them with the coffee. Maria rose suddenly. 'I think it is my doorbell I hear,' she said. 'I think I must go.' She went across the room, out the door and down the stairs.

'What the hell is this all about?' he demanded.

'Quite simple, really. Maria is living downstairs.'

'Off the streets?'

'And much happier for it,' Eleanor said aggressively.

'All right, all right. I didn't say a thing.'

'If you only knew what that girl has been through. All the people who lived off her.'

'You surprise me. And what is she doing now?'

'Well, she found things a little difficult at first, you know. But then she had an idea. Thought of it all herself. It wouldn't have occurred to me.'

'Really?'

'Yes. She's become a model. Apparently there's quite an extraordinary demand for models in London, you know. I didn't know about it. All a girl does is put up little notices advertising herself on notice-boards around the city. It's quite a thing.'

He looked at her incredulously. Only Eleanor could be so naïve. 'And is she doing well?' he said.

'Wonderfully. Her rooms are directly underneath here; she's fixed up a kind of studio. She has her own telephone on that floor, fortunately. It's ideal. People come to her—she doesn't even have to go to them. Amazing, isn't it? It's just because there is such an extraordinary demand. In the last couple of weeks she's had all sorts of customers.'

'I bet,' he said. 'All sorts.'

'Nothing ever moves you,' she said. 'Does it? I think it's absolutely wonderful that a girl can make such a sudden, clean break.'

'I must confess it is incredible.'

'There you are,' she said. 'Even you have to admit it.'

He found he had to stand up and walk about the room to prevent himself laughing outright. 'You must feel very proud of yourself,' he said.

'Of course I am,' Eleanor laughed, bouncing off the couch to pour more coffee. She looked very pretty and absurdly young today. 'But just the same, you know, you've got to give her credit. After all, I hardly had to do anything, apart from giving her encouragement at the right time. Basically she's a nice girl.'

'I'm sure.'

'I'm glad you think so. Try to be a little more pleasant to her, won't you? Remember she's been through such a lot. Underneath she has really a very sensitive nature.'

'You must see quite a lot of her now.'

'Of course. She's in and out of here all the time when she's not working. Insists on cooking me paella and all kinds of things. She's teaching me Spanish. We might even go to Spain together for a while towards the end of the year. She comes from a little fishing village near Alicante.'

'You're certainly having a jolly time together.'

He circled the room again, noticing some new drawings of Maria on the workbench, and then finally sat beside Eleanor on the couch. She was suddenly self-conscious; she looked down into her coffee, idling the sugar-spoon around in the cup. He reached out and turned her face towards him; he held her chin tightly cupped between thumb and forefinger. 'And how is Eleanor?' he said. 'Do you still remember old friends?'

'Why should I?' she said, shaking his hand from her face. 'I've never had friends.'

'Come, now,' he said persuasively. 'Wasn't I a good friend?'

'You?' She laughed. 'You and all the rest.'

'I did my best to help you. Didn't I?'

'I was always under the impression it was some kind of competition,' she said. 'To see who could first deflower the silly virgin from the cow-country and boast about it. And all that happened, so far as I could see, was that you came nearest to winning.'

'I think you're unkind, Eleanor. Really unkind.'

'You don't think I came twelve thousand miles to have all this over again, do you?'

'Didn't you expect to see me?'

'Oh, I knew I'd probably run into you again,' she said. 'Sometime or other. Unfortunately.'

He lay back on the couch, sliding an exploratory arm around her. 'Why don't you just relax?' he said. 'Just relax. It might do you good.'

But she still sat stiffly

'If you want to try again, after five years, the answer is still no,' she said. 'Understand?'

'You're as cold as ice,' he said. 'My God you are.'

But when he drew her down beside him, she did not at first resist. Her head rested on his shoulder; her widened eyes stared up at the ceiling.

'You've been terribly lonely, haven't you?' he said. 'I've been lonely too, you know.'

Her eyes were still wide and staring, as if in surprise at herself. She said nothing.

'Why can't we be friends? Instead of pecking at each other?'

'That's for you to say.' She closed her eyes, almost in pain, as she spoke.

'Why me?' he said softly.

He was stroking her hair, turning her face. Her body, still stiff, fluttered against him. And then, just at the moment he thought he had her at last, she jerked away and a slap jolted his teeth together. She stood erect, hands on hips. He looked up at her in dismay.

'Why you?' she said. 'Because you've got to learn to stop playing with people. Playing with their feelings for the fun of it. That's all.'

'But--'

'But nothing. You know something? Behind that suave mask of yours there's nothing left. Nothing. The person who fashioned that mask died a long time ago. Talking to you is like knocking on the door of an empty house.'

He rose clumsily, angrily. 'If you don't want—'

'No. Stay by all means. But don't expect me to be fooled.'

'Fooled?' He laughed. He zipped his jacket and made for the door. 'Fooled? That's rich, coming from you. Fooled? Oh my God.' He stood, for a moment, in the open doorway. 'You really believe that crap about your precious trollop being a model, don't you?' He laughed again, in her face. 'Don't you?'

'You're a pig,' she cried. 'A dirty-minded pig. God damn you.' She rushed at him, trying to thrust him through the door. Then she swung the door shut on him, bruising his shoulder. 'Get out. Go on. Get out.'

'You know something?' he smiled. 'I think I will.' He went heavily down the stairs, two at a time. The door slammed behind him.

It was on the third notice-board he found, below Patsy (36-22-36) and above Dixie (34-20-34): Maria, new Spanish model, now available. The neatly typewritten card had only one spelling mistake. There was a telephone number.

My God, he thought. How easy.

His face still burned. He went into a pub and sat over scotch. How easy, he thought, how ridiculously easy to finish her. He sat a while longer, and then went out to telephone. There was no answer. He rang again, later that night, but received only the engaged signal: the 'phone was apparently off the hook. When the pub closed he rang from a booth on the way home: still the engaged signal.

The next day, resentment still hot, his mouth still sour, he rang and Maria answered. 'But,' she said, her voice tiny in the receiver, 'no more do I make appointments. I am sorry.'

'Since when?' he said.

'No more do I make appointments,' she repeated.

'Come now,' he said. 'That's not right. I saw your card only yesterday. You can't do that.'

'Please?'

'You can't do that. You can't get away with that. It's unfair.'

'Unfair?' she said vaguely.

'I want an appointment tonight,' he said. 'Understand?'

'Please, I do not,' she said. 'I do not understand.'

'Tonight,' he said. 'Expect me.'

'But you cannot,' she said. 'Because you do not know the address.'

'Oh, yes I do,' he said, and went to replace the receiver.

'No more do I—' she appealed, before her voice was chopped into silence. He strode out of the telephone booth, the door bang-banging behind him; he walked a little way, circling a few streets, and then halted in mid-pavement, astonished at himself. It was easy; too easy. He would never be able to look Eleanor in the face again without laughing. He felt a curious excitement.

Someone—a face, a handshake, a voice—led him off the pavement into a coffee-shop and talked to him. About something; it could have been anything. He wasn't listening; he was thinking of Eleanor, of the way her face would twist and fall.

He idled away the time drinking and arrived at the place after eight. He looked up the stairs climbing to Eleanor's room, and then knocked loudly on Maria's door. The door chinked open and Maria peered out. Eleanor's door remained aloof and shut.

Maria, recognizing him suddenly, tried to close the door again. Her eyes were large and luminous with animal fright. He insinuated himself deftly into the room. 'I made an appointment,' he said. 'Remember?'

'You?' she said, her eyes still huge. 'You?'

'Why not?' he said. 'I saw your card. I didn't bring a camera, but that doesn't matter, does it?'

'Please,' she said. 'You must go. You must.' She pushed him back towards the door : she was quite strong.

'Why?'

'You must go,' she said, still pushing at him.

'What's wrong? Don't you want Eleanor to know?'

'Eleanor knows nothing,' she said. 'Now go.'

'But she is suspicious?'

'A little,' she admitted. 'But from yesterday only. From yesterday I am good. For Eleanor. Now please go.'

But he did not go.

Then he flung open the door and shouted up the stairs. Maria watched him silently, sullenly.

'Why don't you come down?' he was calling. He climbed the stairs slowly: this was his moment. 'Why don't you come on down and see who your friend has for a visitor?' Maria still watched silently. She stood in her doorway and drew her kimono tightly about her shoulders. 'Come on down, why don't you?' He rapped sharply on Eleanor's door. 'Come on down. You find real hospitality down here.'

There was silence within. Only silence.

He paused, and then looked foolishly down at Maria. She was smiling quite distinctly; quite unmistakably. 'What the—' he began.

'Eleanor,' she said, 'is not at home. She is at the theatre.'

'You knew?' he said stupidly.

'But of course. Since it was I who today purchased the ticket for Eleanor tonight. For a play by a Mr O'Neill which she has for a long time desired much to see.' She paused. 'And I shall tell Eleanor that her friend called.'

'You bitch,' he said. 'You pair of bitches.'

Maria still smiled. He raced past her, down the stairs. *'Adios,'* she called.

It was the end of summer before he called at the old house off Portobello Road again; he found empty rooms, and the landlady. 'They've gone, that pair,' she said. 'Gone. And I can't say I'm sorry. Where did they go? Off to Spain, of course, where that dark one come from. She was no better than she should be, that one; don't think I didn't know. They went off together.'

'Together?' he said.

'That's what I told you. Off to Spain they went. The pair of them.'

'Together,' he said, to himself this time.

The landlady retreated into her dim, scrawny Victorian living-room and returned with an envelope. 'You might be the one

this is for,' she said. 'That other one left it. She told me someone might turn up to get it.' She handed him the envelope and
he saw his name scrawled.

'Thanks,' he said, tearing it open. The landlady, still watching
him, regarded the note with curiosity. 'Thanks,' he said again,
and left.

Suddenly he was laughing.

He read the note as he walked: he read it and laughed.

*Maria told me you called once when I was out. A pity I
missed you. I thought you might have called again but you
didn't so I guess you must have been busy or something. All I
can do is leave this note and hope you get it. Anyway what I
really want to do is apologize for being so absolutely disgusting. I said stupid cruel things and I'm sorry. Maria and I are
on our way to Spain. She has arranged a place to live in her
village. A little fisherman's house by the sea. Maria has not
been at all well; but she is recovered now. Poor girl. If I
remember right the euphemism is a social disease; a pity all
things which could easily run under that appropriate heading
cannot be treated so decisively and effectively. She needs sunlight and clean air again; as do I. Think of us this grey
English winter. Regards, Eleanor.*

He might even have read it through again had he not, after a
while, noticed an odd thing.

It was his silence. He had stopped laughing.

THANK YOU GOODBYE

THEY SAT in the large-windowed café at the corner of the square. Outside, empty tramcars banged, autumn wind scattered coloured leaves over yellow cobbles, strollers dawdled. The new pale buildings walling the square were stiffly formal and austere. Fixed above the tallest building, in the corner directly opposite the café, a large five-pointed red star printed itself against the faint gold evening sky. The couple had only just taken their seats. The man was thin and pale, dressed neatly in charcoal suit and pastel tie. He appeared strained or nervous. Twice as they waited for service he glanced at his watch.

'There is time,' said the girl calmly. 'Much time. More than one hour. A taxi will take only five minutes to the railway station. If that is what worries you.'

'I'm not worried,' he said, without conviction. 'About that, anyway.'

'Your suitcases have all gone from the hotel to the station?' she asked. She spoke an unemphatic, almost accentless English; the syllables, accurately pronounced, seemed to sculpt their own emphasis.

'They've gone.'

'Good,' she said. 'Then there is nothing to worry about, is there?'

'No,' he said. 'Nothing.'

'You have only to remove yourself to the station now,' she said. 'It is quite perfectly simple. And this time tomorrow where will you be?'

'I don't know. Vienna perhaps. I don't study timetables closely.'

'But you should,' she observed. 'Travel is adventure. I should.

I should study timetables all the time I travelled.' She paused.
'But then,' she added wistfully, 'I have never travelled.'

'No.'

'In two days' time,' the girl calculated, 'you will be in Paris.
In three days, London. You will be among friends again.'

'Please,' he said suddenly.

She raised her eyebrows.

'Please don't,' he said.

Though there was only a sprinkle of customers, service was
slow. The girl glanced over her shoulder at the solitary old grey-
haired waiter who moved methodically among the check-linened
tables. She caught his eye presently, and he ambled amiably over
to their table.

'*Molya*,' he said. He stood ready to pencil the order.

'Cognac?' the girl said to her friend. 'Or *rakia*?'

'Anything,' he said. 'Except Czech beer. That I can't stand.'

'*Edna malka botilka cognac, molya,*' the girl requested. The
waiter went away.

The man began to drum his fingers on the table. The girl
hummed a tune softly to herself; she seemed perfectly serene.
She was petite, lightly built, with smooth brown slender limbs and
an expressive, delicately-boned Slavic face of dark complexion.
Her hair was black and short cropped; she wore a light grey
skirt and a black short-sleeved sweater with a thin white peasant
motif woven about the neck. She stopped humming suddenly
and, as she reached out to quieten his impatient hand, a chunky
gold bangle slid down her arm. There was a moment's silence;
they could have heard, if they wanted, the rattling of leaves in
the street outside.

'Then we will not look into the future,' she said. 'Perhaps the
immediate past is the more satisfying. Two hours ago—'

'Not that either,' he said abruptly.

'You are very difficult.' She hesitated. 'And, besides, that
reminds me. I left my cigarettes by the bed. Have you—'

He took cigarettes from a pocket and, after she had taken one,
he rested the packet between them, at the centre of the table. He
lit her cigarette, plucked another from the packet, and lit his
own.

'You are very difficult,' she repeated. 'If we cannot discuss the future or the past, then there is only the present.'

'Only the present,' he agreed.

'And the present,' she said, 'is always so difficult to fix. It always escapes before you can discuss it. Is that not so?'

He appeared not to hear.

'Everything escapes,' she observed quietly.

The waiter returned with a small bottle of cognac and two glasses. He set them down on the table, smiled at the girl, and nodded towards her companion.

'*Angliski*,' he said. 'Eng-lish I speak.' He paused impressively. 'How you do,' he said. 'How you do. I love you. Thank you goodbye.'

'You see,' she said. 'He is showing he can speak some English.'

'Tell him he speaks very well.'

'*Mnogo dobré*,' the girl said to the waiter.

He chuckled, performed a jerky little bow of pleasure, and withdrew. 'How you do. I love you,' he laughed to himself as he went away.

'His vocabulary is limited,' the girl remarked. 'But adequate and effective.'

The man looked at his watch. He lit a new cigarette.

'There is still time,' she said. 'Much time.'

The evening sky was darkening. Lights winked about the square. Above the tall building the giant red star was suddenly illuminated. On one side of the square, screened by thin-foliaged trees, a theatre opened its doors and a queue formed. Lights picked out the words *Narodna Kultura* and the smaller word *Teatr*. The night came to life; people scuffed past the café windows, crunching over the fallen leaves. The girl poured the cognac carefully. They took up their glasses.

'*Nez dravé*,' she said as they drank.

'*Nez dravé*.'

'You learn my language so quickly,' she said jestingly. 'It is a pity you go so soon. Perhaps a few more weeks and you would be speaking like a native.'

He was silent.

'You are not amused,' she said. 'You are not amused at anything tonight.' She lit a cigarette for herself and sipped at the
cognac. 'After all it is I who should be sad. Is that not so? My
room will be the same. My streets will be the same. It is your
streets which shall be different. It is you who are going away. Is
that not correct?'

'I don't want it like this,' he said. 'I mean—'

'Yes?'

'I mean I wish it were different.'

'Different?' she said. 'How different?'

'Much different. I wish it weren't necessary. My going away,
I mean.'

'It need not be necessary. You could stay. It would not be
impossible to arrange.'

'Please,' he said. 'Be realistic.'

'Ah, yes,' she said. She paused and inhaled smoke softly. She
turned the side of her face to him and looked out the window at
the lights in the blue evening. 'We must be realistic. Always.'

'Please,' he said. 'You're just trying to hurt yourself.'

'Trying?' She laughed. 'Surely there is no need to try.'

'You're making it worse. For both of us.'

'Can it be so worse?'

'I mean you must see the impossibility of it all. Of everything.'

'Of course,' she said. 'Naturally.' Without haste, she reached
for the bottle and refilled the glasses. 'I must see.'

'We can't persuade ourselves that it could be any different.'

'It was not I who was just now wishing it different.'

'It was in a manner of speaking.'

'Naturally. But then it was not I who was trying to persuade
you either. I only suggested that if you meant what you said, it
would be possible to arrange for you to stay. There is always
the possibility of work for someone like yourself. But I was not
to know that you did not mean what you said, that it was only
a manner of speaking.'

'I see you don't understand,' he said.

'There are difficulties. When you only talk to me in a manner
of speaking.' She studied a speck of ash on the table-cloth and
rubbed it away with a finger. She was silent.

'Blast it,' he said suddenly. 'Why does it have to be like this? Words don't touch you.'

'I am sorry,' she said. 'If it is I who make it like this.'

'You become so cold,' he said. 'You're different.'

'Then you must forgive me,' she said.

'I don't think you really want to understand.'

'I understand you cannot stay. It is quite simple.'

'Besides,' he added, 'I do not belong here.'

'Of course. Now you say what you mean. Now you do not talk in a manner of speaking.'

'It's important,' he said.

'If you wish to make it important, then it is so. But you are not political?'

'If you mean in the shrill sense, no.'

'Then it is perhaps not so important. Many people live here who are not political. Like you, they are indifferent.'

'You don't speak of yourself.'

'If I am, it is not important. I am a person.' She paused. 'If you mean—how was it you said it?—in the shrill sense, no.'

'And if I mean any other way?'

'If you mean that it has been necessary, yes. If you mean it has been necessary because otherwise I might have been illiterate and barefoot in my village, yes. For you it has not been necessary.'

'But now?'

'It is necessary also. But that perhaps you would not understand. If one suddenly discovers one is the parent of a bad child, one does not run away. One must take responsibility. Someone must take responsibility. It is necessary.'

'Rhetoric,' he said.

'Rhetoric is sometimes necessary also. And so?'

'So I am not.'

'It seems to me that with all things it is more important to you not being something than being something. Would you not agree?'

'Whatever you say.'

'Please do not be hurt. I mean only that you always make the greatest importance out of not being something.'

'I understand you perfectly.'

'It is nice,' she said, 'to end on such a note of perfect understanding.' She saw him glance again at his watch. 'Yes, it is
almost time. At the station there will be people waiting to say
goodbye. Anton and Stefan and Marguerite and your other
friends. They will all wish to shake your hand. You must give
them time, and not disappoint them. I will not come to the
station. After all, what is one goodbye among so many?'

'You won't come?' he said.

'You will observe that there is almost one glass of cognac
remaining in this bottle. It would be a pity to leave it, don't you
think? I shall sit here and perhaps order a plate of peppers to
eat with it. Then I shall walk back along the streets to my room.
Perhaps I shall listen to the radio, or read a little, and then it
will be time for sleep. If I sleep early, then tomorrow I will wake
refreshed for work.'

'Are you sure?' he said suddenly. Rising, he reached across the
table and touched her hand lightly.

'Now go,' she said, not looking at him. 'I will say only the
correct things.' She began to recite in a flat voice. 'I hope you
have liked my country. I hope you have found much to interest
you, and enjoy. I hope you will write pleasant things about us,
and that if you must write unpleasant things you will balance
them with the pleasant. I hope—' She stopped. 'Politics,' she said
suddenly. 'I hate politics.'

'We must write,' he said.

'If you wish,' she said. 'But it is not necessary.'

'I promise,' he said. He looked quickly about the café. 'I must
pay,' he added. Just at that moment there was no sign of the old
waiter. 'Before I—'

'But it does not matter. I will pay the bill.'

'I insist. I mean I—'

'But it is I who am in a position to insist. And after all have
you not the saying—in jest, naturally—that it is always the
woman who pays?'

He pulled on his coat.

'Now go,' she repeated. 'Go quickly.'

She did not raise her eyes to see his back vanish out of the door of the café into the pale evening. She did not even see if he looked back. She heard his footsteps hit evenly up the street.

After a while she lifted her head. The queue had gone from the front of the theatre; the plate-glass doors were shut against the gathering chill of night. The wind had dwindled, and leaves rustled gently on the cobbles now. The lights were cold on the empty square. Above the tall building, above the illumined red star, stars of a different kind were sharp in the dark sky.

She filled her glass and beckoned the waiter.

'*Piperki—edna chiniya piperki, molya,*' she said.

He looked at the empty chair, then towards the door. '*Zamina li toi?*'

'*Da,*' she said tiredly. '*Zamina.*'

Presently he brought a small plate of peppers. They were red-coloured and covered with a thin film of oil. She ate with a fork, slowly, chunking off the seedy tops and picking stray seeds from the flesh. She ate only a very small portion of flesh at a time. Occasionally she sipped from her glass. When she had finished she beckoned the waiter again.

'*Smetka, molya,*' she asked.

He stood above her to make out the bill, adding two figures in his notebook. He tore out the page and placed it down beside her. She fed out the money from her frayed leather pocket purse carefully, several notes and coins to pay the bill exactly, and beside them a small heap of coins as a tip. He thanked her and helped her into her coat. It was a light, pale-coloured trench coat and she fastened it tightly about her slight figure. She picked a short fallen curl of hair from her forehead and patted it into place again. Then she went to the door.

'*Dovishdane!*' she called suddenly to the waiter, swinging back on her flat heels as she opened the door.

'*Dovishdane!*' he returned. Then he paused a moment, looked puzzled, and remembered. '*Da,*' he said. 'Thank you goodbye.'

The door closed, feet clipped away, and as he stooped to clear the table he talked to himself, repeating a long-ago lesson. 'How you do. I love you,' he said softly. 'Thank you goodbye.' Now and then, remembering something, he laughed quietly to himself.

THE WATERS OF THE MOON

I

Te waiotemarama is at the end of a long white road looped through the trees of a kauri forest. Among thick trunks, tangling creeper and spiky foliage, sun reaches feebly into the forest in late afternoon: it is then that the bus, rumbling and jerking, coughs through the dust to Te Waiotemarama.

Bill Waugh, a taciturn man by nature, drove that afternoon with one passenger. They did not converse until Bill stopped the bus in the approximate centre of the forest and, with his thumb, indicated the place where a track rose in umber from the dust of the road and climbed, vanishing, into a recess of the forest.

'Get off here if you like,' he said. 'It's a regular stop. There's a monster kauri back there. Hundreds of years old, they say. Worth seeing. Most people have a look on the way through. Please yourself.'

That man's sick, he added mentally.

Bill, with discretion, had been observing the passenger in his mirror. He was a middle-aged man, dry and pale-skinned; he reminded Bill of nothing more nor less than a rabbit. A startled rabbit, with sharp little teeth and rolling white eyes. He was dressed in a suit of indeterminate grey colour, a shirt patchy with dust, and a quiet-coloured tie. He considered the world through thick, hornrimmed spectacles. Watching him, Bill had seen pain twitch the rabbit features. Pain and then slow, softening bewilderment.

'Yes,' Bill said, ramming a handkerchief on his sweaty forehead, swinging in his seat, cocking back his hat and thumbing a cigarette into his mouth. 'Take a look if you like.'

In the silence of the forest the birds sang.

'Thanks,' said the passenger, groping slowly down the aisle. He lowered himself gently from the bus and climbed the track into the forest. His dwindling figure, down a corridor of hundred-foot trees, was lost among fern and shadow.

Bill, who studied mankind with a melancholy compassion, noted that the man was probably sick enough to die. Yet he felt no pity. We all had to face it; sooner or later. For Bill, when El Alamein lit the desert night, it had almost been sooner. To-morrow, the next day, each day given to road and dust and forest and the sharp taste of bottled lager at the end of the ride, was a gift bestowed. Bill was sorry for no one; and everyone. We all had to die.

Presently the man returned along the track with that same groping step. He lifted himself into the bus and edged down the aisle to his seat. 'Been this way before?' Bill enquired, without interest.

'No,' the man said. 'Not this way.'

'It's a fine trip,' Bill said. 'Pretty. The forest. Then the harbour. We hit the harbour in a minute. She's a great sight. You see.'

The passenger was silent, locked in sickness again. The motor thudded with a crack of exhaust: they climbed to the top of a hill, the forest gone and the harbour unrolled. Heaped yellow sandhills jumbled about it, creeks with twisting mangroves and shining mudbanks, shacks with unpainted weatherboards, white beaches, ragged farmland, tall stands of cabbage trees. The road slid downwards, curled away from the gaunt cliffs at the head of the harbour and ran trapped between rock and hill.

Te Waiotemarama is solitary on that part of the coast.

Contrast clumsy macrocarpas with delicate Norfolk pines along a pleasant white beach. Erect a long jetty on uncertain foundations, so that the slopping waves of a winter storm will see it jerk like a stiff-jointed centipede; add a dangerous hand-rail, a creaking landing stage and a slapping-roofed shed, vacant now the steamboats have gone, and a repository for dead fish and odd empty fertilizer sacks. Build about the jetty a long patchwork building containing pub, post office, butcher (three times a week) and general store; and a boardwalk on which can be set broken boxes and discarded chairs so that tattooed, pipe-smoking old Maori women sometimes sit and rest and edge forward into winter sun or retreat into summer shade as they gossip in a language almost forgotten. In time the place may or may not acquire character: the dusty yellowing postcards, hanging in strings outside the general store, certainly will not tell you.

The bus lurched to a stop outside the pub. The engine clumped once, twice, and was still. 'This is it,' Bill said.

He watched the passenger, weighted with two suitcases, move slowly across the road, up over the verandah, and in through the pot-planted pub entrance. Then, licking down a rolled cigarette, he shrugged, pocketed the ignition key, and walked to the bar.

2

On the morning of the third day, a Saturday, he met the teacher. The first two mornings he had taken walks in different directions along the sea road. He breathed salt air, found shade to rest, and returned to the pub in time for a pony-beer before lunch. The third morning only one more avenue of escape remained, and that was a road which ran inland from the township, ledging above the shops and jetty and running gently parallel to the sea road until it struck violently into the hills, through a raw gash in landslid clay, turning from the town and climbing.

Beyond the cutting, overlooking the harbour, stood a small schoolhouse and a white cottage. The schoolhouse was empty and quiet. The slender, proud-necked woman in cotton frock and sunhat watered the flowers in her brilliant garden.

'Good morning,' he said, politely.

'Good morning.' She smiled.

He hesitated before walking on: her friendly smile held him.

'I expect you're the mysterious stranger,' she said. 'Mr Fail, isn't it?'

'That's right,' he said. 'You know about me already?'

'It would be difficult not to.'

'And I expect you're the schoolteacher?'

'Whom you've no doubt been told you should meet.'

'How did you know that?'

'Everyone new, for some reason, is told they should meet me. I imagine that makes me local colour, or something.' She laughed, and he saw the intricate roll of her tongue behind white teeth. Her arms, legs and face were clear-skinned and the colour of summer. She had good legs.

'There's colour there,' he said lamely, looking at the garden. About thirty-five, he thought; about thirty-five or forty, and marvellously well preserved. Perhaps a widow.

'Yes,' she said. 'Until the summer burns it out.' She smiled ruefully. 'The summer's hot here. Have you been here in summer before?'

'I haven't been in this part of the country before.'

'Well!' she said with delight. 'That's something, isn't it? You've chosen a good time to see it. Early in the season, before all the campers come. It's still quiet. Yes, you've made a good choice.'

'Choice?' he said. 'Yes, I suppose it was a good choice.' And then he added, 'Though there wasn't much choice about it. I had to have a holiday now.'

'Oh?' she said. 'Then you've been ill, I take it.'

'Something of the sort,' he said, reticent again. 'Well, I shan't burden you with my company; I'll get on with my constitutional.'

'Please don't feel obliged to go. I was just going to ask if you'd like a cup of tea.'

'Well—' He hesitated. The bright garden, the burning harbour, momentarily blinded decision.

'Please do,' she insisted; and the decision was made. She reached deftly to turn off the tap, disconnect the hose.

Inside the cottage there was colour of a more studied kind. Walls of pale yellow and light blue enclosed contemporary furniture set with sprays of flowers from the garden; paintings of style unfamiliar hung from the walls. Modern art, he thought, without any feeling on the subject. He remembered his landlady, while serving dinner, informing him that the schoolteacher was something of a poet and sometimes had her name in the papers; perhaps, it appeared, a painter too. The interior of the cottage was pervaded with a cool delicate dancing light. It was a surprising place to find in this wilderness of decrepit farmland and crumbling homes. Yet he contained his surprise. 'It's a pleasant place you have here,' he observed mildly.

'I'm glad you like it.'

He turned to the wide windows and the view of the harbour heads; the spray feathering up from the stolid rocks.

'And how do you find Te Waiotemarama?' she added, moving into the kitchen and setting the kettle to boil.

'It has a certain natural beauty,' he said with caution.

'But it's quiet.'

'Yes. Quiet.'

'What made you choose it? For a holiday, I mean. If you'll pardon my rudeness in asking.' She smiled disarmingly as she set out cups and saucers on the table. 'Or didn't you have a reason?'

'There are always reasons.'

'Really?' She raised her eyes with a flicker of delight and astonishment, as if the platitude deserved surprise. 'Please do sit down. And tell me.'

He sat awkwardly, looking at his pallid hands. 'Of course I wanted quietness. That was one reason. And I wanted to get away.'

'And other reasons?'

'I wanted to see something new. To get away from the touristy places. And see something of the country I hadn't seen before. I was born here and I've lived most of my life here. But I'm just beginning to realize how little I know about it.'

'An admirable reason,' she said. She made the tea and poured it.

'So I thought I might take the opportunity while I still had it,' he said. Each movement he made, each word he spoke, seemed loaded with weariness; he reached to receive his tea. 'To see something new, I mean.'

'And why not?' she said softly. 'This, for me, is the real part of the country. The rest is a confection. But this is real.'

'What makes you say that?' he said. He was curious, discerning behind the soft voice, the tranquil features, something suddenly passionate.

But her words, her gestures, were casual again. She shrugged. 'Oh,' she said, 'the life, the people, the landscape—everything.'

'It's all vivid enough,' he said. 'But I can't see—'

'Can't you?' she cried; and he saw he had successfully drawn her again. 'Can't you? But look around. You know that this part of the country was the earliest settled—you know that, don't you? Of course you must. It was here that the ship of civilization ran ashore and foundered. Foundered utterly. Here, within these hills. And so they tried again, in the south, leaving the big old homes to crumble here. In the south they made their feeble patchwork among other hills, building into it all the rot of older civilization. This they forgot, in time, almost entirely. Here, perhaps only here, with the two races mixed, something new, altogether new, can grow up; only here, given the chance. Like fresh flowers growing from the ruins. Can you see that?'

'Yes,' he said. 'But—'

'Of course it's impossible that you should,' she said. 'One would have to give one's life to this part of the country, and love it, to see that. It's a truth one doesn't stumble across in a day. But you'll see, even if you only stay here a short time— you'll see that this place has a very special quality, a very special character.' She rose. 'I talk too much. More tea?'

The room rippled with a peculiar yellow light, as if underwater; the serene woman glided through it.

'I'm sorry, Mr Fail,' she said, 'if I bore you.'

'Not at all. Quite the contrary, I assure you.'

'I hardly know a thing about you.'

'There's little enough to know.'

'You might at least tell me that.'

Mr Fail crossed his legs and tried to relax, but found only discomfort. 'I'm a journalist,' he said finally.

'Oh?'

'The rest is detail. There's little more than that to say.'

'Surely not. Tell me more. You've lived here, in this country, all your life?'

'Not all. I worked ten years in England. In Fleet Street.'

'Aha. You see, detail has its interest. And what have you done since you returned?'

'At first I was a sub-editor in the South Island. Since I came north I've been editorial-writing.'

'Aha. Meditating on the state of the country.'

'A country I know nothing about, in the end.'

'You're honest anyway.'

'There's no special merit attached to a disease which is honest about itself.'

'I'm not sure. At least, if the symptom is plain, there is greater potential for cure. Wouldn't you say so? Come, now. More tea? After all, Te Waiotemarama is an excellent place to begin a cure.' She paused. 'Even if, in your case, it happens to be a twin cure—mind and body; isn't that so?'

'You could say that.'

'You're married, of course.'

'I was; I left my wife in England. She developed an infatuation for English life.'

'So many do. It's a lack of self-sufficiency and self-assertion in the national character, of course; little else can be expected. The surprising thing is that many do return unimpressed; surprising and encouraging. You apparently, for example.'

'You flatter me. There was no intelligence behind it. Only the desire for retreat.'

'Retreat?'

'To safety, if you like—or mediocrity; though that's a word I dislike and distrust. Life is lived at an easier pace in these islands; and that's a fact. I happen to prefer it.'

'And why not?' she asked rhetorically.

'And so I came back, not impressed or unimpressed; without judgement. I was merely grateful to be back.'

'But you know more than before?'

Mr Fail, on his feet now, walked to the window and studied

the view. 'I think I know less,' he said finally. 'And that might mean less than nothing. I don't know.'

That afternoon Mr Fail slept badly. In a dream he floated effortlessly, weightlessly, down long tunnels of darkness with the sound of wind in his ears. His eyes throbbed in his head as, like a swimmer seeking land, he looked vainly for illumination. He danced in the seething claustrophobic darkness like a strung puppet. Then he woke to the pain in his side, the cicadas singing in the late afternoon, the shadows crawling across his carpet. He was exhausted and sticky with sweat. He reached for the small bottle of pills on the table beside his bed.

And it was still early summer. The summer was hot, the teacher had reminded him.

He considered the teacher.

He recalled her, built her face again, only with difficulty. Her presence, her wholeness, commanded attention; not detail. There was something odd there, something beyond experience, something he could not define. If he had met her in other circumstances it would have been perhaps easy to pin her down, dismiss her without further thought. If, for example, he had met her among the people in this country who were so pathetically and self-consciously arty; among the kind of people he often distrusted and more often despised. Divorced from them, a solitary, almost a hermit of her kind, her entire presence seemed to say: Look at this. Not, as one might have expected in those other circumstances: Look at me.

She had a mild but quite definite arrogance; there was certainly little humility. And no restlessness, no discontent, no retreat. Only certainty, confidence, assertion. There was harmony there; a strange harmony.

He hoped they would meet again soon.

Odd, though, that her face blurred so quickly. Next time he must concentrate on it, and not be distracted by delicate hands, swivelling body.

He expected they would meet again soon. After all, when he left, they had been calling each other Isobel and Douglas.

3

Actually her face was not extraordinary. The features were fine enough; the lines firm. There was perhaps a hint of something alien to the Anglo-Saxon in the cheekbones, the slightly lengthened eyes. But really, Mr Fail thought, there was nothing very startling about the face; except its tan, its rich colour. Why, he thought, she could almost be a Maori. She must have followed the sun like a pagan to acquire that colour.

He had met her again in the schoolyard. He saw her, as he drew near the school, surrounded by children, children in shades from pale coffee to dark chocolate; girls in bright print frocks and boys in check shirts. Looking up from her brood, she saw him. 'Why, hello, Douglas,' she cried, the children still eddying about her, tugging her skirt. Laughing, her teeth flashing, she scattered them homeward and went to the gate to greet him.

'I was hoping I'd see you again today,' she said.

Talking, she led him across the playground, up through her garden, to the cottage. 'I think we might take tea on the verandah this afternoon,' she reflected. 'It's pleasant there, in the shade.'

They took tea there; below, beyond the garden, the land sloped away to the schoolyard and schoolhouse, and then dropped sharply to the strung-out rooftops of Te Waiotemarama, the white beach, and the sea. In the sunlit afternoon a fishing launch puttered peacefully down harbour.

'And how are you finding Te Waiotemarama?' she asked, as the cups and saucers chinked.

'I think I'm finding the rhythm,' he said. 'Perhaps, in a day or two, I'll begin fishing off the jetty like the other idlers.'

She laughed. 'I look forward to seeing that.'

'By the way,' he said. 'I don't know Maori. What does it mean?—Te Waiotemarama?'

'The waters of the moon,' she said. 'Rather a pleasant name, don't you think?'

'Tell me,' he said, leaning forward, 'what do people *do* here?'

'Why,' she said, 'they perform essential functions with dignity and non-essentials with difficulty.'

'Take the land as an example. It could be utilized in a much better, much more productive fashion. Thousands of acres, running just a handful of cows when it could run hundreds.'

'But why?' she exclaimed. 'Why hundreds?'

'For money. Just for argument's sake.'

'But if they live a good life already,' she said, 'what's the point?'

'Indeed,' he said. 'In that case, what *is* the point?' He sighed.

'Poor old Douglas. Things still bewilder you. Perhaps you should go a little south, where you'll find farmers running big herds and dying at sixty.'

'And here?'

'It's different. As you see.'

He shook his head.

'Don't worry,' she said cheerfully. 'You'll get used to it.'

At that point a figure emerged from the schoolhouse. The figure of a tall boy in tight navy shorts and patched flannel shirt; a dusky-skinned boy, with firm brown legs and long arms, lithe and soft-footed with the body of an athlete. He came out across the schoolyard, eyes blinking in the sudden sunlight, and looked up and saw the woman on the verandah; he raised an arm in stiff salute. She waved back, a small fluttering of the hand above the teacups. Then he turned and walked out the gate and down the hill to the town.

'That's Kuru,' she said in explanation. 'My biggest boy. And my star pupil.'

'Oh?'

'He works late, quite often. By himself. After the others have gone home.'

'Conscientious.'

'And conscious of his lack. You see, he didn't begin school till late, for one reason and another. So he's old for his class—a giant among pygmies. He has a remarkably receptive mind and a quite extraordinary intelligence. He could go a long way, given help at the crucial times. He's preparing for a scholarship. If he wins it, he'll be going away next year; rather sad for me, but it can't be helped.'

'You love your work, don't you?'

She didn't answer immediately : he sensed not so much embarrassment as a reluctance to slice too deeply, to reveal too much. He would never draw her there. It was too easy for her to escape with simple assent; as she did.

'I do,' she said. 'As a matter of fact.'

So they did not talk of that again.

'Oh, by the way,' she said. 'I have an invitation for you. To tea on Sunday night at the Hicksons' place.'

'Who are they?'

'You must have noticed their place—that big old pioneer house behind a row of Norfolk pines, all lawned and gardened in front. They're a quaint old couple; you'll like them, once you're used to their idiosyncrasies. And it'll be a chance for you to see inside one of the few original homesteads remaining about here.'

'It sounds interesting.'

'They're quite a scream, the Hicksons. An anachronism. But you'll enjoy them. I visit them regularly, as a rule. Mrs Hickson was, I imagine, quite a cultivated woman once; though she's gone to seed here. Actually she's English in origin; Hickson himself is the one of pioneer stock. He's, well, deteriorating quickly now. He's gone cranky. He seems to sit out on his verandah all day, looking out through a telescope for non-existent steamboats. And, by the way, he's a cripple; some disease of the bone as a child. I think it best to warn people in advance. He's always been a burden, now more so than ever. That's why I visit them so often. It helps her keep her end up. They've one child. He's twenty-three, and a beer-swilling, brawling imbecile. Quite the worst influence around here. It was a relief for us all when he cleared off to the city a month or so ago. But you'll like the old couple. They're quaint. But you'll see, anyway.'

'I expect I shall,' he said.

'Oh,' she said, patting back her corn-coloured hair, 'I know you'll enjoy the Hicksons.'

But he did not enjoy the Hicksons; though he would never have told Isobel. He did not enjoy their gloomy cavern of a house, either; he scented decay rather than history in the rooms cluttered with heavy dusty furniture. He could find no interest in the mahogany desk where the first Governor of New Zealand had sat, the bed where the colonizer Wakefield slept, the room in which the missionary Samuel Marsden conducted a service. He wanted to escape to where hard clean winds drove from the west, and the sun flashed from the sea. But he was patient and listened quietly as he was led about the house. He could not relax even at the meal; for that too was an ordeal. Hickson, misshapen and spidery across the table, fixed him with an idiot eye and talked about the ruin of the country, the calamity of inter-marriage between the races; and about the steamboats, the old days that would never return. Mrs Hickson, a prim and plump grey-haired woman, retailed the collected gossip of the week to Isobel; and once, unwinding some frail and tenuous link of memory, led herself back to girlhood, and the neat green fields and hedges of the English countryside. While she talked, Mr Fail found himself studying a photograph of the son which squatted, in a heavy gilt frame, on a sideboard. It was a raw, unfinished face, thin with discontent. A face which belonged nowhere.

It was, finally, a relief to escape out the front door; to walk with Isobel down the white crunching sea-shelled path through the cool garden and into the pale beauty of an evening with the harbour moonlit.

'You didn't like it,' Isobel said quietly.

'No,' he lied. 'I liked it. It was pleasant. An experience, you might say. It gives one a perspective on all that one sees here.'

'It does,' she agreed, as they walked.

Not long after the visit to the Hicksons he received something in the post: a thin book which a friend had hunted down through a half dozen city bookstores. Sitting in his room, his french windows open to sea and sunlight while a cool breeze flicked the curtains, he turned the crisp new pages slowly, noting passages of interest here and there.

He could not have said, with truth, that he liked her verse. The lines were measured, cautious and exact; almost entirely without artifice. Even the images had a kind of brittle austerity. He sensed, behind the cool words, the supple intelligence lacing them together; and something else, which entirely eluded him. Something odd, tantalizing, erratic, which bathed landscapes in a limpidly, almost directly physical glow; there was something there he had not suspected before. Something which intrigued him, fascinated him as much as the woman herself, and finally led him back to her; he could find no answer, turning and re-turning the pages. For the thing, whatever it was, escaped him with the ease of a tiny whirring-winged fantail in the thick sunlit depths of the bush; when he seemed able to reach out for it, it darted away and left him empty-handed and alone in a profound silence.

So at length he placed the book beside his bed, dressed, left the pub, and climbed up to the school.

On his way he passed the Hickson place. Behind the trees he glimpsed old Hickson, alone and small in the wide sweep of the verandah. He seemed to sit there all day, his distorted body twined about the telescope, watching the empty sea, the sky, the seabirds careening. Mr Fail hailed him, but Hickson did not seem to hear.

He found Isobel that afternoon not at the cottage, but in the schoolhouse, coaching the boy Kuru for his examination. Teacher and pupil sat alone in the dim empty schoolroom, side by side at a ridiculously small desk, among the smell of linseed and chalk. Standing in the cabbage-tree shade of the yard, he watched them through the large windows. Patiently she explained; patiently the boy listened. Once she laughed, a high bright sound; and the boy smiled. Then they worked again, Isobel talking and the boy nodding his head in understanding. They worked together in a peaceful, quite perfect intimacy which Mr Fail found beyond him to disturb. He waited until they appeared finished. Then he walked slowly across the yard, into the sunlight, and up to the door of the room.

Isobel gave a small cry of delight on seeing him; she introduced him to Kuru.

'I've heard all about you,' he said. 'I'm very pleased to meet you.'

But the boy greeted him with a suspicion and reluctance near surliness; but a surliness sprung more, perhaps, from shyness than arrogance. All the same, though, there was a stiff dignity about the way he shook Mr Fail's hand, gathered his books, and left the room. An unusual boy, Mr Fail observed. He was left with the memory of a striking brown face lit with two large liquid eyes; strange eyes, curiously gentle.

'And that's Kuru,' Isobel said, tidying her desk.

They took tea on the verandah again. It seemed to Mr Fail that they were nearer each other that afternoon than they had ever been before. And for the first time it occurred to him that he was already actually courting Isobel. After all, she was a woman of a kind who could command much more from him than mere respect and admiration. She was, in fact, a woman of a kind he wished he had met long before. He found himself marvellously relaxed in her company. And entertained by the flash of her wit, the precision of her thought; he never had wish to broach his own opinions when with her. He was content always to listen.

The next Sunday they picnicked at the head of the harbour. There was a shambling old ruin of a house there, now over-grown with bush, which had once belonged to men who piloted the steamboats over the seething sand-bar into the still waters of the harbour. They lunched in the shade of a tumbling wall. Salad, sandwiches, fishcakes; and a bottle of dry white wine Isobel had packed into the basket.

The day was perfect. Nikau palms framed the vivid harbour, and in the distance the yellow sandhills glittered. After lunch Mr Fail remained in the shade while Isobel edged out into the sunlight, full-length on the grass, surrendering to the warmth and closing her eyes. Conversation drifted, thinned, and ended; and, as the sun turned her legs an even deeper brown, Mr Fail discovered himself, in a solitary moment of embarrassment, admiring the long loose body, so wonderfully preserved it might have belonged to a girl of twenty. She seemed so natural there, flung carelessly upon the dry grass in the heat and scent of summer; she was suddenly, for him, part of the summer, part of its rich-ness, its green, its quivering golden light. She gave the summer its peculiarly restful and healing quality.

Why, he thought, she's a regular pagan; a regular little

pagan the way she drenches herself in sun. And then he felt the
odd, scratching edge of disquiet again; the thing he thought lost
when he put aside the book of verse. What was it, he wondered,
that so disturbed him? What was it about this woman, so splen-
didly relaxed in the sun, that should cry an alarm, a warning?

She stirred lazily, voluptuously, easing herself into a soft nest
of crackling grass; and, raising a hand to shadow her eyes against
the brilliance, she looked up at him, her mouth wrinkling a little-
girl's smile. And Mr Fail sat stiffly in the shade.

4

People spoke of the summer. Hot dry November became hot
dry December. The old Maori men, nodding their wise heads,
turned leaves over in their large withered hands and predicted
drought. It was ten years since the north had known a summer
so fierce. Mr Fail, his face colouring with sun, kept more to the
shade, and stayed indoors in the bitter heat of noon. When he
went out, he always went now in loose open-neck shirt, and
sometimes in shorts. It was a real summer, people said. A summer
of shrivelling grass, of crystal mornings, inflamed afternoons, and
nights rising like smoke from the raging land. Mr Fail thought
sometimes, in moments of weakness, of the mountains and cool
green lakes of the south; but in the end did not regret his choice
of a place to holiday, not even when tents flowered along the sea
road and campers crowded the beaches. There was still quietness
enough; pleasantness enough. There was the dazzling sweep of
the harbour beyond his windows in the morning; the brilliant
evenings when stars and moon lit the water. There was his chair
in the shade of the upstairs verandah, his collection of books
arranged neatly beside it; there was the tonic glass of beer at
noon, and the siesta after lunch; there were the days when, after
sunset, in the falling dusk, he dropped his fishing line off the end
of the jetty and yarned with his new friends, the idlers.

And there were the evenings which belonged to Isobel.

Sometimes, on these warm evenings, he tried to steer conversations in mid-flight, tried to circle them down to something more
specific, more personal. Why, for example, had she never

married? Why had she stayed here? Was she really so content? But they were questions he never, in the end, asked : for, if he made approach to them, he slammed against a quite formidable wall of reticence.

So he began to formulate his disquiet. So at length he told himself : There is something odd about that woman. She was, after all, a flagrant violation of the rules. She should not be happy and sufficient, alone. Solitary, she should not retain that marvellous capacity for delight. Yet she was entirely impenetrable; there was no chink in the bright façade through which he might glimpse doubt or defeat. He was as empty-handed as ever he had been. So he thought : There is something odd about that woman. Something unnatural.

That they spent so much time together did not go unremarked. The loungers saw it, the idlers, and the publican and his wife; and the Hicksons, when he accompanied Isobel on her regular visiting chore. They saw it : and made comment. And the boy Kuru saw it, and his eyes made comment.

Summer blistered through Christmas into the new year. Mr Fail felt himself stronger, prided himself on his rather weak tan, and walked with more confident step. The nights of the sharp pains in his side were gone; he had not touched the bottle of pills beside his bed for three weeks.

Calling up at the cottage one evening, he discovered a visitor. Someone had come to stay with Isobel.

'Really, Izzy, I just can't understand how you put up with it here, year in and year out. How do you do it? What is it? What makes you stay here? Don't you wish you could see the theatre sometimes? Or hear good music? Or see a good movie? How do you manage it? Tell me—what is it?'

Isobel smiled wryly at Mr Fail. 'These young people,' she said.

The girl pirouetted across to the cabinet and poured herself another drink. She was an altogether startling creature, clad in black, in tight sweater and matador slacks; she clinked and clacked with adornments, beggars' beads from India, beaten gold bracelets, hoop ear-rings. She had long hair, a short boyish figure and a face which, if attractive, was rather imprecise in character.

'And don't, Izzy, give me any of your stoic philosophy,' she declared, falling on a couch and curling her legs beneath her. She fiddled, drank from her glass, and lit a cigarette. An extraordinarily restless girl, Mr Fail observed; she couldn't seem to sit still for a minute. 'No,' she said. 'Don't tell me. I don't want to hear it all again.' She looked at Mr Fail. 'Do *you* understand her?' she asked. 'Do you?'

'Sometimes,' said Mr Fail cautiously, 'I imagine I do.'

'Well, then,' the girl said, 'you're a remarkable man, Douglas old boy.' She sipped from her glass. 'Maybe you can give me one or two clues. I've been trying to persuade Izzy down to the city for the last five years. Damn it all, this is no place for her; she needs to be with people like herself. Stimulating people. The kind she never meets here.'

'You forget Douglas,' Isobel pointed out. 'He's been stimulating company this summer.'

'But Douglas, after all, is a drop in the bucket,' the girl said. 'If Douglas will forgive the expression.'

'I will,' said Mr Fail gravely.

The girl laughed. 'You know, Douglas, you're a pompous old thing,' she said. 'But I rather love you.'

Mr Fail smiled uncertainly.

'It's really all right,' the girl said provocatively. 'I shan't eat you, you know.' She came to sit on the arm of his chair; and nudged him. 'But you're really terribly lovable. Isn't he, Izzy?'

'Douglas is like me,' Isobel said. 'Impervious to the wiles of the younger generation.'

'You're just a pair of old fogeys,' the girl said, winking at Mr Fail. 'A pair of fogeys meditating in the wilderness. What brought *you* here anyway, Douglas?'

'Douglas came to spend the summer here for his health,' Isobel interposed. 'Which I think a perfectly good idea.'

'Well, you met Izzy, didn't you?' the girl said, turning to Mr Fail again. 'Don't you think Izzy's rather charming?'

'Please, Cheryl darling,' Isobel pleaded. 'Do leave Douglas alone.'

'But Doug and I are getting on like a house on fire,' she appealed. 'Aren't we, Doug? Of course we are. And Izzy's just an old meanie, spoiling our fun.' Her black arm appeared around Mr Fail's shoulder. 'We could have fun. Couldn't we, Dougie?'

'Really Cheryl,' Isobel said. 'Let Douglas relax a little, darling. You're making him dreadfully uncomfortable.'

Mr Fail felt twice trapped: trapped by this brazen girl and trapped by Isobel's eyes. He must not make it appear he was playing up to the girl; why, at his age, it would look ridiculous. Without thinking, he began to loosen his collar in a profound gesture of embarrassment, and then discovered he was already wearing an open-neck shirt. It was suddenly hot: sweat beaded his face.

'But really, Dougie,' the girl insisted, 'don't you think Izzy's charming?'

'Isobel has many fine qualities,' Mr Fail replied. 'Many fine qualities.' The girl was positively like a snake, the way she insinuated herself around him. He mopped his face.

'I think you're so right,' she said. 'I wonder why it is Izzy hasn't married?'

'I think,' said Isobel, rising, 'I am going to make a cup of tea.'

'Apart from the fact that Izzy's a fourth generation New Zealander, she's a perfect Englishwoman,' the girl observed. 'In face of adversity, she makes a cup of tea.'

Mr Fail often saw Isobel and Cheryl together after that evening. But he did not accompany them when they asked him along on their rambles about harbour and coast. It was only partly due to the fact that he preferred to remain indoors in the sticky heat of January; and chiefly because the girl persisted in causing him considerable embarrassment.

He could not understand it.

What could a woman of such fine temperament find in the company of such a cheap little baggage? He could not find one redeeming feature in Cheryl; not one at all. What, exactly, was it?

He met them in various circumstances. Quite often in the

village, in the early morning, he saw them as they were starting off for a tramp out to the head of the harbour. Isobel would be carrying picnic basket and swimming costumes; and Cheryl a sketchbook and a box of water-colours. 'Another excursion in the interest of art,' Isobel would protest. 'Cheryl goes crazy over this scenery.'

What, exactly, was it? Mr Fail wondered as he watched them walk away.

This intruder had wrecked the summer. And, waking to the wreckage in the hot empty afternoons, Mr Fail was left with the solitary question.

What, exactly?

5

Towards the end of January there was a patch of cooler weather. The days were still warm, but swift breezes rose out of the Tasman sea, rattling the bush, jolting the dry trees in the heat-laden land. Mr Fail, who for some reason had taken to reading the slender book of verse again, tried to trace the flight of a lonely, plaintively crying bird across fathomless landscapes of the heart, but with no success. Restless, he walked again. He walked often in that patch of cooler weather, wondering if it was not after all time to return to the city. Wondering if after all everything had once again only turned to nothing in his hands.

On one of these walks he met the girl Cheryl quite by accident. Apparently even Isobel had forsaken her now, for she sat alone in a clearing, drawing a tumbledown farmhouse; alone in the clear liquid light of late afternoon, the cicadas droning about her. She appeared suddenly and surprisingly to Mr Fail in that pool of light crowded with lengthening shadows; she sat working on the stump of a tree, clad only in brief sunsuit. He had already gone half-way across the clearing before he saw her; she had not seen him. Even then, at the risk of seeming ridiculous, he was about to retreat, to hurry back into the bush again before her sharp tongue claimed him. But a dry stick cracked beneath his feet; she looked up and cried out.

'Why, Doug, you are a roamer! Fancy meeting you here.'

He felt his legs quivering in anticipation of the assault. He still had the impulse, despite the chance of appearing totally demented now, to turn and flee. His mouth worked dryly; but no sound emerged. So he nodded to the girl.

'You didn't follow me, by any chance?' she said cheekily.

'No,' he said. 'I did not.'

'Why, Dougie,' she said. 'I believe you really are frightened of me.'

Again his mouth worked with that dry, numb sensation; but this time words did presently emerge. 'Do you think so?' he said very steadily. He went to move on. 'Well, I shan't disturb your work.'

'Oh, but you're not. You're not disturbing me at all.'

'I'm sure I must be.'

'Please don't go. I'm finished now. Really I am.' Her voice became oddly wheedling.

He could not help seeing her drawing. Mr Fail knew little about art; but then one only needed to know little to realize that this inexpert piece lacked even the elementary graces of form and perspective. He glanced at it only once, and did not look again. Then Cheryl laid the sketchbook aside.

'See? I'm really finished.'

'Yes.'

'Really, Doug, you are awfully coy. Please sit down.'

'I prefer to sit in the shade.'

Cheryl, plainly, was a creature of the sun; for a city girl she had gone brown very quickly. Her arms were almost black already.

'Well, the shade it is, then.' She gathered her things. 'I don't mind.'

Mr Fail felt a choking despair. 'I think I really should be getting back to the hotel.'

But it was no use. He found himself sitting in the shade of pines at the edge of the clearing while Cheryl chattered beside him. Like two empty tin cans hitting together, he thought.

'We haven't seen much of you lately,' she said.

'No. I've been keeping indoors.'

'I think Izzy misses you.'

'She does?' He tried not to show excitement.

'You don't sound very interested. You're holding out on me, Doug. You do really like Izzy, don't you?'

'Isobel is very pleasant company.'

'Oh, come off it. More than that, isn't she?'

'I'm not sure what you mean.'

'Really, Doug, don't give me that.' She laughed, yawned, and stretched herself lazily on warm pine-needles. 'Wouldn't you like to sleep with Izzy?'

'Really, I don't think—'

'Don't be so damn stuffy. Of course you would. Izzy's a marvellous person. Anyone would want to sleep with her.'

'I hardly think it's relevant.'

'Of course it's relevant, damn it all. Why else have you been hanging round this dump so long? Not really for your health, I bet. But really because you want to tumble long-legged Isobel in the hay. Isn't that right?'

'If you'll excuse me—'

But Cheryl grabbed him as he rose and brought him to ground again. 'You don't get away as easy as that. Not from me you don't. Now don't start getting excited; just relax. There's no need to break out in a sweat just because I ask you a perfectly simple question. I believe in honesty; don't you?'

'Up to a point.'

'Well, that's interesting. Honesty up to a point. An interesting comment on the state of journalism. And you were an editor or something, weren't you, Doug? Well, well. So I guess you were only honest up to a point with your readers. Yes. That's most interesting indeed.'

Mr Fail was silent. For some reason he was breathing heavily. Cheryl still held him.

'Come on, now; loosen up. You like Izzy, don't you?'

'Naturally I like Isobel. She's a very attractive person.'

'And you'd like to sleep with her?'

'I told you before; it's not relevant.'

'Of course it's bloody well relevant. I would.'

Mr Fail was not sure he understood. Bewildered, he said, 'Would what?'

'Like to sleep with Isobel.' She paused. 'Really, Doug, I do believe you're shocked.'

But Mr Fail was feeling, at that moment, only a great relief. He was like a tree still quivering loosely in the wake of a roaring gale. He mopped his face and a sigh escaped him.

'But you don't,' he said quietly.

'Of course I don't,' she said. 'Worse luck. No one can say I haven't tried. God knows where she gets her love life. Perhaps she gets it vicariously from the raped landscape or some damn thing. I don't know.'

But Mr Fail scarcely heard a word. His nerves were still settling.

'I've known Izzy five years and sometimes I think I don't know any more about her now than I did at the beginning. She likes having odd kids coming to stay with her from the city. Helps her keep in touch, she says. That's one of the reasons why I've collected the invitation so often. And, as a matter of fact, I like coming up here for the summer with Isobel. But I can't be blamed, can I, if I feel a little frustrated sometimes?'

Mr Fail felt more favourably inclined towards the girl. After all, she was only being frank about herself; and frankness was, decidedly, a rare and admirable virtue. He felt he could cope with her now.

'No,' he conceded solemnly. 'You can't.'

'You know,' she said, laughing, 'you're not a bad old stick, Doug. I might have known you had it in you. We understand each other now, don't we?'

'Well,' said Mr Fail, smiling faintly. 'I suppose we do.'

That evening when, for a change, he visited the cottage, he found himself relaxed there for the first time in weeks; and even discovered himself regarding Cheryl, and her garish appearance, with a tolerant affection. Once or twice Cheryl winked at him when Isobel's back was turned: why, he thought, they were almost fellow-conspirators now.

Cheryl excused herself early, saying she was tired, and so he found himself talking to Isobel till late.

Isobel was excited that night, and in the mood for prolonged conversation. Her protégé Kuru had passed his examinations and won the scholarship he had worked for; had, in fact, topped the list. It was an evening for congratulation.

The next morning, looking out from his verandah, he saw Isobel walking with the boy near the sea. The campers had begun to leave, and the beach had a deserted appearance now; Te Waiotemarama was shaking off the canvas trimmings of summer, and returning to normal. They walked beside the rising tide in the crisp morning. Isobel was explaining something; he saw her lips moving, her hands working vigorously. Even from some distance, he imagined he saw the pride in her face. And the boy walked silently beside her.

In the afternoon Mr Fail happened, not entirely by accident this time, upon the clearing again. Cheryl was there. This time she was lying on the grass, sunbathing in the nude, her colour so close to that of the sunburned land that he did not see her at first; so that, if she had not called his name, he would probably have walked out of the clearing without seeing her at all.

When he did see her, he started back. 'Perhaps you'd like to dress,' he said, turning his eyes.

But she made no attempt to cover herself. 'Nonsense,' she said. 'I'd only spoil my tan. Sit down there, on that log in the shade, and talk to me.' She was plump and evenly brown the length of her body; with shock, Mr Fail realized she must have made a practice of sunbathing in this fashion. He sat down, as instructed, but could find nowhere comfortable to place his eyes.

'You're a let-down,' she said. 'An absolute let-down. Hey there, are you so ashamed of yourself you can't even look at me?'

'What do you mean?' he asked, at last looking at her; and finding the experience not altogether unpleasant. 'I don't understand.'

'Last night,' Cheryl said. 'I go to great pains to leave you alone with Izzy—and what happens? Oh, you don't need to tell me. I listened. You talked to her. You bloody well talked to her. My

God, man, what's wrong with you? Can't you persuade her out to look at the moon, or something? Instead you say, yes, you will have another cup of tea, thank you. You're a real let-down. A proper let-down. Don't talk to me.'

'I think you misunderstand my relationship with Isobel,' he said.

'In that case, I can only conclude you misunderstand yourself. Pull your finger out, man. Get her into bed. There's no time like the present.'

'I'm afraid I don't really understand why you should be so concerned.'

'My reasons, dear Douglas, are purely selfish. I'm curious. I want to see if it's possible. I might tell you I'm out of the race now, so you don't need to worry your head about me. You've got a clear field. So what do you do? You bloody well talk.'

He was silent.

'I mean to say,' she added, 'it's not even as if you talk to her about anything interesting. No, it's always about this godforsaken hole, this godforsaken countryside, and the goddam Maoris. Are you really so interested?'

'Isobel makes me interested, as a matter of fact. I like people who are passionate about their interests; her passion is with this country, and its people. She's absorbed in what she's doing here. So I like to hear her talk.'

'Oh God,' Cheryl cried in dismay, rolling over in the grass. 'A bloody great pair of soul-mates.'

'I think you're being rather unfair,' he said.

'What are you trying to tell me now? That you looked after a harem in your youth? That *would* be the unkindest cut of all.'

'I don't think, really, there's any need to be crude. Isobel and I just happen to be very good friends. I'm not sure there's need for more.'

'My God,' she cried, rolling from side to side in the grass again, convulsed with laughter. 'Hark at the man.'

There was a silence. A sea breeze chattered the pines. A tui sang, high and clear, from a burnt-out flax bush. Mr Fail felt a tickling beneath his chin. Instinctively he slapped at it; and found not a mosquito or sandfly, but a piece of straw. Cheryl held the

8—TNZ

straw; she sat curled at his feet now. She had slithered quietly across the grass when he was not looking.

'I'm trying to wake you up,' she announced.

'Really?'

'Doug, I think you're a very frustrated old thing. And half your trouble is you don't know it. You know that?'

'You seem very concerned.'

'Oh, but I am, really, you see. I'm very concerned about you. You know why? I think you're rather nice.'

'You're very flattering.'

'Don't you think I'm nice?' she said pertly, wide eyes blinking. She was so round and soft and brown, her eyes so huge and her eyelashes so spectacularly long, she seemed more like a doll than a person; a quaint, dumpy brown doll. Really, he thought, she was a terribly funny little creature.

'Of course I think you're nice,' he said.

'Well,' she said, 'that's fine, isn't it?'

There was a pause.

'Well,' said Cheryl, making the same pert inviting face, 'is that all you have to say?' She tugged at his arm like a persistent child, tumbling him off the log. 'Is that all you have to say?' she said again as he floundered on the grass. She insinuated herself against him, so that he felt the gentle pressure of the hard little breasts; a brown arm circled his neck and she fingered his face.

'You're not still frightened of me, are you, Dougie? Don't tell me that. No, of course you're not. Because we understand each other, don't we? Of course. And we won't be frightened any more, will we?'

'Really, I think—' said Mr Fail, but it was the cry of a drowning man.

'Don't think, Dougie. Thinking's dangerous. Thinking spoils everything,' she said as she lifted his spectacles. 'You mustn't think.' There was a considerable pause. 'I'm real, you know. Truly. There's nothing extraordinary about me, really. I'm fitted out the same way as everyone else, only more adaptable than most. There, you see. Touch me. See if I'm real.'

Mr Fail, surrendering to the game finally, touched her tentatively. It was astonishing. At that slight touch her head snapped back and her entire body jolted into motion; her mouth drove against him, her tongue flicking hungrily. She caught him, pulled him down, he felt the earth peel away from him. Everything peeled away, shredding like a chrysalis, and he was adrift and drowning.

And then he was no longer drowning. He was sucked upwards slowly, and he found himself gliding in strange currents; gliding without knowledge, without sensation, as she slipped away.

'You see,' she said, 'it wasn't so bad after all, was it?' Her tongue licked gently at his ear as she lay beside him. 'No,' she said presently, 'it wasn't so bad. Only we're just a bit comic, aren't we? Here we are both wanting someone else, and we make do with each other. Sad, isn't it?'

In a little while, kittenish, she added, 'Don't you think I'm nice, Dougie?'

6

Cheryl returned to the city at the beginning of February. Mr Fail was sorry to see her leave; he imagined he felt towards her in a fatherly fashion. Since Mr Fail was childless by his first and only marriage, experience did not contradict him. But certainly he would miss Cheryl. Before she left, she gave him her address in the city; and made him promise to visit her when he too returned. 'But don't get any ideas in your old bonnet,' she said. 'This is strictly friendship from now on.' She laughed. 'This other was for the hell of it. A bit of summer silliness. But then we understood that, didn't we, Dougie?' Well, he had understood it : up to a point.

She pinched him under the chin and shook his hand. 'And good luck,' she said. 'With Izzy, I mean. I think you'll need it. I hope you make good, anyway. There must be a key to unlock that door, somewhere.'

Of course there had to be a key, somewhere. Mr Fail had tried many keys; and the door remained closed. The first week in February, with school about to begin again, Isobel already slipping into the skin of the new year, he tried more. He tried now with urgency, with desperation, always convinced that one more twist should set the tumblers clicking free, release the complex combination, roll open the door on swift hinges, reveal the wonder within.

And yet, without Cheryl, he felt lost and emptied. The girl, oddly and briefly, had given him confidence of a kind.

Though the sun still fired the rainless days, the long bright hours of summer were dwindling; soon it would be autumn.

'I hope,' said Isobel one evening, 'that Cheryl didn't pester you too much, Douglas.'

'Not at all.'

'Really? I had the queer notion she completely unnerved you at the beginning. She's a sweet child, but rather hard to take in large doses, don't you think?'

'That's true,' he said.

'Yet after a while you seemed to cope with her quite well,' she observed.

The observation had more truth than was comfortable. But when he looked at her, he detected no flicker of knowledge in her eyes. 'Yes,' he said. 'I managed. Young people bewilder me these days. They live by different rules. I imagine it's just a question of getting used to them.' He hesitated. 'Actually, after a while, I found Cheryl quite entertaining.'

'Well,' said Isobel, smiling, 'I could see you enjoyed each other's company. I must say I was quite pleasantly surprised the day I saw you come strolling back here with her. I'm pleased you liked her, in the end. For a while I thought she might drive you away.'

'Would that have been so terrible?' he asked quickly.

'Of course. I should have been very sorry indeed, Douglas.' Swiftly she parried him : swiftly she rose and cleared away the tea things. And he remembered it was late; and that tomorrow school began. He rose wearily.

'I shan't keep you up. I'd almost forgotten tomorrow was your big day.'

'There's no need for you to go yet, Douglas,' she said politely. 'The new hordes don't terrify me all that much, you know.'

'But I will go,' he insisted. 'I know you'll be tired.'

He went to the door.

'Oh, Douglas,' she said suddenly.

'Yes?' He turned quickly, expectantly.

'You haven't forgotten the wedding?'

'The wedding?' he said bleakly.

'On Saturday.'

'Oh, yes,' he said. 'The wedding.'

'You do remember, don't you?'

'Yes. Of course. I promised to go, didn't I?'

Of course he should have remembered. After all, he was almost a resident member of the Te Waiotemarama community now. But he had forgotten, entirely forgotten, until Isobel reminded him.

The wedding was an event in the district. The Hickson boy, having got a girl three months pregnant, had been persuaded by his mother to return from the city and marry the girl to salvage the family honour. The girl was a Maori and the sister of Kuru. Coffee-skinned children would inherit the house of Hickson.

In the days before the wedding, Mr Fail strolling past the school, saw Isobel with her new hordes; saw the small hands clutch at her skirt as she led the children in tiny straggling crocodiles across the playground and read them stories in the shade of the cabbage trees. An odd spasm of pain burned his throat when he saw her so disposed; she was even more remote behind this new screen of admirers.

One afternoon, on his way to take tea with Isobel, he met Kuru emerging from the cottage; the boy, unsmiling and unresponsive as ever, greeted him briefly and continued down the hill.

'I see Kuru hasn't gone yet,' he said.

'No,' Isobel said. 'He should have gone off to his new school last weekend. But he's staying on for his sister's wedding. Then he'll go.'

'You'll miss him,' he observed.

'Naturally,' she said, busying herself, 'I miss all my children as I lose them, one by one.'

The night before the wedding Mr Fail woke with a twinge in his side, and came to the conclusion that he was an idiot. It was an idiot business altogether, proceeding from nowhere to nowhere. All night he had been disturbed by trackless, heavy-weighted dreams. And so he had woken, at this morning hour, with the twinge; and the thought that it had all, in the end, been quite pointless. He swallowed two pills and then walked barefoot across the room and peeled back the curtains from the french windows. It was still dark, and faint moonlight glimmered on the harbour.

He could of course finish it quite simply. There was a bus back to the city tomorrow morning, Sunday.

The more he considered it, the more attractive the thought became. He could say something quietly to Isobel, this afternoon, at the wedding. And if he chose his moment carefully enough, chose his words carefully enough, then it might become the moment for which he had waited so long. Surely then he would be able to prise some response from her; something to put her off guard long enough for him to take his chance and say what he wanted to say. He padded back to bed and slept till late.

In the afternoon he went to the wedding.

7

Isobel wore white gloves. The Hicksons shuffled in bewilderment through the crush of Maori guests. Hickson grated along on his walking sticks; Mrs Hickson darted glances to right and left like a startled bird. Kuru, surprisingly sleek in a dark suit, guided the preacher through the guests; and listened attentively to what the preacher, a dry sad little man, had to tell him.

The ceremony was brief. Kuru's sister was plainly pregnant, though not grotesquely so; young Hickson wore his surliest expression and looked suffocated in suit and tie. The preacher spoke his solemn words and they, the recipients, bowed their heads; and were joined.

The Hicksons soon escaped the wedding breakfast, before their drunken son began bawling bawdy songs with his friends. They went meekly down the hall, Hickson hobbling, Mrs Hickson leading gently. They shook hands and vanished.

And Mr Fail felt an unexpected choke of pity.

The preacher was next to leave; and the party raged. Kegs thundered across the wooden floor; feet battered the boards in wild dancing. Voices bellowed and glasses crashed monotonously. Occasionally he glimpsed Isobel, so suddenly elegant, moving lightly and easily through it all, talking to the bride, reproving the groom, chatting to up-country guests; he could not get close to her. Certainly not close enough to talk to her. Perhaps afterwards, he told himself placatingly. For urgency possessed him; already he could see the dusty bus rolling out of Te Waiotemarama. It was a thought he could not tolerate.

Presently he found the heat and racket of the smoke-laden hall altogether too much to endure. He went out, for a moment, on to the verandah of the hall; and then, feeling a slight palpitation in his side, concluded that he was probably over-excited and, on reflection, walked down the road to the pub to get his pills. He was away from the hall longer than he expected, for when he reached his room he felt his head still spinning from the liquor and smoke, and the need to sit and rest a while.

When he returned to the hall eventually he found Isobel gone. His first thought was that perhaps, like himself, she had merely escaped the place a few minutes; and would return. But with the passing minutes ransacked for sight of her and found empty, he realized she must indeed have gone.

Urgency became panic; he hurried out of the hall, up the hill, to the cottage.

The cottage was empty.

He could not imagine where she had gone. Why she had escaped so quickly. He sat, breathless, on the edge of her verandah a minute, shading his eyes against the sunlight, looking down at the harbour, the white sand ribboning beaches among the rocks. The clamour of his body settled, leaving a slow burning of mind; he took a deep silent breath, and found himself watching two figures diminish along the long thin beach which curved around to the harbour heads. Idly, irrelevantly, he thought that one of the pair might be Isobel, while scratching with the active part of his mind at other possibilities; then suddenly, when the thought became relevant, his body snapped into motion like a fish on a hook.

Of course. Her bathing costume was missing from the place where it usually hung to dry. She must have decided, fleeing the heat of the hall, to go swimming. Why not? It was natural. She was not to know he was leaving tomorrow.

Quickly now, he hurried down the hill, through the village. He passed the Hickson house. Hickson was back on his place on the verandah, fastened about his telescope again. He had it trained somewhere in the direction of the heads. As he swivelled it slowly before his eye, his laughter rang across the lawn and summer-dead garden. He was laughing for no reason plain to Mr Fail.

But that shrill lunatic laughter pursued him out of the village, across the crisp, tide-washed sand. Sometimes he could see the figures ahead; other times he lost sight of them behind dunes and toi-toi. Their direction seemed erratic. At times they moved inland to no clear purpose, following not the line of the beach, but the straighter line their own feet took them.

And when he saw Isobel was walking with Kuru, he knew his own time was badly chosen. Naturally she would want to have a few words with her pupil before he left. Tomorrow Kuru would leave in the same bus Mr Fail planned to take. Today was the day for goodbye to Kuru : distracted, Isobel would have no time or thought for another. Why hadn't he thought of it? It was too late now; too late. And Mr Fail plodded steadily behind the couple who every now and then receded beyond his vision; receded and then appeared again, even more distant, so that he soon realized his own pace was slowing. He would never catch them at this rate; and they were always too far ahead for him to call across the sound of the sea. They would never hear him.

Then he lost them.

He walked and saw no more of them. And at length he rounded the heads and came to the ocean beach where giant surf hammered, found it empty, and climbed the sandhills above the beach, through tussocks of lupin and marram, to see if height would bring new sight to him. For a time it brought nothing. He saw only a line of empty ocean beaches stringing the long shoreline against the Tasman sea. White sand and blue sea and hard sunlight. A landscape austere and rock-strewn. Exhausted, he collapsed to the sand, his breath thumping his lungs.

He had lost them. It was ridiculous.

He lay there a very long while. Seagulls wheeled in the sky and wind purred the dry grasses. The sun, retreating across the sea, sprinkled grass-shadow like cool water over his heated body. A little while longer and he might have slept.

The voices seemed to swim up from great depth, through layers of sunset heat and dusk coolness, through layers of wind sound and sea sound, erupting like tiny quick bubbles against Mr Fail's ear. At first he thought he only imagined them; and absurdly he dismissed them.

But they persisted, faint and distant, until they could no longer be ignored. Presently he rose, under the burning clouds of sunset, and scanned the shore.

They were not really far away. Actually he found himself looking directly down on them. They were in a place where the sea spilled into the sandhills, a tiny rocky lagoon, quiet and concealed, circled with toi-toi. They must have only recently arrived, for they had not been there when he looked before; they must have arrived, dawdling their way, since he had fallen on the sand among the lupins.

They were swimming, the two, the tall summer-coloured woman suddenly blonde and slight beside the lean glistening brown boy; swimming and laughing and splashing, gay in the antic water. Sometimes they spun down into the clear depths, so that there was only the swift flash of underwater flesh as they swam side by side, intimate and altogether alone in that queerly silent remove from the world. Again and again they began to descend, sometimes for so long that it seemed they might never rise at all, and then exploded to the surface, silvery water rustling from their bodies.

He called to them. He cried out. They did not hear.

As the pain came beating up his side Mr Fail, sliding in the sand, had half-fallen to his knees, hands lifting in supplication. Then his hands dropped suddenly, as if to catch the pain, wrench it away. Then they jumped to his eyes, to tug apart the curtains gathering there.

And when he fell, he rolled over once or twice, until caught on a ledge of sand, and lay quite still.

RIVER, GIRL AND ONION

FOR JENNY BOJILOVA

1

That saturday began badly for Lila.

That Saturday began with the bird. Or, to be more precise, with the absence of the bird.

The bird was a yellow-green canary which sang from a square wire cage in the courtyard below her window. It was an old courtyard, unevenly paved, with three walls where plaster peeled, like torn rag, from bleached brick. At the open end, facing the street, there was an iron railing and a flight of worn stone steps descending into a dark cellar. Above was a predictably smoky patch of London sky. Five battered garbage cans stood there; and there also, in mild and middling weather, the caged canary sang. Quite often a mid-point in the morning, bringing some vagary of wind or rain, would see the old spinster owner of the bird hastening to make safe her pet: the cage would be withdrawn, a window would close, and thin lace would curtain the canary within a dim, drawing-room world. Of that Lila could see little: a cabinet stocked with fragile china, a corner of faded carpet, and two potted plants. Her only real contact with that remote, melancholy world was in the distinctly favourable circumstance of flinging her window wide on a sunlit morning to hear the thin, sweet voice circling the courtyard. At that hour Lila was receptive to sweetness, rather than melancholy.

In exactly this circumstance, in exactly this receptive mood, Lila one sunny spring noon discovered the absence of the bird. She was alarmed and horrified. The day seemed quite unreal. For there was the courtyard, painted pale gold, without a song, without a bird; and the spinster's window was fast. Lila shivered in her thin nightdress and distractedly drew a thick woollen dressing-gown over her shoulders.

It seemed, certainly, a symptom of some tragedy : the bird had escaped and flown; the bird was dead; the spinster was dead; or both, the woman and the pet, were dead. These seemed to Lila the limit of possibilities; but as an omen in Lila's life the event seemed to have unlimited possibilities. And not even the news, which she heard later in the day, that the spinster had merely taken her annual holiday with a sister in Devon, and had given the bird into care of a neighbour, rescued Lila from her intuition of impending disaster. It did, however, jolt her into the realization that she was thinking in Russian; and had, in fact, since she had risen to the songless courtyard, been thinking in Russian. The thoughts coming so swiftly, so darkly, had demanded the language. For once, however, she made no effort to revert to English; moodily she tidied her small room and drew the curtains on the shining afternoon.

When Cecil arrived at five, he found her dramatically arranged upon the bed in a darkened room. This did not surprise him : he was used, by now, to what she called her peasant moods. He was used also to dramatic arrangements of her body, and darkened rooms. He shook off his duffle-coat and sat silently on the end of her bed. He lit two cigarettes and handed one to Lila. '*Spaseebo bolshoi*,' she murmured.

'*Pazhahlsta*,' he returned and fell silent, since he had already reached the limit of his ability to converse in Russian. His eyes became accustomed to the dark. She was dressed simply; she wore a loose roll-neck black sweater and her long legs were sheathed in tight slacks which veed above her bare ankles. One leg was crooked delicately, while the other cut a straight black line down the pale bedcover. At the head of the bed was an effective arrangement of arms, enhanced now by the cigarette idly burning between loose fingers. The pillow was awry, and her head rested crosswise on it; her face was an oval pale and withdrawn in darkly fanning hair. He admired the complete picture and wondered if he should make love to her. He finally rejected this idea on grounds of expediency, since it was plain that a bout of love-making, however minor in dimension, would delay them over-long in the room; and they had to meet Paul at seven. And, the situation considered, it was clear that he would have difficulty getting Lila there on time anyway.

2

Lila was considering Cecil not as a lover; but as an adviser in the matter of love. The fact that Cecil had already served fitfully as a lover only enhanced his possible value as an adviser.

Her friendship with Cecil had not been of long duration. They met on a long sea voyage, from New Zealand to Southampton. Lila had lived in that country since she was four; Cecil was a fourth generation New Zealander who claimed a small percentage of Maori blood. This had entered his family, he said, as a result of a primarily spiritual relationship between his great-grandfather, a Christian missionary, and the daughter of a Maori chief. This girl died giving birth to a half-caste child, which his great-grandfather adopted. The great-grandfather was eaten in the latter stage of the Maori wars by the *Hau Hau*, that fanatic group which combined Christianity and cannibalism with apparent success, and who reported, after the feast at which he was the *pièce de résistance*, that they had observed the Angel Gabriel in full flight; but his half-caste child was spared to become Cecil's grandfather. So Cecil could fairly claim a blood relationship with the country going back to 1350, the year of the great Polynesian migration.

All this Lila learned from Cecil, a vague-eyed young man with rumpled clothes and woolly black hair, on the long haul up the Pacific to the Panama canal. Her own relationship with the islands they were leaving behind was far less complex. She had simply been taken there as a child after spending her first years in Europe. She had, she once calculated, been conceived in Warsaw, seen out most of gestation in Leipzig, been born in Paris, and then shipped to the Pacific before war or revolution once again overtook her family. Life in New Zealand had a schizophrenic quality; she was always a solitary traveller between two worlds separated neatly by language.

The world of her native language was one of wistful

evenings at the family fireside, and of bleak-eyed old people at Orthodox services praying for the deliverance of holy Russia; the world of her adopted language was one of lazy colonial accent where, at least in her parents' view, there was an unhappy and disrespectful attitude towards questions of breeding. Though they might hold aloof from this world, there was after a while no question but that they must surrender their daughter to it as a kind of hostage for the privilege of living in the sunlit quiet and freedom of this new country.

There was in this, naturally, reason for distress; at times cause enough for them to speak of a return to Europe, where there would be a proper respect for traditional values. Sometimes events, the end of the war or the death of Stalin, spun two-sided coins of hope and despair in their lives: there might yet, they hoped, be a return to the old gentle life of their own land. But Lila, growing taller, recognized that that life had gone as if it had never been.

At seventeen, overcoming reluctance and distaste, her parents began to equip her with the facts of life; Lila, however, had learned them in a more practical fashion, with a good-looking boy behind a clump of toi-toi, at fifteen. When she began to attend university, they were happy; when she failed her units two years in succession, they were unhappy. When she announced that her current boy friend was secretary of the university Communist Party, they were distinctly unnerved. And when at last she took a serious interest in drama, their feelings were mixed; they reasoned that it was good that their daughter should find something positive to interest her, but their gladness was tainted with a long-held suspicion of the theatre, and the fear that their daughter might mix with loose women and homo-sexuals. They were fortunately not able to see the ease with which their daughter mixed with these people. Rejoicing in her apparent success, they were even able to conceal their squeam-ishness when she appeared in a Saroyan play as a prostitute, and in a Sartre play as a lesbian; her mother, in fact, conceded that in the latter play she would never have known her little girl, her *malenkaya dyevotchka*.

Actually it was no longer adequate to call Lila even a *bolshoya*

dyevotchka. At the abnormal height for a Russian girl of six
feet and half an inch (the climate, her parents explained)
she had every appearance of a mature woman. Certainly she
was afflicted with all the discontents of womanhood. Even her
parents now seemed to agree that a girl of her age should find
the other sex a major preoccupation; indeed they began to seem
eager that life should soon bestow the twin blessings of marriage
and childbirth upon her. Two boys from the White Russian
community became regular visitors, though never at Lila's invitation, to the house; they seemed anxious to actively co-operate in
bestowing blessings. They might conceivably have been less
anxious had they known, when one or other of them visited the
house on a Sunday afternoon, that Lila had the night before
drunk whisky and gone to bed with a highly neurotic but rather
brilliant young artist who threw the whisky bottles out of his
attic window and sometimes said very obscene things to Lila.
These two polite young men had arrived on the scene altogether
too late; their only actual hope, had they known it, was that Lila
might one day tire of having obscene things said to her. Not that
she was particularly fond of hearing these things, or of the artist;
it was just that he gave a reasonable impression of being human.
Also she was not anxious to become the recipient of twin
blessings.

Already it seemed to her that she squandered far too much
of her dramatic energy upon life, rather than the stage. So she
abandoned the artist, worked hard, and won a scholarship to
study in London; and one rainy autumn day found herself waving farewell to her tearful parents from the deck of a ship. Only
then, as the tangling streamers snapped across the widening
water, did she remember to be surprised at herself.

She met Cecil at meal-times; they were placed at the same
table. He was very lost and moody among all the strange people;
since she was the only one who seemed prepared to listen to him,
he followed her about the ship. His sombre face waited for her
whenever she came up on deck or turned away from a game;
he was very persistent. She supposed him brilliant, since he
talked profoundly about life. After some time, however, it
emerged that his great regret was that he knew so little about

life. 'All the twenty-four years of my life I have been sitting in classrooms and lecture-rooms having things told me,' he explained. 'Nobody gave me a chance to know things.' He had finished university with honours in philosophy; now he was going to Paris. He was vague about precisely why he was going to Paris. He might study; he might write. Paris seemed the place for a good many things. Two difficulties which he discounted as minor were that he had no money, and spoke no French. But he was perfectly confident. 'I read once, in a magazine,' he said, 'about a man who went around the world with twenty pounds and one language.'

After a while he thought fit to say, 'I hope, Lila, you do not think I am pursuing you from some concealed physical motive. My motive is purely intellectual.' Lila was relieved. Presently, however, she felt distinctly dowdy and unattractive; she also began to feel self-conscious and silly. She powdered her nose frequently, studied her clothes carefully, and ensured her head was at the right tilt for a pleasing silhouette when she spoke to him on the deck at night.

At length, the night after Pitcairn, he kissed her, more by accident than design. And the night after Curaçao, where they drank iced beer on a cool white terrace overlooking the sea, there was a more compromising incident under a lifeboat on the upper deck. Nevertheless, the voyage between Pitcairn and Curaçao had been a long, slow one.

After the incident under the lifeboat Cecil felt obliged to pro- pose marriage. Lila suggested Cecil have more experience before marriage. 'I am thinking of it only for your sake,' she explained. She added that she believed their affair very Lawrentian; for Cecil's benefit, however, she was unable to specify precisely what she meant since her artist friend, from whom she had acquired the word, had used it in rather an undiscriminating fashion. 'No doubt, Cecil,' she said, 'you will in time understand what I mean. With experience.'

They were in London three days together. After they dis- covered Piccadilly Circus small and grubby, St. Paul's pigeon- spattered, and the Thames marvellous, Cecil left for Paris. Two weeks later, when Lila called at New Zealand House for her mail, she found an urgent note from Cecil which informed her, among other things, that he was back in London. 'I am desperate', the note concluded.

Hoping to save him from self-destruction, Lila took a taxi to the cheap Bloomsbury hotel where he was staying temporarily. He had no patience for her bright message that there were still beautiful things in the world, and that tomorrow the birds would sing. 'It was terrible,' he said. His money dwindling, he was forced to sleep on boulevard benches and slowly nibble long loaves of bread to outwit hunger. He was friendless and alone and twice, while he was sleeping outdoors, it had rained. He had endured dreadful experiences. Once a querulous and incomprehensible gendarme actually seemed about to arrest him. Another time, in hope that he might glimpse someone famous or perhaps even hear English spoken, he recklessly spent sixty francs on a small coffee at the Café de Flore and fell into conversation with a very nice young American who bought him two glasses of beer and talked about Gide. Both these, Cecil admitted, had only very nearly been dreadful experiences. Once again friendless and alone, he met a strange woman in a dim street one night. They were unable, beyond a certain point, to understand each other. 'It was very Lawrentian,' Cecil said. They went down beside the Seine; and it was an altogether remarkable experience until the woman, in a sudden frightful fit of anger, pursued him along the river bank, striking him on the head with a parasol and demanding, he gathered, a certain number of francs. He had not stopped running until he found the staid old buildings of London walling him in again, and people speaking a substantially understandable language. He was about to cable a friend for money to return to New Zealand.

Since Lila was at that time feeling lonely in London, disliking her drama school, her fellow students, her landlady and the weather, and most of all the fact that she went alone to the theatre, she was glad to see Cecil and tried to persuade him to stay. After two expensive weeks of coffee, beer, meals and double theatre tickets, she eventually persuaded him; and forgot to be lonely.

After Cecil took a job at eight pounds a week caring for

rabbits and guinea pigs in a hospital laboratory, and could pay
for his own theatre tickets, Lila suddenly found him a liability.
For she met a personable young man at the drama school who
seemed more interested in her than in other personable young
men, and who took her to cocktails before and after the theatre;
consequently she wanted to see less of Cecil.

On lonely Sundays, however, when Cecil trudged bleak streets
and tired of looking at the paintings in the galleries, he usually
ended his wandering by knocking at Lila's door. In time Lila
began to find this irritating. She suggested Cecil should make
other friends in London. 'I am thinking of it only for your sake,'
she explained. Cecil tried very hard, after that, to make friends.
At the hospital, though, where he was ordered about by crabby
nurses and severe doctors graded in an hierarchy baffling in com-
plexity, he only had time to make friends with the cockney boy
who swept the floors. This cockney boy, who had a pimply face
and a sweet nature, had never heard of Kant or Hegel and
privately thought Cecil bloody queer. He took Cecil rock 'n'
rolling at the Palais. Though Cecil escaped with only bruises
and abrasions of a minor nature, the evening was sufficiently
alarming for him not to take Cecil again.

Cecil persevered in his quest for friends. But not until a Sunday when Lila was away, weekending in Somerset with her
young man, did he find any. That afternoon, at Speakers'
Corner, he found two. He was afterwards very grateful to Lila,
for had she not so often reminded him of his duty to himself to
make friends, he would obviously not have spoken to the two
young men with strange accents who seemed to enjoy arguments.

They were students, these two, and they shared a room in
Gower Street. Jose was from Venezuela and Paul was from
Hungary. Jose had been a wanderer ever since he had gone into
exile after leading a student strike in Caracas; he had studied in
Mexico City, Berlin and Paris. Paul had been in London since
late 1956; he also had been some kind of student leader. Both
spoke English of an erratic variety. They had only really been
speaking it since they had come to England and, talking to each
other in English all the time, they had evolved a strangely
private idiom. Certainly they confused Cecil. They confused him

even more with their arguments. To these arguments Cecil could contribute little since no one had told him anything about Marx. In his first year at university a lecturer had introduced his subject by saying that all philosophy was bad, and the worst was Marxism; in his last year a professor made passing reference to a forgotten and discredited philosopher named Marx. Cecil had paid no great attention.

Jose was handsome, his skin richly coloured by Indian and Negro blood; he had a neat moustache, brilliant white teeth, and astonishingly vivid eyes. He wore bright check shirts and a leather jacket. Cecil could imagine a pistol tucked carelessly in Jose's belt; in fact, Jose's personality so much appealed to him that he immediately stopped writing a rather long and complicated story about a young man who looked after rabbits and guinea pigs, and began writing another about a young Latin American revolutionary with quick wicked eyes. Cecil worked on this story for some months while at the same time, under the guidance of Jose and Paul, studying internal contradictions and dialectical leaps. His real difficulty with the story was that he could find no ending. He ignored those who advised him that it was no longer necessary for short stories to have endings. Cecil was one of those brave pioneers who fly in the face of literary fashion. 'It is cheating to have no ending,' he said.

Paul was a contrast. His face was thick and heavy; he smiled rarely, and dressed darkly. He suffered prolonged moods of depression; and, so Jose once told Cecil, often cried out in his sleep.

Paul's father, a socialist veteran and ally of Bela Kun in 1919, had after the second world war been prominent in the new Hungarian government until arrested and shot as a fascist Titoist-Trotzkyist and imperialist agent. Paul, a student activist, was asked to denounce his father; since he declined to do so, he was expelled from university and went to work in a factory. He was there four years until, after his father's corpse was rehabilitated, he was readmitted to university. When the trouble in Hungary began he had spoken with some authority about the nature of the government. He was not able to speak with much clarity about what happened after the tanks blasted into

Budapest. His last clear memory was of participating in a radio broadcast before some of his remaining friends, fearing for his safety, pushed him into a fast car headed for the border.

He was tumbled about from bed to bed, from place to place; people kept trying to make him say things he didn't want to say. He wanted to say different things, but when he said different things, no one seemed to be listening. Naturally, because of his father's name, a large number of journalists wanted to talk to him. He should have been a gift for any journalist; instead of a gift, he was a problem. For example, when asked to outline his disillusionment with Communism, he unreasonably persisted in saying he was still a Communist, and that Rakosi, Krushchev, Stalin and the rest were not really Communists at all; and the journalists fiddled, talked among themselves, and lit cigarettes. In the end, then, he began to say nothing with a fair degree of success; and the journalists lost interest. When he reached London he met Jose, with whom he had corresponded since Jose visited Budapest for a youth festival. He was ill for a while, and Jose looked after him. He found Jose would listen to what he wanted to say; and he felt better. Jose could sometimes even make Paul smile.

Jose usually entertained Paul by persuading him to laugh at the English. Jose once said he hoped Cecil didn't mind them laughing at the English. 'You are English colonial, no?' he said.

'Please do not worry,' Cecil said. 'I feel my inherited English blood must have undergone some vital chemical change under the South Pacific sun. It is probably something dialectical. For I have no longer anything in common with this tribe of strange castes and rituals. I am not an Englishman of the colonial variety. I am a Polynesian of the pale-skinned variety.'

'You are an angry young man, yes?' said Paul.

'No,' said Cecil. 'I am an unhappy young man.'

Lila, while Cecil dutifully developed new friendships, had begun to give herself to prolonged twilights of the soul, and wandered at dusk through streets and parks. Her young man had left her for a baronet's daughter who would one day inherit a fine estate and several large companies. Lila could have competed against this girl, who was actually a silly brazen creature,

but she could not compete against the fine estate and large companies. She was also disillusioned with the theatre. Her unusual
height apparently proclaimed her unfit for consideration in any
serious dramatic role. Plainly a woman with such difficult
statistics could only hope, at best, to play comedy. Also she
objected to the methods of tuition at the school. These seemed
more concerned with displaying the body than displaying the
soul. She deduced that the school was more akin to a training-
ground for a slave-market than a school for the theatre. Lonely
and depressed, she resented the fact that Cecil no longer came
to see her. 'He is mean and disloyal,' she told herself sulkily,
'after all I have done for him. But I have my pride. I will not
seek him out.'

They met again by accident in a book shop in the Charing
Cross Road. Lila was reading a life of Stanislavsky, and Cecil a
novel well reviewed in the Sunday papers. Cecil often did this.
After a study of the Sunday papers he selected the novel most
favourably reviewed and read it on Saturday afternoons all the
way down the Charing Cross Road. He read an average of forty
pages in each shop; then moved on to the next. Cecil acquired
a vast knowledge of the current literary product.

On that afternoon, when he met Lila, he ignored his cool
reception and took her to an espresso bar where he gave her a
long and exhaustively detailed analysis of the contemporary
literary scene and assailed a prominent new writer. 'He ignores
the role of the cash nexus,' he said. Lila, with the memory of
the baronet's daughter still fresh, was inclined to agree with
Cecil's view of the cash nexus but, preserving her frigid front,
did not say say. Instead, five minutes later, she burst into tears.
This interrupted the point Cecil was making about the decisive
nature of the Hungarian revolution.

Cecil was embarrassed. When they left the espresso bar he
perceived the most obvious way of ridding himself of his embarrassment. 'I will take you home,' he said. Lila sprinkled fresh
tears on the busy footpath. 'You are only trying to dispose of
me,' she claimed. Lila wanted not to be disposed of; but to be
loved. 'I have a suggestion to make,' Cecil said finally. Lila was
by this time relieved to know Cecil was capable of making any

suggestion whatsoever. 'I will take you to meet two good friends of mine,' he said. 'The company may do you good.'

They ate that night in a little Italian restaurant just off the Tottenham Court Road. This became a habit; every Saturday the four met to eat in the same place. Afterwards they wandered Soho or went to a Thames-side pub. Sometimes, though rarely, their number was increased by a stray Latin American, Hungarian or New Zealander. The most definite feature of their group, however, was that there was never an Englishman included. They all vaguely regretted this. 'Maybe,' said Paul, 'we should better know England if we knew just one Englishman.' Lila said she knew an Englishman once and didn't like him anyway; but Lila was prejudiced. Each week they exchanged new stories gathered from observation of the native population of London. For example, Lila once reported, 'Today I saw a bowler-hat kissing a girl.' This story, however, was generally disbelieved.

Lila departed suddenly and stormily from her drama school. It was actually the result of a tutor describing Russian character so that the students might better involve themselves in a Chekhov play. Lila quarrelled with this description as superficial, and indeed stupid; but the tutor countered with the remark that Lila could scarcely profess to know a great deal about Russian character since she had never lived in Russia. Lila, who felt the truth of this keenly, was dismayed and angry. 'If I am not a Russian,' she demanded, 'then what am I?' 'Very probably,' replied the tutor coolly, before proceeding with evaluation of the Russian character, 'you are a New Zealander.' Lila walked out of the class. 'I am a woman without a country,' she told them sadly the following Saturday. 'I am a lonely voyager on a strange sea.'

'We are all voyagers,' Paul observed. 'All lonely voyagers on strange seas. Even,' he added significantly, 'even Cecil.' This was to reassure Cecil and include him in their company since, though Cecil was the only one of them who felt free to return to his own country, he still lacked the money to do so.

'What can I do?' Lila appealed. 'Where will it all end?' She tried to get work in repertory; she finished working as a waitress.

She received a large number of tips and propositions from the customers she served. Lila took the tips and ignored the propositions; they nevertheless disturbed her. 'I am sliding down,' she declared. 'I shall be on the street in a few weeks.' However, Jose, Paul and Cecil promised to save her; they would, they said, keep her as collective mistress. Lila did not think this idea amusing. 'Where will it all end?' she said.

One Sunday afternoon she walked with Jose through Kensington Gardens; afterwards they passed along the street which held the Soviet embassy. Up and down the street small children played, jabbering in Russian; their parents promenaded and gossiped in the sunlight. Lila was excited; she had never heard so many people talking Russian around her before. All at once she began to shiver. 'I feel queer,' she said. 'Quickly, I must sit down.' Jose was alarmed and attentive. 'Have you one ache in the head?' he said uncertainly. No, said Lila. It was not a headache. 'It is nothing,' she added. 'It will probably go away very soon.'

But, whatever it was, it did not go away very soon. Some days later Lila returned to the street and talked to a cultural attaché at the embassy about going to Russia and working in the Soviet theatre. The attaché discussed socialist realism. This upset Lila. 'I am an unsocially realist person,' she said the following Saturday. 'There is no place for me.'

Lila, who was a head taller than short chunky Jose, had fallen in love with him. This presented some difficulty. Lila liked to give the impression of being a very loose woman. She gave a very good impression of being a loose woman. Also she liked to give the impression of being in love with everyone; in this she was entirely successful too. That was the difficulty. For when she told Jose she loved him, Jose naturally presumed she told Cecil and Paul the same thing; and felt no urgent and personal concern in the matter.

Lila on principle disapproved of revolutions. Yet she managed to listen without protest when Jose announced, in a fit of frustration, that instead of studying philosophy, it would be far better if he learned to use a tommy-gun. Lila soothed him; and he told her about his father, a colonel in the Venezuelan army who, since late adolescence, had had a pouched pistol swinging against his thigh. When a disagreement with the current dictator sent him into brief exile in Mexico, his father, without his pistol for the first time in twenty years, felt naked, and constantly slapped his unadorned thigh in bewilderment. He stayed indoors, fearful of open streets in daylight and dark streets at night. With such a father it was not surprising that Jose should have begun life a pacifist. But now he was convinced pacifism was useless. 'I have dead pacifist friends,' he said, to clinch his argument. 'Maybe,' he added presently, 'I am no right to say the tommy-gun is superior to philosophy. Combining the tommy-gun and philosophy is one big problem.'

Lila was alarmed when Jose spoke of returning to Venezuela. 'What will become of you?' she cried. Jose answered the question coolly. 'Maybe for me only more exile,' he said. 'I think I will no be dead. They make dead only big men. I am one little man.' Lila was not reassured. When she said 'What will become of you?' she really meant 'What will become of me?' Jose appeared to think life a risky enough proposition without marriage too. Lila tried to become pregnant; Jose studied the calendar and successfully averted this possibility. Lila indulged in obvious liasons with Paul and Cecil in hope of making Jose jealous; since Jose had not minded this situation at the beginning he saw no reason why he should dislike it now. Actually he found a greater degree of comfort in this less demanding situation.

Lila became despondent. To console her, Jose read her Lorca as they lay in her room, or sat in the pale yellow sunshine among the falling autumn leaves. Lila listened with impatience; she liked the sound of Spanish, she explained, but she couldn't understand the words. Jose bought her a book of English translations and she followed him through the *Romancero Gitano*. 'Is beautiful, no?' said Jose. 'I like much the poem of the gypsy and the woman who was no a maiden.' 'It was a very ephemeral affair,' said Lila. 'Russians do not have ephemeral affairs. They love with the soul.' Jose was very silent and thoughtful.

'Jose, darling,' Lila said, 'why don't you take me away somewhere?'

'I will take you to Brighton,' Jose said. Jose had heard of the English custom of weekends at Brighton. But Lila really wanted to be taken to Paris. When they went to Paris Lila found herself miserable; Jose insisted on visiting all his exile friends and discussing, in rapid Spanish, the political situation up and down the Americas while Lila sat silent and dismayed in corners of crowded, smoky little Latin Quarter hotel rooms. Jose's friends all seemed to find Lila, and her height, very amusing; she became tired of hearing them refer to her, when they talked to Jose, as *su amiga alta* and *su amiga loca*. 'I wish we had gone to Brighton,' Lila said after three days. Jose came to the reasonable conclusion that women were impossible to understand; and even more impossible to please.

Paul and Cecil saw each other often. Paul was still unhappy about people trying to make him say things he didn't want to say. One friend of his had gone back to Hungary safely by saying all the things they wanted said there; another had made himself prosperous, writing and lecturing in America, saying what they wanted said there. Both had written him letters. One called him a traitorous counter-revolutionary; the other called him a traitorous stooge. 'I want only to be left alone,' Paul said.

Cecil was persevering with literature. He had found no ending for the story about a character like Jose; and, abandoning it, he returned to his story about the young man who looked after rabbits and guinea pigs in a hospital. After some deliberation he attached an ending to this story; it showed the young man being taken to a mental hospital and, in his cell, proclaiming himself a guinea pig. Cecil thought this story very ironic and very symbolic of the human condition. He read the story to Paul. He explained that the young man in the story had only a passing resemblance to his own character. Paul said he understood perfectly; but suggested the end of the story sounded contrived. Cecil began writing a new, rather bitter story about a Hungarian.

On New Year's Eve Jose and Paul gave a party. Their room had been conscientiously tidied : coloured streamers tangled down from their ceiling : the table was set with wine and beer, bright paper hats, salt biscuits and potato crisps. When they

arrived, Lila received flowers and kisses, and Cecil a large glass
of beer. They sang away the time before midnight. The landlady came upstairs to complain about the noise. 'Why,' she
declared, 'it must be possible to hear you half-way down the
street.' Cecil, who had been drinking considerably, suggested
she get all the way down the street. Jose, with Latin charm,
pacified her and sent her downstairs with a gin and tonic.

At midnight, wearing their bright party hats, they stood holding hands in the centre of the room. Cecil and Lila taught Jose
and Paul how to sing *Auld Lang Syne*.

After midnight, fallen separate in their chairs again, Jose
revealed he was returning to Venezuela. Since everyone had been
drinking, and everyone spoke frequently of returning home, only
Paul, who knew already, took the announcement seriously at
first. But when Jose went on to explain that he had received a
letter from Caracas which told him a movement was afoot
against the régime, and which urged him to return as soon as he
could, Lila, who wanted to hear no more, rose to her feet with a
stricken face. 'This room is very stuffy,' she said. 'I want to open
a window.' Jose said he hoped to get a post lecturing at Caracas
university; it would be a good cover for clandestine political
activity. 'Even with the window open,' Lila said, 'this room is
still very stuffy. Why don't we go for a walk?' The other three,
drowsy with drink and chilled with the rush of frosty air into
the room, were not enthusiastic. But when Lila became insistent
they pulled on their coats and followed her down into the street.

At Piccadilly the crowds were thinning and dissolving into the
cold evening, leaving the Circus webbed with streamers and
strewn with confetti. Now and then a song spluttered like a spark
in a dying fire. There was a man being sick on the footpath;
another asking passers-by if they were Irish.

By the time they found coffee in a dimmed Soho, they were
all quite miserable. 'In New Zealand,' Cecil said, 'it is summer.
After midnight we go swimming.' Paul said he was going home
to bed. 'That,' said Cecil, 'is the most sensible idea I have heard
for a full hour.'

Jose took Lila home. When they were alone together, walking
the emptied streets, Lila said, 'It is terrible. The new year is two

hours old already.' Jose was silent. 'When are you going?' she said finally. He was not sure. 'But soon,' he added. She took his arm tightly. 'Will you remember me?' she said. Yes, he would remember her; and Paul, and Cecil. But her particularly? Yes, her particularly. 'How could I forget?' Jose sighed. And—who knew?—maybe after the revolution she would come to Venezuela, he said; she, and Paul, and Cecil.

But Lila only said, 'Wouldn't it be a wonderful thing if we could just go on walking like this, arm in arm, on and on, for ever and ever?' Jose, who really thought the night rather too cold to enjoy walking, agreed that it would be a wonderful thing.

At the airport, the morning he left, there were gifts and tears. They would all, he said, have to come to Venezuela one day. Jose embraced all three dispassionately and strutted jauntily across the tarmac to the waiting aircraft. *'Salud!'* he cried before a door sealed him from sight. A hand waved at a window and the aircraft rose up into a cloudless winter sky. Lila, in the restaurant, said she wouldn't have coffee. 'I want English tea,' she said. 'Very weak, with milk and sugar.' The next morning, opening her newspaper, she read about tanks racketing through the streets of Caracas.

3

'It is getting late,' Cecil said. To verify this remark he rose from the bed, crossed the room, and peeled back the curtains to reveal the darkening courtyard.

'Of course,' said Lila. 'It is always late.'

Cecil let the curtains fall with a swish. The courtyard depressed him. He turned to Lila; and discovered she depressed him too. 'We shall be keeping Paul waiting,' he said.

'We are always waiting,' Lila said. 'In our different ways. All of us are waiting.'

'Lila,' said Cecil gravely, resuming his place on the edge of the bed, 'you generalize too much from particulars.' He paused and sighed. 'But I know,' he added, 'that you are very miserable just now. I mean about Jose and everything. So it is scarcely fair to expect you to be in a logical state of mind.'

'It is more than eight weeks,' Lila said. She meant since she, Paul and Cecil had each received postcards which showed Caracas in colour, and told them Jose had arrived. 'And I have written sixteen letters, and there is still no answer. After all, he can't be busy now, can he? The revolution was over almost as soon as he arrived.'

'Perhaps,' said Cecil, 'they are consolidating. And preparing against the counter-revolution. Who knows?'

'God knows,' Lila said firmly. 'He could have sent another postcard at least. Don't sixteen letters deserve something?'

Cecil admitted they did; and shrugged. Presently he took Lila's long slender hand and rested it gently on his palm, as if measuring it for weight and size. He spoke carefully. 'You must bear in mind, Lila, that Jose may have a girl friend, or a fiancée, or even a wife, in Venezuela.'

'Impossible,' Lila said with sudden vigour. 'He hasn't been there for years.'

'Nevertheless,' Cecil said, shrugging again, 'such things are not unknown.' He was content to leave it at that, knowing quite well that the seed planted in Lila's imagination would in time, watered by discontent, grow and flourish. He meant, however, no cruelty; he wanted merely that Lila should reconcile herself to her fate, and so become herself again. She was playing her present role with too much conviction.

'I want to ask your advice,' she said at last. 'Do you think I should go to Venezuela? There are planes flying all week, and I have almost enough money. It is perfectly safe now there is no revolution.'

'I think it would be unwise,' Cecil said. 'To say the least. Apart from all the more obvious reasons, if you spent all your money flying to Venezuela, you would have none left to pay your fare back to New Zealand.'

Lila abruptly withdrew her hand from Cecil. 'Who said I was going back to New Zealand? I didn't.'

'I was coming to that,' Cecil said quietly.

'Anyway,' Lila continued, 'why New Zealand? It is not my country. The world is my country.'

'No one has said that seriously since Thomas Paine,' Cecil

observed. 'He also said mankind was his religion. But that is, of course, beside the point.'

'You annoy me,' Lila said. 'How can I go back? To go back would be to admit the world has defeated me.'

'You are failing to adapt yourself to the English language,' Cecil said. 'There is no longer such a word as defeat. There are only tactical and diplomatic withdrawals. Such as Suez, for example.'

'I don't understand why you should talk about New Zealand.'

'I was coming to that,' Cecil repeated patiently.

'Then I wish you would come to it. And stop—what is it?— beating about the bush.'

Cecil took Lila's hand again. 'Lila, why don't you come back to New Zealand with me?'

'Is this another proposal?'

'You might consider it one.'

'Very well. You astonish me, Cecil. But I have just one decisive question to ask : how can you possibly expect to keep me in the manner to which I am accustomed?'

Cecil made a thoughtful survey of the room, and the meagre collection of belongings within it. 'It should not be too difficult,' he said. 'To keep you in the manner to which you are accustomed.'

'How can you understand?' she cried. 'How could you possibly understand?' She pointed an accusing finger at him. 'You are a materialist. So you can think only in material terms.'

Cecil felt helpless.

'And when,' Lila continued, 'I asked if you could keep me in the manner to which I am accustomed, it would not occur to you that I meant in a manner quite other than material : that I meant in the manner of inner life.'

'I am aware,' said Cecil, 'of your spiritual inclination.'

'Do you seriously expect me, Cecil, to surrender my rich inner life to become the wife of a New Zealand petit bourgeois?'

'On the contrary,' Cecil said indignantly. 'My background is working-class. My father is a truck-driver and very proletarian. I am not petit bourgeois.'

'In New Zealand even the bourgeoisie is petit bourgeois,' Lila said, rising from the bed. 'Now, shall we go?'

They met Paul a little after seven in the restaurant. His face was no more grave than usual; but he was strangely quiet during the meal. Afterwards, while they sipped coffee, he revealed the cause. He had a letter from Venezuela.

'Why,' Lila protested, 'haven't I got one?'

Probably because, Paul said, she had not taken the precaution of writing her return address on the back of her letters. In any case, the letter had not been from Jose, and was written in Spanish. Since Paul knew little Spanish, he had been forced that morning to go out and purchase a cheap Spanish-English dictionary and a grammar. He had spent the rest of the day preparing a translation.

'Well?' Lila said.

The letter was from Jose's wife. It appeared that Jose and some other students had been involved in a skirmish with militia during the closing stage of the uprising; because they were poorly armed, most of the students, including Jose, had been killed. The concluding part of the letter expressed some moral and religious sentiments which were very idiomatic in expression and too difficult for Paul to translate.

After some time Paul suggested they walk a little. Lila, confessing a headache, agreed it might be a good idea. Cecil, saying nothing at all, followed them out of the steamy restaurant into the cool night.

They wandered in no particular direction, through bright streets and dark streets, streets crowded and streets empty, until a late hour of the evening found them on the embankment. Nearby was a pub, its windows lit yellow; noise came to them faintly. Lila watched the river and shivered. A criss-cross of lights glossed the dark running water.

She turned to the others. 'I think it is now necessary for us to have cigarettes,' she said. When cigarettes had been lighted, she added, 'What is wrong with you two? I am the only cheerful one.' She laughed, almost successfully.

'Yes,' Paul said. 'You are the only cheerful one.'

'We shall be philosophical,' Lila said. 'It is very comforting, being philosophical.'

'Yes,' Cecil said.

'We shall,' Lila said, 'smoke our cigarettes and look out upon the river. If we wish to be philosophical, we may reflect on how life is like a river, lazily twisting and sharply plunging, a river of many currents interwoven. If the image is too tired and outworn, forgive me. It is convenient and near at hand. Sometimes good images are hard to find. We have not yet learned to package them in cellophane and put them into deep-freeze so that they may be purchased fresh and ready-made—though that day too may come. However,' she finished, shivering again, 'I think we could find a better place to spend the evening.'

Cecil and Paul watched Lila with steady curiosity. It occurred to Cecil, as they began walking again, that he had an ending for at least one story.

Presently they found a place where they could drink more coffee. It was a gloomy little cave of a place with shiny espresso machine, juke-box jazz, and bare wooden tables. At the next table a number of bearded young men swarmed about a girl with long yellow hair, black sweater and corduroy slacks; the girl's face, while not particularly pretty, had a very clear, serene expression. There was an absolute and perfect stillness in the way she sat at the centre of the bubbling young men.

'What are you watching her for?' Lila asked Cecil. 'Am I not so interesting?'

'I was just thinking,' he said. 'There, if you still want one, is your image. But I will not elaborate.'

'Nonsense,' Lila said. 'You want to make it glamorous suddenly. Young men flirting with a fair muse. But there is nothing glamorous. Life is about as glamorous as an onion. Peel it down, skin after skin, and what have you got in the end? Nothing. Only tears. Only the tears.'

'You are being very brave,' Paul said, reaching for her hand. 'You have been very brave all the evening.'

'We are all being brave,' Lila said. 'Or trying to be. And who knows? Perhaps we are.'

After a long silence, they all at once began to talk. Paul thought that, after all, he might return to Hungary soon. Perhaps he could escape having to say anything; perhaps not.

Perhaps he could escape gaol; perhaps not. 'There is no longer profit in running away,' he said. 'Countries are much like suits of clothes. I think it is better to wear only the dirty suit of one's own country than to keep covering it with the dirty suits of other countries. Eventually one could suffocate in such dirt.' He shrugged, turned his empty palms upwards, and smiled sadly.

It was very late. The music had subsided, and the girl with yellow hair had left with one of the bearded young men. Cecil talked about returning to New Zealand, where nothing ever happened : Lila wondered tiredly what it would be like married to a New Zealand petit bourgeois.

When the shop closed, they went out into the crisp night and found a slender quarter of moon risen. A peace had descended on the quietening city, the shining river, the tall murky buildings.

Cecil was telling Paul that in New Zealand there were no revolutions. 'Sometimes,' he added, 'I think that it is a good thing, and sometimes I think it is a bad thing.'

Lila took their arms and fell into step between them.

'And sometimes,' she said, 'you don't know what you are saying.'

MAURICE SHADBOLT

Maurice Shadbolt was born in Auckland, New Zealand, in 1932. After graduating from the University in Auckland, he worked as a journalist and documentary film director. Now a free-lance journalist, Mr. Shadbolt divides his time between his assignments and his own writing. In 1957 he received the tenth anniversary prose award of *Landfall,* a literary magazine in New Zealand. For *The New Zealanders* he received the New Zealand State Scholarship in Letters, 1960, and the Hubert Church Prose Award for the best prose work published by a new Zealander in 1959. The story, "The Strangers," included in this book, has appeared in *The New Yorker.* Mr. Shadbolt has traveled in China, the Soviet Union, and throughout Eastern and Western Europe. He has lived, as well, in England and Spain. He now lives in Wellington, New Zealand, with his wife, Gillian Heming, also a journalist, and their son.